HUNTED

THE UNDOING

BOOK THREE

ABOUT THE AUTHOR

Donna Collins was born at home in Romford, Essex, England. Five minutes later, she was one-hundred-per cent a bookworm. Her favourite novel, Enid Blyton's *The Children of Cherry Tree Farm*, was a gift from her parents and now the most worn book on her bookshelf.

It was this book, and her love for 70's and 80's TV shows such as *Hart to Hart*, *Charlie's Angels*, *Hunter*, and *Dempsey and Makepeace*, that lured Donna to the dark side of mystery and thriller writing. Since then, Donna has racked up many favourite authors, including Paula Gosling (*A Running Duck* is the second most worn book on her bookshelf), Jonathan Kellerman, Patricia Cornwell, and A.J. Quinnell.

Although Donna loves to write, she also loves crime - and her career proves it. Having founded her school magazine, her professional career includes not only working at OK! Magazine but also for Essex Police, Ormiston Prison Services, and Essex Offender Services. With publishing credits for freelance and commissioned magazine articles under her belt, Donna has now turned her attention and imagination to what she is best at – storytelling.

In her spare time (what spare time?), Donna loves anything scary that will get her adrenaline pumping, including storm chasing, fright nights, zombie-infested shopping malls, and séance panic rooms - with her all-time goal involving the open sea, a cage, and a whole heap of great white sharks. Donna also proudly boasts finishing the 2010 London Marathon, but you'll have to ask nicely if you want her to tell you where she was placed and who overtook her.

Dead in the Water is the first in the Jason Wade Thriller series.

Contact

admin@donnacollins.co.uk
www.donnacollins.co.uk
Facebook /DonnaCollinsUK
Instagram @DonnaCollinsUK

Also by Donna Collins

<u>The Hunted Series</u>

The Sacrifice

Resurrection

<u>The Jason Wade Series</u>

Dead in the Water

HUNTED: THE UNDOING

Donna Collins

Willow Books

First published in Great Britain in 2017
by Willow Books.

All rights reserved.
ISBN: 9780992782733
Second Edition

Cover Art: Jackie Elliff
Cover Design: Will' Terran

AUTHOR'S NOTE

This is where I like to tell you about some discoveries I made while researching and writing my books.

And this book is no different.

I have two places in mind. One, which appeared briefly in The Sacrifice, is much more a part of this book. I am of course talking about the Catacombs underneath Paris, which I found through a fantastic little video on YouTube called *A Man Gets Lost In The Catacombs*. The video is in two parts, and you'll see many similarities with what I have written. I was so excited when researching this place and, even more, I loved visiting it. I cannot recommend it enough - but pre-book to avoid the queues!

The second place I have to share with you is Morwenstow in Cornwall. I needed an out-of-the-way church and, oh boy, did I find it. The Church of St Morwenna and St John the Baptist is tucked away behind a wooden stile and lychgate and surrounded by tombs and gravestones. The church is swallowed in history and, if you take a short walk past the church – dodging the minefield of cowpats as you go – you reach the cliffs.

For Mum
Who steals coats and dances like a drunken Monkey.

CHAPTER ONE

SUNDAY
Cairngorms National Park, Scotland

Everything was quiet.

The wind didn't rattle through the trees. Birds didn't chirp happy songs from high above. And Roman's voice, asking if she was okay, never came.

Eliza opened her eyes. The shed door stood open. Apart from Jacob's lifeless form, nobody was inside. She crawled to her feet, not bothering to brush the forest floor from her legs, and approached the tiny, wooden building.

Nothing inside indicated where the Sheriff could have taken Roman.

Back outside, the trees swayed in the breeze. The coolness hit Eliza's bare legs and she shivered. She had no idea what to do. She had no idea where she was. And she had no idea how the hell she was supposed to find a way back to civilisation.

She hung her head and past events resurfaced. Moments earlier, she and Roman had killed Jacob and then unsuccessfully engaged the Sheriff in battle. And now the Sheriff had Roman back in Purgatory.

Find my brother.

They'd been the last words Roman had spoken to her.

It was an impossible task. Roman had barely ever spoken about his brother. So how was she supposed to find him? She couldn't even remember his name. Heck, come to think of it, she couldn't remember Roman's full name.

She stared at her feet. Dried blood and mud darkened what had once been sand-coloured, suede boots. The blood could have belonged to any number of people. So many had died around her. The waitress at the diner. The police at the motel. The teenagers in the car. Tears filled her eyes and she crumpled onto her knees. She wanted Roman back. She *needed* him back. This was not how they'd planned their ending. She should be on the run right now – with Roman by her side and the Sheriff defeated.

The Sheriff. What if he returned for her like he'd promised?

At the rear of the shed, the narrow path she'd slid down earlier that day looked twice as hard to climb back up. She glanced around for an easier route but couldn't find one. Taking a deep breath, she dug the toe of her boot into the mud and reached for a branch.

Behind her, the shed door slammed shut.

Eliza froze. She listened as someone paced around inside the small, wooden building. Had the Sheriff returned?

Eliza forgot the hill and fled towards the trees, finding cover behind a nearby trunk. She crouched and watched through the branches.

The Sheriff stepped away from the shed door. His coat was stretched tight across his shoulders, and he was tall enough to reach the roof of the shed even with his upper body hunched over.

He sniffed the air, like he had in her father's driveway. "Eliza, I can smell you're close."

He couldn't smell her. Jacob had been the one he'd tracked. And Jacob was dead.

"Make yourself known to me, girl, and, in return, your brother shall go free."

Eliza dug her fists into the loose dirt. Tears blurred her vision. If she thought there was the slightest chance the Sheriff would keep that promise, she'd willingly give herself up to him this very second. But she'd be a fool to believe him. She clenched both handfuls of dirt, afraid that if she let go, there would be nothing to stop her from walking out into the small clearing.

The Sheriff turned and began to slowly inspect the woods. His scan reached Eliza's position in the trees and she held her breath, too frightened to move. He stared in her direction for ages. Then he moved on, completing a full 360 of the forest around them.

"Your brother will pay dearly for your betrayal."

The Sheriff grabbed a log from the pile and hurled it into the trees opposite. It smashed against a bough and splintered into pieces.

Birds scattered into the sky. A scream built in Eliza's throat and she covered her mouth. She turned her back to the trunk, both hands pressed hard against her lips. The Sheriff shouted out her name and Eliza squeezed her eyes shut. The echo had only just about died when he bellowed her name again.

Time ticked by, but Eliza didn't hear the Sheriff call out for her again. She opened her eyes and loosened the grip on her mouth. New tears replaced the dried ones and she told herself she had to move. But her paralysed body wouldn't follow her command.

Minutes ticked by like hours. Her brother and Roman had sacrificed so much for her –their very lives – and how did she repay them? By hiding pathetically behind a tree.

Nathaniel. That was the name of Roman's brother.

Okay, she had a name. But it still didn't help her any.

She grit her teeth and wiped her eyes dry on the back of her hand. If nothing else, the last few days had taught her that she was better than this…snivelling wreck. She was a fighter. The Sheriff could be anywhere – maybe back in Purgatory, maybe somewhere in the woods waiting for her. But she'd fought him – not once, but three times. And she'd survived every encounter. In fact, he was the one who should be worried about her. Because the next time she saw him, she would kill him.

She stood and peered out from behind the tree, her determination to find Roman and Billy sparking her inner strength. The clearing was empty. But wherever the Sheriff was now, Eliza was under no illusions; he would return.

She twisted round the other side of the tree and looked at the hill behind the shed. Her hands clenched into fists and she evaluated the surrounding forest – her only other option of escape. But where would that lead her? She could walk for miles and never find a way out.

A sour taste filled her mouth and she wrapped her arms around herself. It wouldn't be long before daylight faded. She needed to find help. She needed to head back up the hill.

Giving the area one last scan, she stepped out from behind the tree and crept towards the shed. Twigs snapped under foot, louder than the crack of a whip. She reached the shed window and peered inside. Jacob still lay dead on the floor. A desire to rejoice at the death of the man who had lived inside her and made her life a living hell was short-lived. She turned to the hill.

The sweat she worked up climbing soon cooled. She rubbed her legs, warding away the afternoon chill. The forest was growing darker with every passing minute. Freezing conditions would accompany the darkness, and her inadequate clothing would do nothing to keep her warm. Her brisk pace quickened to a jog. Trees and foliage passed in a blur. She had to figure out how to track down Nathaniel.

So, what did she know? She didn't know where Roman lived. Nor where he liked to hang out. Nor what his job was. Nor who his friends were, if he even had any.

Then, an idea sprang to mind.

She might not know who Roman's friends were, but she knew who his acquaintances had been...her father and Davis.

A newfound bounce in her step, she quickened her pace. Both Davis and her father were gone – one dead and the other lost in the depths of Purgatory. Asking them for information was out of the question. But her father had kept impeccable records on everything. Surely that included Roman. All she needed was a phone number or an address. Anything.

Finally, she had a plan. Now all she had to do was find that road.

It must have been an hour later that Eliza reached the A9 at Killiecrankie.

Her feet hurt. Billy's boots had been rubbing the backs of her heels since Roman had put them on her the day before and it was becoming unbearable.

Eliza hugged herself and rubbed her arms. Since she'd stopped running, the heat she'd generated had rapidly vamoosed. She started to jump on the spot. Her feet screamed, but she kept going. She hadn't seen a car since earlier that morning, when she and Roman had purposely hidden from them. Now she'd give anything to have one pass by.

When a pair of bright headlights finally appeared in the distance, she uttered a soft cry.

She moved to the side of the road and waited. When the vehicle's beam eventually found her, she waved her arms and prayed the driver would stop. The vehicle – a lorry – rumbled past, and her heart stuttered. Then brake lights illuminated the darkened road.

The engine growled to a halt and Eliza let go of the breath she was holding.

The passenger door swung open and a middle-aged man leaned out. "Ye okay? Dae ye need some help?"

"I need a ride."

"Where're ye heading?"

"Cornwall."

The driver chuckled. "Wee bit too far for me, love."

"How about a train station? Somewhere that'll get me to London."

The driver scratched his head. "Edinburgh will git ye to Kings Cross. Though it's a tad oot ma way…"

"Please. I'm desperate."

The driver paused for a second, then motioned for her to climb aboard. "What kind o' man wid ah be if ah left ye oot here?"

Eliza hurried to the lorry. It took all the strength she had left to haul her tired body into the cab and pull the heavy door shut behind her.

"So, ye gunna tell me how ye came to be oot here alone in the dark?"

Eliza looked at him. With only the dash lighting his features, he looked a little like Wolverine – minus the white vest and metal claws.

"My car broke down."

"Uh-huh." Wolverine sat back in his seat. He reclipped his seatbelt and pulled back onto the road. "Ye in some kind 'o trouble, gal?"

Eliza glanced down at her clothing, suddenly conscious of the way she looked. She straightened her shirt – ripped at the shoulder and stained with dried blood and mud and…oh, heck, just about everything. She put her fingers to her matted hair and tried to flatten it. She couldn't tell him the truth – that she'd fought the Purgatory Sheriff and killed pretty much everyone she'd come into contact with over the last few days. The driver would either die laughing or kick her to the kerb. Still, given her current attire, her broken-down-car excuse didn't cut it either.

"I had a fight with my boyfriend." She cringed. The words had passed her lips before she'd had time to think up something more plausible.

Wolverine did not look convinced. He released his mobile from the holder and passed it to her. "Ye wanna call someone?"

A phone sounded good, but even if she had a direct line to Hell itself, who could she call? "No, thank you."

"There's a jacket in the back. Put it on." The driver slipped the phone into his shirt pocket and hesitated. "So, yer boyfriend did this tae ye?"

"Kind of." Eliza leaned over the seat and grabbed the jacket – a black, donkey one. She pulled it up under her chin, like one would a blanket.

"Then ah should be taking ye tae the police station. Or a hospital."

Eliza turned to argue, but the driver didn't appear to be listening anymore. He stared through the windshield. A crease formed across his brow. Now he really did look like Wolverine. He reached for a switch just left of the steering wheel and the road brightened under the full beam.

"Is that yer boyfriend?"

Eliza looked ahead. The Sheriff stood in the middle of the road, in the same guise as she'd last seen him. The same pale, haunting features; the same black coat; the same black hat sitting proud on top of his head.

He smiled, lips wide and lacking any warmth whatsoever, and ran his bony fingers across the hat's rim.

CHAPTER TWO

Roman opened his eyes.

The guard's size-nines booted him in the stomach.

He rolled onto his back, stalling to give his newly cracked rib a chance to heal. The cloaked guard stood over him, his face hidden in the hood's shadow. But Roman knew who it was. The gold medallion that hung from the chain around his neck identified him clearly.

Roman raised himself onto his elbows. "Well, well, well. As I live and breathe. Thomas Blood."

Thomas removed his hood. He looked remarkably tanned considering life down here in the pit meant the sun hadn't touched his skin in centuries. He smiled but said nothing.

"Still not much of a talker, eh?"

"Words waste time."

A catch pole rested against the cave wall. Not the worst of torturous instruments to encounter while down here. More of an annoyance because once it clamped your neck it never let go. Thomas reached for it.

Roman flipped onto his front and sprang to his knees, ready to run, but Thomas booted him in the side. Using the pole, he pushed Roman onto his back again.

Roman coughed and pain exploded around his ribs.

Thomas planted a foot either side of his chest and twirled the ten-foot pole one-eighty so two iron jaws pressed against Roman's throat. Then he jammed it downwards. The arms inside the jaw detracted and slithered past the sides of Roman's neck until he felt cold iron press hard against his throat. Only then did the arms spring out, trapping his neck inside. Roman twisted, but the tip of a two-inch spike at the base of the iron jaw pressed deep beneath his chin. He had little choice but to quickly relax.

Roman had been here before and knew the drill. The arms inside the jaw clamped his throat and when Thomas lifted the pole, Roman had no option but to rise with it.

"Is this really necessary?"

Thomas gripped the middle of the pole, about five feet from Roman and well out of arm's reach. He stepped forward, forcing Roman backwards.

Roman instinctively grabbed the pole for balance. He took another step backwards, yanking the pole – and Thomas – towards him. Thomas stumbled forward and fell. The far end of the weighted pole dropped with him. At the other end, the iron jaw elevated and the spike impaled Roman's chin, its tip puncturing his mouth and finding the underneath of his tongue. Roman grabbed the pole and pulled it from Thomas's grasp. It slipped through Thomas's fingers. Its sheer length made it heavier than it needed to be, but Roman raised it as high as he could, leapt over Thomas, and bolted.

He didn't get far.

Six cloaked guards cut him off a mere fifty metres along the passageway. Roman tried to turn but the pole whacked against the cave wall and stopped him.

Roman stopped, held up his hands, and surrendered. The pole dropped and the spike elevated and pierced the underside of his mouth again. He flinched and waited for Thomas to duck beneath his arms. He waited even longer for Thomas to raise the end of pole off the ground. When he did, the spike slithered free from his chin.

Roman lowered his head – at least, as far as he could before the spike started to pierce his mouth again. He'd tried this same move once before, centuries ago. This was the second time he'd failed to pull it off.

"Use the shackles," Thomas said irritably.

A guard bent before Roman and did as he was ordered. Roman couldn't see – he couldn't look down, the spike ready to pierce his chin again if he did. But he heard the chains. And he felt their heaviness around his ankles. The guard stood, but there was no eye contact, no matter how much Roman willed it. He added two more shackles, one for each of Roman's wrists. Heck, even Houdini would struggle to escape this.

Without uttering another word, Thomas jabbed the pole forward for the second time. Roman stumbled backwards. He tried to balance, but the shackles restricted his movement. Instinctively, he reached for the pole for support again. The chain linking the cuffs to his shackles pulled tight. His hands failed to reach the stick and, powerless to do anything else, Roman toppled.

The iron jaw around his neck inevitably went with him. As did the pole. The spike stabbed the roof of his mouth and, this time, Roman cried out.

"Get him up," Thomas said.

The guards dragged Roman to his feet. Thomas's eyes sparkled with satisfaction. He pushed the pole forward, nudging Roman backwards, his tiny steps scampering along the passage to keep pace with his captor.

Deja vu.

A chill descended and Roman clenched his fists. He didn't need to be facing front to know where he was heading. The prisoners couldn't be heard – yet. But their screams lived inside his head and had woken him every single morning since his escape.

Thomas kept walking and Roman had no choice but to scurry backwards in sync with him – straight into a stalagmite. The iron jaw pressed against his throat and the spike embedded his mouth further. Blood oozed over his lips and Roman tensed.

Thomas grinned.

Roman grinned back, the pain subsiding. "I'm surprised the Sheriff isn't here to personally welcome me, seeing as it's taken the best part of a few hundred years to finally catch me."

"He has other matters to attend to first, but he'll be here. Don't you worry about that." Thomas smiled, revealing stained teeth, and the stench of centuries-old plaque polluted the air.

Roman tensed. "He's still in Cairngorms?"

The thought of the Sheriff pursuing Eliza caused adrenaline to surge through his body. His pulse pounded inside his ears and he attacked, hands stiff, fingers curled – just the right shape to squeeze around Thomas's neck and rip his head from his shoulders. The cuffs pulled the chain tight and Roman reached no further than a foot. A guttural roar bellowed past his lips and he attacked again. The same restriction stopped him.

Thomas smiled. "Careful. You'll give yourself a heart attack."

"I swear, if he's hurt her, I will kill everyone down here." Spittle caught in the corners of Roman's mouth.

Thomas's smile widened. "That would be a neat trick."

"Remove these chains. I'll show you a neat trick or two."

"Now where's the fun in that?" Thomas steered Roman around the stalagmite and forced him backwards again.

Roman shuffled along with him and tried to calm down. Tried to gain control. But he wanted to scream. His vision clouded and the image of Eliza's mutilated body took hold of his mind. He needed to know whether the Sheriff had caught her. He clenched his teeth and tried to stem the tremors that dominated his body.

He was awash with memories of the torture chamber. He'd be there soon. Did the Sheriff have something up his sleeve? Would Eliza's strung-up body be there to greet him? Sweat drenched his skin. He tried to turn, suddenly convinced the Sheriff was standing somewhere behind him ready to inflict his torture, but the spike forced him to face forward.

Thomas manoeuvred Roman around another stalagmite and Roman fought to keep his balance. His legs couldn't move the speed he needed them to go and his hands couldn't reach the pole and hold on for stability. Roman was fucked.

Back he went, his fairy steps moving at such speed his heels barely had time to touch the ground. The passageway was an endless parade of identical rocks. Thomas shoved him around further stalagmites and sometimes he forced Roman straight into them.

Finally, the screams came.

Roman's blood went cold. Gurgled cries echoed along the corridor as a whip cracked down upon bare flesh. Roman saw it. Not physically – he hadn't quite reached the torture room yet. But the familiar sound brought with it images from scores of buried memories. He struggled against the jaw clamp. Inside his mouth, his tongue ran across the tip of the spike. He tilted his head but couldn't lift his chin off the pointed spear.

Thomas pulled on the pole and Roman halted. He heard a handle turn and a door creaked open behind him. He was here. His final destination: The dungeon. The prison. Purgatory's hell hole. There were many names this room went by. Roman preferred to call it the torture room, because that was exactly what it was – a room where fucking torture happened.

He readied himself. Even if he did fight for freedom and make it to the waiting room, he had no idea what souls, if any, were due to be returned.

Thomas pushed again on the pole, but Roman dug his heels in. A guard grabbed his shoulder, but Roman struggled and resisted. Slowly, the men pushed him backwards. Roman's feet slid through the dirt. He pulled on his restraints and stretched for the doorframe. His fingertips brushed the aged wood. The spike ripped through his chin and a rush of blood filled his mouth, seeping down his throat and into his lungs. Roman coughed and spluttered, gasping for breath. His fingertips managed to grab the frame. Another guard joined the scuffle and pried Roman's hand from the wood.

Thomas pushed on the pole again, shoving Roman backwards. The guards clamped Roman's upper arms and together they dragged him through the doorway. Roman struggled for air, coughing the blood from his lungs. His fate was inevitable.

He closed his eyes and the Lord's Prayer whispered from his lips.

CHAPTER THREE

The driver lifted his foot from the accelerator. "Is that even a man?"

"Don't stop. Keep going," Eliza urged.

"Ah'll hit him."

"He'll kill you if you stop."

The lorry slowed to no more than a crawl, then stopped. The driver pulled the handbrake. He leaned across her, reached under the seat, and pulled out a baseball bat.

"Stay here," he told her and reached for the door.

Eliza pulled him back. "I'm begging you. Don't go out there."

Wolverine didn't listen. He opened the door and jumped down onto the road.

Eliza looked back at the Sheriff. He lowered his face, letting the rim of his hat hide his horrific deformity from the light. But he still watched her, like he had back in her father's driveway. She'd defeated him then – with Roman's help. But now, on this desolate road, Roman wasn't here. She was all alone.

The cab door closed and the Sheriff turned his attention to the driver.

"A'right, pal," the driver said. "Ye wanna git oot the road?"

Eliza scrambled into the driver's seat. From this angle, she could see the top of the driver's head. He stood by the corner of the lorry, beside the headlight. He was a sitting duck out there.

The Sheriff stepped forward and the driver nervously raised the bat chest-height. "Ah suggest ye stay where ye are, pal."

The Sheriff looked up, allowing the light to finally find him. He blinked, his eyes dark pools.

The driver stepped back, but it was too late. The Sheriff smiled again, his stained teeth too dull to shine, even with the brightness of the full beam upon them.

The driver stared at him for a moment then spun back to the cab. He went for the door at the same time Eliza pulled on the handle and pushed it open. The driver jumped onto the step. He reached for her and Eliza grabbed his hand. He'd made it half-way into the cab when the Sheriff appeared over his shoulder and grabbed him. He wrapped his hand around the driver's neck and dug his fingers deep into the poor man's throat until his eyes bulged.

"Leave him alone. He has nothing to do with this." Eliza pulled the driver towards her, but the Sheriff's strength far outweighed hers.

He smiled and yanked the man from Eliza's grip. The baseball bat fell from the driver's hand and he yelled out for help.

Every instinct told Eliza to close the door and drive away. Instead, she leapt from the cab. The Sheriff lifted the driver into the air. The man struggled, his feet kicking some four feet above the ground.

Eliza grabbed the bat. She needed the movie reel inside her head to begin playing. But it didn't. And she had no idea how to kickstart it. She didn't have the strength to do much damage to the Sheriff alone, yet she still charged towards him. The bat whacked his shoulder. She drew back and swung again. This time she struck the Sheriff's upper arm. The monster turned towards her. He let the driver drop to the ground, ignoring him when he coughed and spluttered and tried to get to his knees.

Eliza wanted to reach out to him, but the Sheriff stepped between them. "Did you think I wouldn't return for you?"

Eliza's breaths came short and sharp and she didn't bother to control them. "How did you find me? You were tracking Jacob, not me."

"There are many ways to hunt someone down. The forest makes for good tracking and you did very little to cover your trail."

"So, you followed me?"

The Sheriff smiled. "And now I'm looking forward to taking you back with me."

"What makes you think I'll let you?"

"Your powers cannot stop me, witch." The Sheriff took a step towards her, albeit a somewhat guarded one.

Eliza retreated, maintaining the gap between them. She glanced past the Sheriff. The driver struggled to his knees, only just managing to stay upright.

"Don't concern yourself with him." The Sheriff took another step closer. "Worry about your own fate."

"Don't come any nearer." Eliza tightened her grip on the bat.

The Sheriff eyed her for a second. He stepped forward again.

Eliza swung the bat. The Sheriff stopped it dead with the palm of his hand, without so much as an eye twitch. His scrawny fingers wrapped around the smooth wood. He pulled it from Eliza's grip and threw it to the ground.

Eliza turned to run but the Sheriff's bony fingers coiled around the back of her neck. He tightened his grip, lifted her off the ground – as he had with Wolverine – and dragged her backwards. She felt him lean into her, and then his voice was in her ear.

"I can't wait to parade you before Roman."

Eliza stamped down hard on the Sheriff's foot and butted her head backwards. It had little effect. He towered over her and she only managed to hit his chest.

The Sheriff spun her around to face him. He tightened his fingers around her throat. Eliza tried in vain to pry them free, kicking out and scratching at the Sheriff's face, her splintered nails tearing away his leathery, white skin.

Finally, the movie reel inside her head began. As if on invisible wires, the bat rose from the ground until it hovered behind the Sheriff's head. It smashed into his skull, knocking his hat away. The Sheriff stumbled forward but didn't release his hold on her. The bat swung again. And again. Pounding into the back of the Sheriff's head.

Crack after crack, Eliza heard his skull break apart, but still the Sheriff clung to her throat. The movie reel continued. It hauled the Sheriff backwards and slammed him against the side of the lorry. Eliza went with him, still trapped in his grasp. The Sheriff met Eliza's gaze and his eyes widened, filled more with anger than pain. He dropped to his knees and his fingers loosened their hold on her.

Eliza collapsed beside him and gasped for breath. But she wasn't finished with him. The bat moved swiftly towards the Sheriff and again hammered down upon his skull. The Sheriff fell forward and sprawled the tarmac.

Eliza got up and staggered towards the driver.

"We need to get to the lorry," she said, her voice hoarse.

"What is that thing?"

"You wouldn't believe me if I told you." Eliza helped the driver to his feet.

"Is it dead?"

"No." She climbed into the lorry.

The driver climbed in after her and closed the door. "How d'ye make things shift like that?"

"I don't know." Eliza couldn't explain it to herself, let alone anyone else. "Let's just get out of here. Are you okay to drive?"

The man nodded. The engine was still running and he found first gear. Then he paused. "It's gone. Where's it gone?"

Eliza's body tightened. She leaned forward, seeing nothing but tarmac. Then, out of the corner of her eye, she saw the Sheriff at her window.

"Drive!"

The driver didn't waste time with his seatbelt. He stamped down on the accelerator. The Sheriff punched through the passenger window, smashing it inwards, showering Eliza with fractured glass. The Sheriff reached in and grabbed her shirt. He pulled her towards him, slamming her against the broken window. Jagged edges scratched her face and shoulders, and she cried out.

The driver stretched over to help her. The lorry swerved across the road and he bolted back upright, fighting to regain control. The brakes squealed. The wheels locked. And everything jolted forward.

The driver head-butted the steering wheel. Eliza's shirt tore free from the Sheriff's grasp and he catapulted across the hood, vanishing somewhere in front of the lorry. Eliza slammed against the dash and crashed into the footwell.

The engine stalled and silence descended.

The driver lifted his head. Blood trickled along the bridge of his nose. He looked back at the steering wheel and turned the key. The engine roared to life and he glanced down at Eliza. A faint smile of accomplishment curled his lips. Then his eyes flickered shut and he passed out.

Eliza scrambled up onto the passenger seat. She couldn't see the Sheriff, but she knew he was there — somewhere in front of the lorry.

She turned to the lorry driver. His head lolled against the headrest.

"Hey!" She tapped his arm.

He didn't respond.

The Sheriff stood. Looking a little unbalanced, he raised his arms and stretched. Rolled his neck, first to the left, then to the right. Eliza took a deep breath and willed him to move. She wanted to swipe him over to the side of the road and out of her way – but the movie reel wouldn't play.

"Shit." Eliza shook the driver again.

He groaned.

The engine still purred. Eliza glanced at the steering wheel. She had no idea how to drive a lorry. Outside, the Sheriff cast his gaze over the ground around him.

Eliza pulled the driver across to the passenger side as far as she could and scooted into his seat. Her feet just about reached the pedals. She searched for the seat adjuster but couldn't find it, so she perched on the edge of the seat and prepared to drive away.

The Sheriff bent down and retrieved his hat. He sat it on his head and glanced up at her.

Eliza revved the engine. Her muscles tensed. She licked her lips and curled her shaking hands around the steering wheel. The Sheriff stared directly at her, his black eyes daring her to take him on. Eliza revved the engine again and attempted to edge forward. The lorry jerked and promptly stalled. She quickly turned the ignition key and the engine growled to life once more. This time, Eliza didn't hesitate. She stamped her foot on the accelerator. The engine revved until it screamed for release. She lifted her foot from the clutch and the vehicle shot forward. The Sheriff dived for cover, but the lorry caught him, clipping his hip and spinning him onto the grass verge. The smashed headlight flickered and the full beam died.

Eliza didn't look back. She didn't slow. She didn't reverse. She just kept going.

CHAPTER FOUR

The quiet tones of Dusty Springfield's 'Son of a Preacher Man' played on the radio.

Eliza's neck ached with worry. She tried to alleviate the tension by tapping her fingers to the tune for twenty seconds or so. The song finished – and so did her tapping. The ache remained in her neck and her thoughts turned to the driver. He was still lying unconscious across the passenger seat. She'd wanted to stop and check he was all right. But she couldn't check. She couldn't risk the Sheriff catching up with them.

On the radio, the DJ rambled on about a looming competition where a lucky listener could win a weekend trip to Italy. A trip to Italy sounded so good right about now. In fact, she'd welcome a trip anywhere. A nice, normal trip. Somewhere she could be with Roman. Somewhere she could telephone her brother just to tell him she'd arrived safely – because he was back home. Alive and well.

The headlights lit up a road sign. She'd finally reached Edinburgh. She pulled over to the side of the road and cut the engine.

The driver stirred and came to. He looked at her but didn't try to move. "Is it dead? Are we safe?"

Eliza nodded and unclipped her seatbelt. "I have to go. Will you be okay?"

The driver sat up, winced a little and glanced out of the windows. "Ah have nae idea what happened tonight and I don't want tae know. Ah just need tae be sure that thing won't be coming after me."

"It won't." Eliza pushed open the lorry's door.

The driver studied her for a moment. "Take the jacket."

Eliza smiled. She reached for the driver's donkey jacket and jumped down onto the road. Glancing down at her sore legs, she saw new scratches and bruises now overlapped her previous ones. Her knee hurt and her shoulder felt like hell, but, luckily, she had no broken bones or fractures.

"I'm sorry for tonight." She turned from him and started to jog towards Edinburgh.

She didn't get far. A couple of hundred yards, in fact. She rubbed the stitch cramping her side. The hairs on the back of her neck spiked and she turned, expecting to see the Sheriff powering up behind her.

He wasn't there.

She pulled her shirt cuffs down over her hands, as though their length might somehow protect her. Cursing her growing paranoia, she walked for a little while before giving running another shot. It took longer than she'd hoped to reach Edinburgh's train station.

It was a grand, golden building – on the outside. Inside was a mishmash of plywood corridors and building work. The disarray didn't deter the travelling crowds, however. They surrounded her in droves.

Up ahead, the departures board hung from the ceiling like a display piece in an art gallery. Eliza found a train leaving for King's Cross in twenty-five minutes. Then she saw the ticket inspectors at the barriers. Panic pinched her stomach and she pushed her way through the waiting crowds until she reached the west side of the station. She had just over twenty minutes to wait, but it might as well have been a hundred and twenty; she'd never find a way past the inspectors without a ticket.

She swiped loose hair from her face and pulled the donkey jacket around her. Its length covered her shorts – just. Remnants of dried blood and filth stained her legs. Cuts and bruises marked her skin. There was nothing she could do to cover her bare legs, though, other than tie the jacket around her waist. Hell, if ever she was in need of a shower and a change of clothes – it was now.

She saw the public restrooms and her body calmed a little at the thought of being able to clean herself up. She crossed the foyer and headed down the stairwell. At the bottom, barriers blocked her path by way of turnstiles wanting to see twenty pence before allowing entry. Eliza glanced around. There was nobody in sight and she ducked under them.

The ladies' toilet was empty and she wasted no time in filling a sink with water and washing what dirt she could from her body. She patted her skin dry with paper towels and stared in the mirror. She looked like hell. When her tears came, she did nothing to stop them.

The door squeaked open and a redhead – eighteen maybe twenty years old – clip-clopped across the tiled floor. She was sozzled. She threw her coat and bag onto the counter and, without acknowledging Eliza, dashed for one of the cubicles. Her stilettoes must have reached a good five inches and almost brought her down mid-run. She pushed open the toilet door and fell through, landing on her knees. Her hair fell around her face, but she didn't move it out of the way before the vomit spewed from her mouth. Some landed on the floor, some over the toilet seat. Very little seemed to make it into the basin itself.

This was where Eliza usually stepped in and helped. She glanced at the coat and bag. It couldn't be this easy. Could it? She removed the donkey jacket and swapped it for the girl's coat – a nice, long one that would easily cover her legs. The girl's bag was open. Lying on top was her train pass. Just beneath was her purse. Eliza looked back at the door. If she took them, she'd be leaving the girl in the same predicament she herself faced now. She thought about Billy and Roman being tortured in Purgatory – and grabbed the train pass. She took only a tenner from the purse, leaving a couple of twenties for the girl. Then she made for the exit, pulling her new coat around her as she went.

Pressing the pass against the barrier's pad caused the two gates that blocked her path to catapult open. A guard stood nearby. He smiled – robot-like – and Eliza hurried past him. She didn't want smiles – of any kind. She just wanted to be on the train to London.

She chose a carriage that only had a few people in it, made it to the toilets, and locked herself inside.

Her face cooled a little when she splashed it with water. She lowered the toilet seat and sat down, wondering how long until the train pulled out. Christ, she was going to have to do this all over again when she changed trains in London.

A yawn pushed past her lips and her eyes glazed over. For the first time that day, she felt tired. A second yawn followed, and her eyelids dropped. She rested her head against the wall, fighting to keep her eyes open. But they soon closed, and it wasn't long before Roman visited her dreams.

CHAPTER FIVE

The shackles locked together above Roman's head and pinched his skin.

It was a short-lived pain that was the least of his worries. He glanced about the room and immediately recognised it. It had been his home for so many years. A lifetime, in fact. Numerous prisoners surrounded him, some of whom were locked in shackles like himself. Others were strapped to the array of torturous devices that filled every available space. Tremors rocked Roman's arms. Each and every one of these implements had been used on him hundreds of times in the past, maybe even thousands, and all of them held a terrible memory that Roman had fought hard to forget.

He glanced away from the prisoners, recognising the majority were people he'd left behind when he'd escaped.

Thomas Blood bent down and tugged on the shackles around Roman's feet. Seemingly satisfied they were secure, he stepped back.

The Sheriff waited in the corner of the room, frustration hardening his eyes. "Feisty girl you have back there in Cairngorms. Puts up a real fight."

Roman pulled at his restraints. He wanted blood. He wanted the Sheriff's blood.

He searched the torture room for Eliza. "I swear, if she's here...if you've hurt her—"

"I must say, I thought it would take longer to break you, Roman." The Sheriff pushed away from the wall.

He stood, hunched and menacing, but still wearing that look of frustration.

Roman forced a tight smile, willing the rage to stay within and not be so evident. He diverted his gaze to the familiar looking man hanging opposite. Went by the name of Ronald, if Roman wasn't mistaken. Like Roman, he was suspended from the ceiling by his wrists. Nothing but mere skin and bones. His head bowed towards the floor and his thin, grey hair dangled loose over his shoulders. Only the slight rise and fall of his chest suggested he still clung to life. He didn't look too dissimilar from the night Roman had broken free all those centuries ago. How would he feel if that were Eliza hanging there?

"What's wrong, Holbrook? You look scared." The Sheriff sauntered forward, the look of frustration gone, the man clearly enjoying every moment.

Roman hardened his glare. "Do I look scared to you?"

"You look like a man with his heart exposed."

Roman scoffed and shook his head. "If you've killed Eliza then she's gone and you can't use her against me anymore. If she's alive then she's smart enough to run."

The Sheriff's smile remained, but its sparkle died.

"And, as I've already endured every torture you have to offer," Roman continued, "I'd say you're back at square one."

"Are you sure?"

"You couldn't break me first time around. You won't break me now."

"Brave words from someone so petrified."

"You of all people should know I don't scare easily." Roman buried his terror and pushed harrowing memories from his thoughts. He dug deep to find some of that cocky sarcasm that had protected him so well over the years, looked up at the shackles, then glanced around the room. "Very thoughtful of you to reserve my favourite spot, though. Best view in the house."

The Sheriff smiled. "Well, then, I guess today is your lucky day. I've arranged some company for you."

Roman's cockiness evaporated. He frantically searched the dungeon again, praying Eliza would not meet his gaze. All he saw were the other prisoners strung up around him and a bloodied body tied to the rack.

"You're bluffing. You don't have her."

"Maybe. Maybe not. What I do with her is up to you."

"Meaning?"

"Meaning, I want to know how you escaped."

"The same way Jacob did."

"I have spent the best part of three days chasing Jacob around. I am well aware how both he and you escaped the waiting room." The Sheriff smiled. "I want to know how you escaped here – this room."

Roman quietened. He shrugged and shook his head.

"Have it your way." The Sheriff backed up towards an iron casket known as the Iron Maiden – a head-shaped mould on top and two hinged doors closed in front.

Tremors spread across Roman's body. The Sheriff reached for the handle and pulled the left door open an inch or so. Roman didn't want to see inside. His pulse raced. Pain filled his lungs. The Sheriff pulled open the door another inch allowing a sliver of darkness to emerge. Roman strained to hear any evidence that Eliza might be inside: a groan, a whimper, her delicate tones pleading for his help. The Sheriff pulled the door open further and Roman's legs weakened in anticipation of seeing her fall out.

The Sheriff grinned. It was obvious he was toying with him and enjoying the anguish he was stirring up. He pulled the door open a little more. Somebody was inside. Roman stretched his neck. He saw material – maybe from a trouser leg – covered in dirt and grime. What had Eliza been wearing? He wracked his brain, but that information was a blur to him now. All he remembered was dressing her in her brother's shorts and boots.

"That had better not be her."

"You're in no position to threaten me. Down here, I am the power. I suggest you remember how to fear me."

"I never feared you," Roman lied.

His arms tensed and he pulled at the restraints, desperate to break free. When he couldn't, he took a deep breath. He ignored the building ache in his biceps as the blood rushed down from his hands towards his shoulders. There was no use pleading with the Sheriff. Torture and pain would come soon. It was just a matter of time.

The Sheriff stared at him for a moment. The glint of enjoyment remained in his eye.

"Then let me refresh your memory." He pulled the door wide open.

Pain seared Roman's left hand and he felt his bones break. It was then that he realised he'd pulled it free from the restraint. A body fell from the Iron Maiden.

Billy lay sprawled across the ground – unconscious, not dead. Holes lacerated his bare torso. The dirty material Roman spied was what was left of Billy's grey police uniform, shredded and torn and covered in blood. Roman's muscles weakened and he slumped as far as the shackle still restraining his right hand would allow him. He closed his eyes and felt tears well behind his eyelids. He'd known the bastard was playing him. Confused thoughts were jumbled inside his head – remorse for what was happening to Billy, but elation that it was not Eliza who had tumbled to the floor in front of him.

He tested his broken hand, which wasn't healing as quickly as he'd like down here in the chamber, and opened his eyes. So far, his newfound freedom had gone unnoticed and he wanted to keep it that way. He straightened, pretending the shackle above his head still held him.

"I knew you didn't have her," he said, letting out a shaky laugh.

"Not yet. But I will."

"She's way too smart for you."

The Sheriff narrowed his eyes and crossed his arms. He stared at Roman, but still Roman's free hand went undetected. Finally, the Sheriff glanced down at Billy.

"String him up," he said to Thomas in a tone that didn't disguise his annoyance.

Thomas waved his hand and two guards rushed forward. Each grabbed one of Billy's arms and dragged him across the chamber towards Roman. They lifted him so Thomas could secure shackles to his wrists and ankles. When Thomas finished, he stood and all three of them backed away, leaving a semi-conscious Billy hanging there.

The Sheriff stepped in front of them. "I have someone I need to go and find." He grinned. Seeming to sense it unnerved Roman, he held it way longer than necessary. "I'll be back shortly." He turned to Thomas. "Until we know how he escaped, I want a guard on him constantly. Under no circumstances are you to let him out of your sight."

Roman wanted to scream. Instead, he just glared and stayed quiet. His free hand hadn't healed – nor was it likely to down here – and he didn't want to draw the Sheriff's attention to the shackle that no longer secured him. He watched the Sheriff leave.

"Stay with him," Thomas said to the guards and he, too, left the chamber.

The two guards remained by Roman, though, to his relief, they stood with their backs to him.

When the large, oak door closed, Roman turned to Billy. He didn't look good. He looked as though he'd died a couple of times already.

"Billy."

Roman reached beneath Billy's chin with he free hand and lifted his head to face him. Sweat-drenched hair clung to Billy's face. Underneath, Roman saw his left ear had been hacked off.

"Billy. Look at me. It's Roman."

Billy tilted his head. He glanced at Roman with glazed eyes. "Where's Eliza?"

His voice was weak. Barely audible.

"Not here."

"That thing didn't get her?"

A guard shifted position and Roman released Billy's chin. He quickly raised his hand back to the shackle. The guard didn't turn and Roman exhaled in relief.

"No," he said to Billy.

Billy lowered his head. Light sobs shook his shoulders.

Opposite, the grey-haired man strung from the ceiling coughed and spat out a mouthful of blood. He registered Roman and a spark of recognition flitted across his bloodshot eyes.

"What is this place?" Billy said.

"Paradise. Can't you tell?" Roman winced. Now was not the time for him to make stupid wisecracks, and he wished he'd given a different answer.

He looked away from the man opposite and turned back to Billy. A good percentage of his blood was pooled around the base of the Iron Maiden. A smaller amount marked the path to where he hung now. He would be dead soon. Blood aside, his ashen skin and mutilated body was evidence of that.

"Just hang in there, mate."

"Am I dead?"

"No."

Roman's plan to escape as quickly as possible was going to have to wait. Billy wouldn't live long enough to make it to the chamber door, let alone the waiting room, and Roman wouldn't get very far carrying him.

"But I've seen..." Billy paused. His eyes flitted from side to side.

It was obvious to Roman that the man didn't understand what had happened to him. Roman wiggled his dislocated hand back through the empty shackle. It was a struggle that hurt like fucking hell, but he couldn't afford to let anyone see he'd gotten one hand free. He continued to force his hand through the clamp until he felt the weighted iron around his wrist. He couldn't escape yet, not without Billy. Eliza would never forgive him.

Billy looked up and met Roman's gaze. "I can't possibly be alive."

"I know, mate. I know."

"Then how?"

"That's what Purgatory is. Living the ultimate death over and over."

"So, am I dead or alive?"

"You're alive. Never forget that."

Billy spoke no more, but Roman had questions. "Where's your father?"

Billy coughed. "Saving his own skin."

"He won't survive in the tunnels for long. The guards will find him and then they'll bring him here."

Billy coughed again. At least he wasn't coughing up blood. Yet.

"Billy, first chance we get, we're outta here."

"How?"

"Same way I did it before."

CHAPTER SIX

MONDAY

Eliza stretched and rubbed the sleep from her eyes.

She got up from her seat and even though her legs felt heavy, she rushed from the train to join the other morning commuters on the platform. A bus crossed over the bridge and she paused. She had no money. The ten pounds she'd taken from the girl's purse had been spent on an overpriced coffee and a biscuit at King's Cross. Of course, she could walk to her father's – if she had a couple of hours to spare.

She didn't.

Without her mobile to look up her contacts, the public telephones were of little use. Besides, who would she call? Everyone who could help her was either dead or in Purgatory.

She pushed through the suits and hurried to the top of the stairs. The suits turned left towards the town centre. Eliza turned right towards the taxi rank.

The first car in line was a Mondeo – scratched up and quite an old car by today's standards. A dark-haired man sat behind the wheel reading the morning's newspaper – The Sun. Said it all, really.

He saw her approach and pressed a button on his armrest. The passenger window lowered. "Where you going to, honey?"

"Fowey. Readymoney Road."

Eliza opened the door and settled beside him. The driver's identification hanging from the rear-view mirror listed his name as David Smith. The picture didn't do him justice and made him look way older than he appeared in person.

The driver folded his paper and threw it on the back seat. "Just got off the train?" He pulled away from the kerb.

"Uh-huh."

"Where've you come in from? London?"

Eliza nodded.

He glanced her way. "Looks like you've had a heavy night."

"You have no idea."

She didn't want to make conversation. She wanted silence so she could think. Her whole body ached for rest. But her mind raced. A quarter of an hour and she'd be at her father's. Maybe the police would be there – maybe they wouldn't. Either way, she needed to gain access and find out where the hell Roman came from so she could track down his brother – whoever the hell he was.

"So, you live in Fowey?"

"My father does."

"You're lucky you didn't arrive a few days ago. Only way you'd have gotten to Fowey would've been by bicycle or on foot. Roads were closed everywhere because of the gas leaks."

"Gas leaks?"

"Cracked pipes underground caused by the tremors."

Eliza wanted to laugh. The government *had* been quick with their cover story. But how they'd managed to dupe the media and the public into believing gas leaks were the cause of such devastation amazed her.

Ten minutes of idle chatter and then the driver indicated and turned left onto the B3269. The view should have been enough to console Eliza. After all, the security of arriving home safely was what anyone else would have craved. Instead, her fists were clenched so tight that her broken nails dug into her palms. Her body stiffened.

"Nice houses down here."

Eliza didn't answer. Her father's nice house held nothing but deathly memories for her.

"What house is yours?"

"Last one on the end."

The cab slowed at the entrance to her father's driveway. An officer stood inside the gates with his back towards the road. Eliza looked past him. Only part of the house could be viewed from here, but it was enough to see several more police cars parked in front of it. Enough to see she'd never get access to her father's house from here without being seen.

"Keep going," Eliza said.

"This is the last house."

"Just keep going." She waited until the cab had almost reached the cove. "You can stop here."

The cab stopped. The driver reached for the digital box that sat on the dash. "Okay, that'll be thirty-two even."

Eliza reached for the door handle. "I just need to go and get the money."

"Hey, wait a minute. You think I'm stupid?"

"No."

"You think you're the first person to tell me they'll be back with my money?"

"I'm telling you the truth."

"So why have I got to stop here, almost on the sand? Why can't I drive you to your door?"

Eliza thought about the police. "Please. I promise I'll be back with your money."

The driver reached for the gear stick. "I'll take you to your house. You say it's the last house?"

"Yes, but..."

"But nothing. These houses are gated. I'll happily drive you through the gates and wait outside the front door while you go get my money."

He didn't have time to put the car into reverse; Eliza opened the door and jumped out. "I'll be back in a bit. If you want paying, you'll wait." She slammed the door shut on him.

The run down to the beach was an easy one. A small, concrete slope and then sand – still firm from where the tide had gone out. Two sets of footprints were the only proof anyone else had been here this morning – one set human, the other set from a dog. Both sets had almost disappeared. Surf gently rolled to shore and the sea appeared calm. Hell of a difference from her last visit.

She glanced up at the cliff. Seeing it was like reliving the crucifixion and all of the horrors her father had inflicted upon her all over again. Did McKenzie's corpse still lie up there? She shivered, suddenly cold, even though there wasn't a breeze. She pulled her coat tight to her chest. The glow of the sun hadn't quite reached its peak and the secret entrance that led to her father's library remained hidden in shadow.

She knew her father's house better than any police officer; it should be easy to get in and out undetected. She started along the passageway. By the time she reached the iron gate, the insides of the cave had swallowed every shred of daylight. She reached out, felt the iron bars pushed flat against the rock, and allowed the jagged wall to guide her forward. When the corridor ended, she turned right. A slither of light pushed beneath the secret door – the bookcase – but it wasn't enough to light up the corridor. She looked down. Davis's body lay at her feet, just where she'd left him. He didn't look dead under the restricted light. There were no signs of maggots or flies, and no smell reached her nostrils. In fact, Eliza wanted to kick him to confirm he wasn't just unconscious. But he wasn't sleeping. He was dead. And, truth be told, he frightened her more now than when he'd been alive.

She sidestepped him. Reaching for the bookcase, she felt around for a handle or a button or a lever –

anything that would unlock the secret door. She found a latch about halfway down on the righthand side.

It clicked when she tugged it.

Eliza waited for the echo to die then slowly swung the door back an inch. Light from the library streamed through the tiny gap and found Davis, highlighting his gaunt, colourless face. He was definitely dead. Eliza turned back to the library. Satisfied there wasn't anybody on the other side, she pulled the bookcase open and hurried to her father's desk. Stacks of correspondence and unopened mail littered the top – definitely not the kind of mess her father would normally tolerate. But nothing about this reality she found herself in was normal. She pushed several rolls of architect's plans to one side and began to sort through the paperwork. Finding no evidence that any of it had to do with Roman, she pulled open a drawer. More paperwork. Still no address for Roman. Another drawer – same old nothing.

Male voices sounded in the hallway outside. Eliza hurried to the bookcase, ready to hide again. She turned back. Beneath the door to the corridor, shadows danced in the light. Eliza listened, trying to make out what was being said. The voices – two of them from what she could hear – were too muffled to understand. Then the shadows moved away and the light returned.

Eliza surveyed the rest of the room. She sure as hell wasn't going to find what she wanted on the drinks cart or down the back of the sofa cushions.

She headed to the library door and pressed her ear against the varnished oak. She couldn't hear a thing on the other side. She got on her hands and knees and eyed the marble floor through the gap. No sign of any police.

Her father's study was just across the way. She stood and slowly opened the door. The officers she'd heard pass by minutes earlier were nowhere to be seen. In fact, the house seemed eerily quiet. She crept across the corridor to her father's study and swiftly entered.

True to her father's OCD, nothing was out of place.

Apart from the telephone, the odd photograph, and a banker's lamp she'd always had a fondness for, the desk was devoid of any paperwork. She pulled on a drawer. It was locked – as she'd expected it would be. On the far wall, an oil painting of her mother grabbed her attention. Her father had commissioned it after her death. The act of a grieving husband who couldn't let their love die – or so Eliza had always thought. But that wasn't the case. Roman had revealed her father's part in her so-called mother's death, and Eliza had no reason to disbelieve him. She stared at the painting. Not a symbol of her father's love, but a trophy reminder of what he – a cold-hearted killer – had achieved.

Eliza swung the painting open like a door. Behind it was a safe – relatively small considering the size of the one hidden inside her father's walk-in closet. This smaller one had a keypad and a display requesting a six-digit code. Eliza punched in her birthday. Figures illuminated the digital display, but the keypad beeped its rejection. She entered her father's birthday, her mother's birthday, Billy's birthday. None of them worked. She started on anniversaries and holidays. Even random numbers in the hope she'd get lucky. None of them opened the safe.

She slammed the painting shut. Frustration shook her hands and she closed her eyes, giving herself a moment to calm down. When she opened them, her oil-painted mother was staring at her, almost as if trying to give her a clue. Eliza stilled. Her father had proven himself a sick bastard, but to use a murder date as a code?

Eliza swung the painting open and punched in the date of her mother's death. With a beep of acceptance, the door clicked and unlocked. A deep loathing for her father bubbled in the pit of her stomach. He had killed the woman she had known as her mother and then paraded the fact in the open, knowing nobody would ever make the connection.

Eliza opened the safe door and stared at the contents: a set of keys – six to be exact, but none she recognised the look of; several passports – all supporting her father's picture, but none listing his real name; and a wad of money – all twenty-pound notes. She put the items on the desk and fanned out the money. Lots of notes. Had to amount to thousands. She stuffed the cash into her coat pocket and turned back to the safe. The only thing left inside was a small, leather notebook secured by a buckled strap. Eliza opened it. Pages and pages were filled with names and figures and company addresses. She quickly flicked through, but Roman's name didn't pop out at her. Regardless, she slipped it into the other coat pocket.

She stared at the desk. Reaching for the set of keys, she rifled through them looking for one that would fit the locked drawer. Yale wouldn't work; it wasn't that kind of lock. But this small, antique, brass one with the fleuron bow?

Eliza inserted the key, muttered a silent prayer, and twisted it. The key turned a full 360 and Eliza pulled the drawer open. At the top lay four files. None of them held anything that would help her. Underneath, there were three A4 manila envelopes. The first one contained paperwork on herself along with passwords, key cards, bank details. Just how long had her father been planning her death? She opened the second envelope and smiled. Information, and lots of it. All on Roman. Eliza quickly scanned the pages until she found an address. Yes. This was exactly what she needed. Making a mental note, she shoved the papers back inside the manila wallet and, taking the other two envelopes, headed to the door.

She listened for the slightest sound. Content she couldn't hear anything, she slowly opened the door. Through the inch-wide crack, the hallway looked vacant. The library was just across the way. A couple of steps and she'd be home free.

She was halfway between the office and library when a policeman exited the kitchen. Eliza froze and the two of them stared at one another. The library door was so close. Eliza could feel the secret passage calling to her.

"Stop right there." The officer walked towards her.

Eliza darted for the library door, but the officer was quicker. His arm reached across the frame and blocked her from entering.

He pulled her back and secured her against the wall. "I'm going to take a stab in the dark and guess you're Eliza Hamilton?"

Eliza's mind raced. She needed to get the hell out of there. The front door was too far away to aid in her escape, as were the stairs. But the library door was still ajar.

"I'm Officer Grimes." Large, round, gold-framed glasses covered most of his face. Behind them, tiredness had drawn lines around his eyes. "Miss Hamilton, I recognise you from the photographs hanging in your father's office."

He relaxed a little and withdrew some of his weight from her, although still not enough for her to attempt a getaway. "Are you okay?"

His question confused her. Why wasn't he placing her under arrest?

"Can you tell me where you've been?"

Eliza glanced at the front door again. Why wasn't this guy reading her her rights?

"Miss Hamilton, there have been search parties out looking for you for days."

"I'm sorry."

PC Grimes smiled. "No, I mean there have been a lot of people worried about you."

His smile faded and he reached across his chest. Pinned just beneath his left shoulder was a radio.

His gaze never left her as he pressed the side-button and spoke into the mic. "I have Eliza Hamilton secured in the hallway. Any officer available to assist?"

He didn't wait for a reply and returned his full attention to her. "Eliza – it's okay if I call you Eliza?" Again, he didn't wait for a response. "We are having problems locating your father. It seems he has disappeared. Do you know anything that could help us find him?"

Oh, sure. He's in Purgatory. Eliza shook her head. "No."

"Can you tell me what happened at the hospital?"

The hospital? That seemed like months ago rather than days.

PC Grimes was waiting for an answer, but what could Eliza tell him? She certainly couldn't start blabbing on about zombies and sacrifices.

"We have a witness who says he saw a man take you from the hospital. We also have a lot of dead patients and staff inside. Do you know who was responsible?"

Eliza remained silent.

"It is vital you help us, Eliza. Who is this man? Is he involved in your father's disappearance?"

"What?"

"Your brother is also missing."

"What?"

"Both your father and your brother are missing." Grimes removed his hand from her shoulder and stepped back. "Does your brother know this man?"

Eliza frowned. "My brother? Why would you say that?"

PC Grimes paused. He pushed his glasses back up on to his nose. "Maybe you need to sit down."

He tried to lead her to the antique chair her father had loved so much. Eliza hated that chair with a passion.

She shrugged away from his grip. "I'm fine."

PC Grimes inhaled and held the breath for a moment. "A witness saw your brother kill two police officers outside his apartment."

Eliza frowned. "I don't know what you're talking about, but my brother had nothing to do with anyone dying."

"The witness seems pretty certain."

"Well, the witness is wrong. My father's the person you want."

The officer lowered his head and glared at her over the top of his glasses. "You're saying your father, the mayor, killed those officers?"

"No, but he's responsible."

"I sense you don't like your father very much."

Eliza scoffed.

PC Grimes raised his head. "We also found two more bodies inside your brother's apartment. One was a police officer your brother worked alongside."

Eddie and his girlfriend. Eliza blinked back the tears that raced to her eyes. She had killed them both – or at least Jacob had – and this idiot copper standing in front of her was blaming Billy for it. "You have it wrong. Billy didn't kill anybody. He isn't even here."

"Where is he?"

"He went away Friday night. He wasn't even here when they died."

The officer stared at her. His face hardened. "Eliza, I never told you when they died."

Eliza's mouth filled with saliva. She desperately tried to hold onto her poker face. "I just assumed."

"Assumed what?"

"That they died more recently than last Friday. Look, I'm telling you it's my father you want."

"I'm going to have to ask you to come back to the station with me." Almost as an afterthought, he added, "Purely to help me with my enquiries."

He gently urged her away from the wall and reached for his radio again. "This is PC Grimes. I'm bringing Miss Hamilton out. Have the car ready."

"Actually, I think I do need to sit down. Could you get me a glass of water?" Eliza turned for the chair, but she didn't sit.

Officer Grimes reached for his radio. "Tim, could you bring a glass of water out into the hallway, please?"

A moment later, a second officer exited the kitchen carrying a glass of water. He promptly handed it to Grimes, who passed it on to Eliza. He turned from her and muttered something to his colleague. The copper looked at Eliza and then towards the front door. There was some more mumbling, which Eliza couldn't quite make out, and then they stopped talking. The officer gave Eliza another look. He flashed a quick smile – very forced – and headed off to the main foyer.

Grimes didn't turn to face Eliza until the officer was out of sight. "Feel better?"

Eliza remembered she'd asked for the water and started to sip.

"Okay, Miss Hamilton. Are you ready to accompany me to the station now?"

Eliza sipped a little more water. She needed to think. She needed to buy herself some time.

Grimes sighed. He wasn't having any of it. He shifted position and didn't even try to hide his impatience. His gaze landed on the envelopes, but before he could ask about them, Eliza threw the glass of water in his face. Water hit his eyes and he flinched, blinking hard. His brief loss of concentration was all Eliza needed. She darted for the library and locked herself inside.

"Eliza?" Grimes banged on the door. "Open the door."

Eliza was already at the open bookcase. She darted inside. Grimes bashed the library door. It didn't open. Eliza grabbed the small lever and pulled the secret door towards her.

Another bash and the library door burst open.

Grimes entered the room with more caution than urgency. He looked Eliza's way and raced towards her. The entrance was inches from being secured when he whipped his hand through the gap and wrapped his fingers around the edge of the case. Eliza tugged on the door, but Grimes had strength Eliza couldn't match. She slid haphazardly towards the library as Grimes hauled the case open, her feet catching Davis's shoulder and tipping his lifeless body onto its front. The smell of death filled the passageway. Eliza wanted to cover her nose, but the tug of war she had going with Grimes wouldn't allow it. She gagged, the unbearable stench overpowering her.

She wished the movie reel inside her head would start playing. Wished Grimes would let go so she could close the door. None of it happened. There was no sensation, not even a tingle. Just the overwhelming urge to puke the rancid odour of Davis from her nostrils.

Grimes pulled the door open and Eliza had no choice but to release the handle and run for the beach. She sprinted through the darkened passage, the uneven floor testing her balance. The salty sea air dampened her skin.

"Eliza," Grimes called out behind her. "Stop."

But if there was one thing Eliza had learned over the last couple of days – it was to run. Grimes would have seen Davis's body when the door swung open and he definitely would have smelt him. Most probably, he'd already put two and two together and assumed she'd killed him.

She fled past the iron gate and found the beach. Her feet squelched through the sand as she ran for the taxi. Grimes yelled out, but it was only the echo that caught up with her.

The cab driver remained behind the wheel, and Eliza yanked the door open.

"Eliza," PC Grimes shouted.

Eliza jumped into the car. Through the windscreen, she watched the police officer racing across the beach towards them.

She turned to the cab driver. "I need to get out of here."

The cab driver hadn't noticed the police officer yet. "Show me you can pay."

Eliza glanced at Grimes. He'd almost made it to the road.

She pulled the wad of cash from her pocket and waved it in front of the cabbie. "Get me out of here right now and there'll be a couple of hundred bonus for you."

The driver started the engine and twisted in the seat. He had the car reversing back up the street and past her father's driveway before Grimes reached the road. Eliza watched him reach for his radio. The police officer who'd been standing guard outside her father's gates ran out into the road. But he could do nothing other than join his comrade and watch the taxi reversing up the narrow street.

David the cabbie manoeuvred into a turning point, used the palm of his hand to spin the steering wheel towards Fowey's town centre, and drove off. "Where am I going?"

Eliza opened the envelope and pulled out the papers. "24 Orchard Lane."

"You know you could have walked that from here, right?"

A woman's voice cackled over the radio. "0-2-9-4, can you give me your location please?"

David reached for the receiver.

Eliza stopped him. "I'll give you another hundred if you turn off the radio and your mobile."

CHAPTER SEVEN

The Sheriff stormed along the passageway.

He opened the door to the waiting room, pushed his way through the crowds, and headed straight for the door on the other side of the room. He didn't bother to knock.

Inside, electric lights led him along a white corridor. At the end, a centurion – armoured up to the hilt – guarded a black, iron gate. His parted feet stood firm, a double-ended flail gripped between both hands.

He blocked the Sheriff's path. "State your business."

"I need to speak to the Elders."

"State your business."

"I have a request."

The black gate swung open and the centurion stepped aside. "The Elders will see you."

The Sheriff shuffled past him, quicker than he wanted to, but slower than he liked. Centurions and unpredictability came hand in hand. They survived on their senses. If they sensed you were a threat, they would slaughter you and remove your soul in a heartbeat. Not even the Elders could really control them.

The Sheriff made it through the gate and into an empty room. He waited for a second entrance – doorless, with a stone surround – to manifest in front of him then stepped into the room on the other side.

Inside, a crescent table curled around him. Five grey-haired men sat in high-back chairs, each spaced exactly a meter and a half apart. The Sheriff stepped forward to where a pentagon was engraved on the marble floor. He waited while the Elders communicated telepathically with one another.

Finally, the Elder sitting in centre spoke. "State your request."

"I need a location."

"We have another escapee?"

"No. I have apprehended Roman Holbrook."

"That was not your order."

"His whereabouts became known while tracking Jacob Witenie."

The Elders conversed silently for a second. "Do we know how he escaped?"

An ache cramped the Sheriff's calf, but he didn't dare move. "Sire, he hitched a ride from the waiting room in a vessel, as Jacob Witenie did."

"And, yet, we do not sense Witenie here."

The Sheriff could bear his discomfort no longer. He shifted his feet, swallowed, and cleared his throat. "No. Holbrook killed him before I had the opportunity to return him."

"Then who is it you request to locate?"

"Holbrook's associate, Eliza Hamilton."

The Elder looked to his left and then to his right. "That name is unfamiliar to us."

"She is the vessel Witenie escaped in. She died and Holbrook resurrected her – without authorisation."

"That is not her crime."

"No, Sire, but she can be used to make Holbrook divulge how he originally escaped the chamber."

Again, the Elder in the centre turned to his colleagues. And, again, nobody spoke.

"Your request is denied."

"But, Sire—"

The Elder held up his hand. "Your request is denied. Her name has not been sent to us. She is not ours to collect."

The Sheriff bowed his head. To argue with the Elders was forbidden. He clenched his fists and nodded. He waited for the Elders to wave him off then slowly backed up through the stone opening. Once in the white room, the opening disappeared. The iron gate swung open and the centurion beckoned him out.

The Sheriff rushed back to the waiting room, but instead of heading to the torture chamber as ordered, he walked into the portal. Going back for Eliza risked his own existence, but his hatred for Roman was something he could not let go of. He knew he would never break Roman's spirit, no matter what devices he used on him. But using them on Eliza would cause pain that not even Roman could bear.

Eliza was Roman's Achilles' heel.

All he had to do was find her.

CHAPTER EIGHT

The cab pulled up outside 24 Orchard Lane.

It looked neglected and rundown. Overgrown grass swamped the front garden, weeds popped up through the cracked pathway, paint peeled away from the sills, and the guttering looked ready to fall at any moment. It was exactly the sort of place Eliza imagined Roman would live.

Although the morning sun had risen, darkness lingered behind the windows. Nobody looked to be home. Roman sure as hell wasn't there. But would anyone else be inside? A woman, maybe?

She turned to Dave the cab driver. "Wait here."

"I do have a home to get to." He paused and tilted his head. "Unless you want to pay me another two hundred?"

"Really? Another two hundred?"

"You gave it to me in Fowey."

"That was a one-off."

"You gave me a hundred just to turn off the radio."

"Which means I've paid you enough to wait for me."

"You don't pay, I'm gone as soon as you shut the car door."

Eliza clenched her jaw. She wanted to tell this idiot where to go, but she needed his car. She reached into the envelope and pulled out five twenty-pound notes. "This is all you're getting."

The driver's face brightened.

Eliza shoved the money into her coat pocket, grabbed the envelopes, and got out of the car.

"Hey," the driver called out behind her.

Eliza ducked her head. "You'll get it when I come back."

She slammed the door shut, heard him shout something, and crossed the road towards the house.

Reaching the porch, she rang the bell. It just seemed the right thing to do. When no bell chimed and nobody came to the door, she reached for the handle, unsurprised to find the door unlocked. She glanced over her shoulder towards the driver. He'd nestled back into his seat, the morning paper once again open across the steering wheel. Behind him, no twitching curtains betrayed nosey neighbours playing neighbourhood watch. The last thing Eliza needed was the police turning up. Satisfied she wasn't being observed, she opened the door and entered.

How the hell could anybody live like this? Pizza boxes and old newspapers were stacked high in the corner of the hallway. Unopened letters littered a small table. Eliza listened for any sound: a television, a running shower, but the house was deadly silent.

"Hello?" she called out. "I'm a friend of Roman's. Is anyone home?"

She waited for an answer, but only the tick of the grandfather clock in the far corner replied, telling her that time was running out. She walked into the kitchen. It was just as messy as the hallway. She glanced around. What the hell was she looking for, anyway? She opened the fridge without knowing why. There wasn't a lot inside: a couple of beers and some mouldy cheese. She closed the door, turned, and leaned against it. In front of her, the wooden kitchen table had a drawer. She pulled it open and began to rifle through a stack of take away menus and old utility bills – each addressed to *the occupier*. Well, all but one, which was addressed to Roman Holbrook. Eliza opened the letter. It was nothing exciting. Just a magazine subscription to Men's Health.

Eliza turned to the worktop. Pulling open several drawers, all she found was cutlery and dirty tea towels. The cupboards were no better – light on food and cleaning products.

She rested her hands on her hips and took a deep breath. For some reason, she had thought her quest to locate Roman's brother would be a little easier. She exhaled, reasoning that nothing about Roman was simple, and left the kitchen.

A couple of old chairs, a bean bag, and a television spruced up the living room. Like in her father's library, she doubted she'd find anything useful down the sides of the armchairs but checked anyway, uncovering some loose change and an empty crisp bag – chicken flavoured. She sighed and dropped it back on the cushion. Yawning, she stretched the tiredness from her muscles. She still had upstairs to check. Her mouth dried. If she found no information up there then it was game over. Roman and Billy would be lost to Purgatory forever.

She hurried back through the hallway and headed upstairs. The first floor was bigger than she had thought it would be. There were four rooms in total: a small toilet, the bathroom beside it, and two rooms that looked out over the street. The first room was completely empty, containing no bed or furniture of any kind. It was just four walls and a light bulb hanging from the ceiling. The second room was how she would have imagined Roman's bedroom to be – devoid of any furniture other than a bed, a small side table, and a really, really old television set.

Eliza waved the waft of rotting food and stale odour away from her nose. This was a waste of time. There was nothing in here that would lead her to Roman's brother. The built-in wardrobe door was open. No clothes hung on the hangers. No secret shoebox was hidden away in the corner. She walked around the unmade bed. No curtains hung at the window and, outside, she saw the cab remained parked by the roadside. She sat on the corner of the bed, the mattress sinking so low she almost slid off. Returning to her father's house was out of the question, which left her with nowhere else to go.

Her fingers tapped her knee. She bit down on pursed lips. What was she missing? Roman had been alive forever. There had to be some trace of his existence somewhere. She lay back on the bed and stared up at the stained ceiling. How many times had Roman laid here staring at that same stain? Eliza closed her eyes. She thought back to the motel room and how it had felt being held in his arms. In that moment, he'd made her feel like the most important thing in the world.

She bolted upright. His Aston Martin – his pride and joy. She'd bet his whole life was in that car. But where in the hell was it? Police impound, maybe?

"Hey, you up there?" Dave yelled out.

Eliza heard him climbing the stairs. "I'm up here."

The driver reached the landing then disappeared. A moment later, Eliza heard the toilet flush.

He entered the bedroom still doing up his flies. "God, what's that smell?"

"Do you have a mobile on you?"

"Yeah, why?"

"Because I need to borrow it."

Dave pulled it from his back pocket. He held it out then thought better of it and snatched it away. "How much?"

"For the phone?"

"To use the phone."

"Are you serious?"

"Hey, I should be home sleeping right now."

"I'm not giving you any more money."

The driver waved the phone at her.

"Fine, another fifty on top of the hundred I owe you."

Dave smiled. He handed Eliza the phone, took it back to unlock it, and passed it over. "Who you ringing?"

"Not ringing. Googling."

Dave sat beside her. She didn't know what smelt worse – Roman's bedroom or the driver's body odour.

She surfed the Internet, finally finding the address for the police impound. "Can you take me to Liskeard?"

"Liskeard? How much more driving are we gonna be doing today?"

"You know you're going to be paid, so stop your bitching."

"Another two hundred?"

"To go to Looe? No. I'll round off the one fifty I owe you to two hundred."

The driver contemplated the offer. "Mind if I go raid the kitchen?"

"Knock yourself out."

Eliza lay back on the bed and settled her gaze on the stained ceiling again. If she tried to talk her way in, she'd be recognised in minutes. Could she send in Dave the driver? She tilted her head and studied the vodka bottle on the bedside table. If it hadn't already been empty, she'd have drained it dry herself.

She sat up again. She'd just have to wing it. She stood and turned for the door and that's when she saw it – the tiniest piece of paper sticking up through the floorboards beneath the TV.

She quickly moved the wobbly stall to one side and knelt. Her nails were shot to pieces; not one had survived the conflict of the last few days. Trying to pick the paper out was impossible; she couldn't get a sturdy pinch on its corner. She looked for the end of the floorboard, found it, and tried to lift it. It wasn't nailed down, but it was wedged between the others pretty damn snug. She searched the bedroom for anything that could impersonate a jimmy or lever. Her gaze swung back to the empty vodka bottle. She grabbed it and hit it against the bedside table. The bottle broke into two halves. She jammed the sharpest point into the gap top right of the board's corner and levered it up and down until the board caught and began to lift. She didn't need it to rise much before her fingers were able to grip it and prise it the rest of the way.

The driver ran into the room. "I heard glass breaking."

Eliza ignored him. Adrenaline buzzed through her like she'd just found buried treasure. She threw the board to one side and reached for the paper. It was nothing but a scrunched up piece of scrap. Her heart sank a little. She unfolded it. No name. No information. No 'X' marks the spot for Roman's brother. Just a telephone number scribbled in red biro. An unrecognisable area code that would probably lead her to the local takeaway.

She dialled the number anyway.

There were four long rings and then an answer machine kicked in.

"You've reached Tavistock Investigations. Nobody is free to take your call, so please leave a message and number, and we'll get right back to you."

Eliza hung up. It could be nothing. But, then, what else did she have to go on? On the one hand, she was close to Liskeard and the police impound, but, on the other hand, she would probably get arrested on sight. If she travelled over to Tavistock, maybe she'd find something to help her.

The impound made more sense, but her gut screamed that Tavistock held the answers.

She tapped the name into the driver's phone and found the address. "I need to go to Tavistock."

The driver sighed. "That's a good hour and a half away."

"And you'll be compensated for it."

Eliza hurried for the stairs. She grabbed one of Roman's baseball caps from the coat hook by the front door – a navy Timberland one – pulled it on her head, and headed out to the car. She was already seated and buckled in when Dave got in beside her.

He opened his mouth to speak, but Eliza held up a wad of cash – the two hundred she owed him plus another two hundred.

The cabbie started the car.

CHAPTER NINE

The large, oak door swung open.

The two guards turned to face Roman, the first time since being stationed to watch him. Thomas Blood led two other guards into the room, their hoods pulled down over their heads, the shadows hiding their faces.

Thomas headed in his direction, which meant only one thing – Roman was next in line to suffer their torment. His stomach tightened and he closed his eyes. Swallowing back his fear, he prayed one of the other prisoners would take Blood's fancy instead. But he knew their orders concerning whom to mutilate and torture next would have come from the Sheriff. In a few hours, like Billy, he would be dead.

Thomas waited while the guards grabbed Roman's shackles and unlocked them. Roman grimaced. His dislocated thumb was nowhere near healed. The iron clamps released his wrists and he clasped his hand close. Endless escape options scrolled through his mind. He could fight his way out of the chamber. He glanced at the oak door. Beyond was a maze of passages and corridors, all of which would be crawling with the Sheriff's henchmen moments after news of his escape broke. He released his hand, not wanting to draw too much attention to it, and looked across at Billy. Even if he did escape and found his way back to Eliza, how would he explain leaving her brother behind? But, then, what was the alternative? To be tortured again and again for all eternity?

The guards unlocked the manacles around Roman's ankles. Before they had a chance to stand again, Roman kicked one over and punched down onto the base of the other's neck. Thomas leapt at him and Roman caught him mid-flight around the neck. Thomas swung at Roman and a glint of silver caught the light. Roman blocked his strike and rammed him back into the rock. He gripped his wrist, kneed him in the stomach, and whacked his hand against the wall. The blade fell from Thomas's grip and Roman punched him in the side of the face. Thomas fought back, but Roman threw him to the ground. He kicked Thomas in stomach and followed up with a kick to his face.

Roman's path to the door was free. No other guards were around to give chase or block his escape. So, Roman ran. Murmurs for help came from the other prisoners, like they had the night Roman had first escaped. And, like that night, Roman ignored them. He reached the door, grabbed the handle – and stopped. He couldn't leave Billy.

Yes, you can.

But returning without him would destroy Eliza.

So, tell her you didn't find him. Tell her he's dead.

Roman twisted the handle. He couldn't leave Billy behind. Having Eliza in his life had changed him; it had changed the way he thought. The guards got to their feet, shaken and disorientated. They saw Roman and their expressions relayed their surprise at being spared having to chase him through the tunnels. Roman released the handle and raised his hands in surrender. The guards stepped towards him – hesitantly. Simultaneously, they reached for him – each grabbing an arm and securing it behind his back.

When Roman declined to resist, their grip tightened, their confidence returning. He glanced back at the door and questioned whether he'd made the right choice. He thought of Eliza and didn't question it anymore.

The guards tried to walk Roman forward, but he dug his heels in. Hours of agonising pain on one of the devices awaited him; he certainly wasn't going to make it easy for the guards to get him there. The guards gripped tighter. One punched Roman in the gut. Roman doubled forward and the other guard followed up with what felt like a chop to the back of his head. Roman fell to his knees, the wind knocked out of him. He coughed and took a moment to suck new air into his lungs. He glanced up, his eye-line waist-height with the guard to his left.

Roman punched through his captor's robe, smashing him straight in the groin. The guard dropped to his knees. He tried to curl over, but Roman grabbed him by the ears. Rage broke through Roman's fear and he smashed his forehead against the guard's nose. The oak door opened and Roman turned, ready to take on whatever came his way. More guards – three of them – ran into the room. They charged towards him and before he had a chance to get to his feet, they were upon him. Two of them pinned down his arms; the third clamped him tight around the neck.

Roman fought their hold but made little leeway. The guard he'd head-butted rose gingerly to his feet. He wiped a trickle of blood from his nose and turned to the table to his left. He reached for the tongue-tearer.

"The Sheriff said the rack." Thomas was back on his feet. "How do you expect me to question him if he has no tongue to answer me with?"

The guard's fingers slipped away from the scissor-like device. He bowed his head and muttered an apology then, along with another guard, got to work untying the prisoner already stretched out on the rack. They let his body drop through the frame onto the ground. With the rack now empty, the remaining guards were quick to drag Roman towards it. Roman tensed and dug his heels into the dirt. He struggled against their hold, glancing around for anything to help him get free. The guards lifted him onto the frame. Roman squirmed and kicked out. It took all four of them to hold him steady while the fifth guard secured the ropes around his wrists and ankles. Roman hung there suspended while the previous occupant was dragged out from beneath him and carried away.

Thomas stepped forward. He leaned over, his stench engulfing Roman. "The Sheriff wants to know how you escaped last time, and don't say you fought your way out."

Roman snorted and turned his head.

Thomas grabbed his throat. His nails dug deep and he forced Roman to face him again. "You will tell me, Roman. The only question you have to ask yourself is how much entertainment you're prepared to provide until then."

Roman pulled on the rope restraints. Thomas smiled, Roman's vulnerability clearly amusing him.

"Prepare him," Thomas ordered his men.

The guards stepped forward, tearing Roman's jumper off him.

Roman tried to relax. He attempted to con himself into believing his immediate fate wouldn't be all that bad. The ropes chafed his skin and his tremors worsened. Pain gripped his chest. Memories of his last experience on the rack resurfaced. Again, he pulled against the ropes that bound him, dreading that first turn of the crank.

It didn't come. What were the guards waiting for?

From this angle, Roman's view was limited. He stretched his neck and searched the room for Thomas. He wouldn't have left – not when things were about to get good.

"Don't worry. I'm still here." Thomas approached Roman from behind. He leaned over the top of Roman's head and held out a silver object. "Recognise this?"

The lead sprinkler. Oh, Roman remembered it, all right. How could he forget?

Thomas handed the sprinkler to a guard and Roman's gaze followed it across the room to where a large fire pit burned. Another guard filled it with molten lead and tremors rocked Roman's whole body. He clenched his fists and grit his teeth, biting back the scream that wanted to escape.

Thomas placed his hands on the crank's handle. His fingers wrapped around the wooden pole. "Last chance to make this easy on yourself."

Roman found a smile. "Fuck you."

Thomas returned the smile – only bigger. "You never fail to disappoint me."

He pulled the handle down. The ratchet turned. One notch. Two. Three.

Roman heard the wooden rollers rotate. The tension in the ropes around his hands and feet tightened. His limbs stretched, having no choice but to go with it. Roman's body lifted in line with the frame, his joints close to popping.

Pain burned his muscles and Roman swallowed back the agony. To cry out now would be futile, especially when there was so much worse to come.

"Come, come, Roman. Everything you make me do to you, the Sheriff has promised he will also inflict on the girl."

"Go fuck yourself."

Thomas turned the crank again.

A scream gurgled in the back of Roman's throat, but he refused to give Thomas the pleasure of seeing him in pain so early on.

"You can spare her this agonising pain, Roman." Thomas turned the crank again. "Just tell me how you escaped."

"I hitched a lift out of the waiting room."

"The Sheriff knows that. We all know that after the whole Jacob episode." Another turn of the crank. "No, the Sheriff wants to know how you escaped the torture room."

"Just lucky, I guess."

Thomas turned the crank again.

Roman's ligament snapped. His shoulder splintered from the socket. He couldn't halt the cry from passing his lips.

"Imagine how the girl's cries will sound."

Sweat trickled down Roman's face. "You're dead when I get off this thing."

"You'll be dead by the time you get off." Thomas took the lead sprinkler from the guard. "This is your last chance to save yourself, Roman. Tell me how you escaped."

Roman took a deep breath but couldn't quite hold it. He released it and sucked in several smaller breaths.

"Suit yourself." Thomas turned to the guard. "Fix the eye clamps."

Two guards came over. One secured Roman's head in a vice-like grip while the other pulled his lids open. Air quickly dried Roman's eyes and he tried unsuccessfully to blink. A third guard appeared holding two metal rings. Wire hooks curled out around the edges like eyelashes around the eye. He pushed the first one over Roman's left socket. The hooks scratched against his eye and curled beneath his lid. The guard twisted a small lever and the clamp secured the lid in place. Then he did the same to Roman's right eye. The hooks felt like pins piercing his eyelids. All three guards stepped back. Roman tried to blink, but the clamps held his eyes wide open.

Thomas stepped forward. Roman's breathing accelerated.

Thomas raised the sprinkler above Roman's face. "You'll wish you talked."

He shook the silver rattle and molten lead dripped out.

Droplets landed on Roman's cheeks, his forehead, inside his mouth.

Roman's body tightened further. He yelled out, thrashing side to side as much as his restraints allowed.

Thomas lowered the sprinkler above Roman's right eye.

Roman tried to turn away but couldn't. He watched the droplet fall from the sprinkler. It landed in his eye and spread out along his lid. Blindness quickly took hold. A scream gurgled past his lips. He heard himself begin to beg for mercy, but pride stopped him from finishing the sentence.

His left eye watched the next three droplets follow the first.

And, finally, he screamed.

CHAPTER TEN

Tavistock was wide-awake and open for business.

Dave pulled off the main road and onto a small industrial estate. It was made up of reasonably sized units – apart from the one he stopped outside, which was no bigger than a residential garage. A small, Perspex sign displaying 'Tavistock Investigations' was screwed to the right-hand side of the entrance.

Eliza unclipped her seatbelt. "Wait here. I'll only be a minute."

"You keep saying that."

"And you keep getting paid for it."

She got out of the car and approached the building. The door was locked, so she pressed the intercom button. There was no answer. She walked to the window and peered inside, but the blinds were pulled and all she could see were several dead flies on the sill.

She walked back to the door and pressed the buzzer again. When no one answered the second time, she picked up a small rock from a neglected flowerbed. She hadn't survived the last twenty-four hours only to be stopped by a locked door. She glanced around. Lucky for her, the industrial estate seemed to be the quietest place on earth and vacant of any workforce.

Eliza turned to the frosted glass that made up the top part of the front door. Like the window, a blind blocked any view inside. She gripped the rock, took a deep breath, and whacked it against the glass. A hairline splinter cracked the corner of the window. Dismal, even for a first attempt. She whacked it again, minus the apprehension she'd felt before. The glass shattered. Shards fell, some landing around her feet but most falling inside on the mat. Eliza reached through, unlocked the door, and swiftly slipped inside.

The reception area was tiny – just spacious enough for the vacant desk, which was by the far wall. A computer lead remained plugged in, but the laptop itself was missing, and a dying plant drooped in a terracotta pot in the corner. Behind the desk was a door. She turned the handle, expecting it to be locked.

It wasn't.

She swallowed. Her heart raced and she knew she should feel scared – or at least a little nervous. But she didn't. She felt exhilarated. Maybe it was desperation; maybe it was fortitude. Whatever the feeling that raced through her veins, it made her hungry to find Roman's brother.

She stepped inside, relieved to have a little more space to think, and headed straight for the filing cabinet. It was black. Four-drawers tall. Would it be too much to ask to find one big, fat file labelled *Roman Holbrook* nestled inside?

The top drawer opened. Security definitely wasn't high on this firm's agenda. Squashed inside, a number of files hung on the runner. They didn't appear to be in a particular order, either alphabetically or numerically. Half were listed by surname, some by forename. Others were arranged by an ID number and the rest were just blank.

Eliza fingered her way through them, her eyes scanning the paperwork inside for certain words: Roman, Holbrook, Nate/Nathaniel. Even her own name or her father's. She finished searching the last file, finding nothing that could help her. Three more to go. She closed the drawer and slid open the one below. Inside were more files, again in no particular order – or at least none that she could see.

Eliza wasn't even halfway through when she heard the front door open. She quietly closed the cabinet and crept to the office door. In the foyer, glass crunched under foot. She pressed her ear to the door and heard someone creeping across the reception. Somebody was out there. Eliza backed up into the room and searched for somewhere to hide.

The handle turned and the office door slowly opened. It was cliché, but Eliza ducked behind the desk. The most predictable place to hide and more than likely the first place anyone would look for her. Shoes squeaked as they walked across the room. Six steps and the squeaking stopped. Then silence.

Eliza waited, but nobody called out. Someone was there, though. She could hear them breathing. She wanted to peer out and see who was in the room. If it was the cab driver then she was wasting time hiding when she could be searching.

Finally, impatience got the better of her. She leaned forward and looked around the end of the desk. Two black, leather shoes stood in front of her, both worn and severely scuffed around the toes. Eliza glanced up.

A young-looking chap stared down at her. "Who the hell are you?"

Eliza crawled out from under the desk. "I need to ask you some questions."

"Forget it. I'm calling the police." He reached over the desk and grabbed the phone.

"Don't," Eliza said, getting to her feet.

The man paused mid-dial.

"Are you the investigator who owns this place?"

"I am."

"Then I need to ask you some questions."

"You need to ask me?" He laughed. "You just broke into my office. I'm the one who needs to be asking the questions."

"I know this looks bad." Eliza motioned for him to put the phone down. "If you just give me a chance to explain..."

"Why did you break in?"

"Because you didn't answer."

The young man raised his eyebrows.

"I need some information."

"I need a holiday in Hawaii, but I'm not going to break into an airport and stow away on a plane to get it." He began to dial again.

"Please," Eliza pleaded, but it was clear the man had finished listening to her.

He held the phone to his ear. "Yes, police please..."

"I just need to ask you about a person," Eliza said. "A man named Roman Holbrook."

The man glanced towards the filing cabinet. The second drawer down wasn't quite closed. "You been going through my files?"

"I just need some help—"

"Yes. I want to report a break-in," he said into the phone. "The thief is still on the premises. My address—"

Eliza slapped the phone from his hand.

His shock quickly turned to anger.

He grabbed Eliza by the shoulders and shoved her back against the wall. "I suggest you stay put." He glared at her then turned to retrieve the phone.

Eliza remained against the wall like she was glued there. She didn't need to move to stop him. Rage took over and the movie reel began to play. Before the man had time to grab the phone, it slid from his grasp and scooted across the floor. He watched it smash against the skirting board.

"Do you know a man named Roman Holbrook?" Eliza asked.

The man didn't move. He didn't speak. He just continued to stare at the broken phone.

"Hey," Eliza shouted. "I need to ask you about Roman Holbrook."

The man glanced up at her, eyes wide, his skin pale. Light tremors shook his hands. "Did you see that? It moved on its own."

Eliza moved away from the wall. "Yes. Now I need to know if you've heard the name Roman Holbrook."

The man turned from her and looked back at the phone. "How did it do that?"

Eliza was getting nowhere. She seized the man by the shoulders and turned him to face her. "I need you to focus on me for a moment."

The man settled his gaze on her.

"Do you know a man called Roman Holbrook? Yes or no."

The man was quiet for a second or two.

"My files are confidential," he finally whispered.

"Yes, but I need to know. Lives depend on it."

"My clients expect full privacy."

Eliza took a deep breath. "If you don't tell me, that phone is going to fly back here and whack you on the side of the head, you hear? Now tell me about Roman Holbrook."

Again, the man glanced warily at the phone. "He said he'd break my legs if I ever mentioned him to anyone."

Sounds like Roman. Eliza twisted the man around to face her again. "Did he hire you?"

"He hired my great grandfather, who passed the business on..." The man shook his head. "You know how these hand-me-downs work."

"What did he hire you for?"

"He'll kill me if I talk."

"He's dead." She wasn't exactly lying.

The man's eyes focused a little. "Dead?"

Eliza nodded. "So, you can talk to me and you'll be fine."

The man swallowed. He gave the phone another glance, probably to check it was still there. Then he got to his feet and perched on the corner of the desk. "I hate this bastard business." He felt his forehead then used his sleeve to pat down his neck.

Eliza didn't have time to play Dr. Phil. "What did Roman hire you for?"

The man sighed. "To find his brother."

Eliza's heart skipped a beat. "And did you? Find him, I mean?"

The man nodded. "My great grandfather did, decades ago. Christ, a century, even."

"A century?" And, just like that, Eliza's excitement died a little. "So, you have no up-to-date information on where his brother is now?"

"No, I do. This Holbrook guy wanted constant updates." The man got up and walked to the filing cabinet. He bent for the bottom drawer and paused. "He's definitely dead? You're absolutely certain of that?"

Eliza nodded. "At this moment in time, he no longer walks this earth."

"Huh." The guy snorted. He opened the draw, reached towards the back, pulled out the thickest file Eliza had ever seen, and passed it to her. "Everything you want to know is in there."

Eliza didn't mean to, but she snatched it from his hand. It weighed a ton. Inside was a collection of paperwork and photos – lots of photos – all featuring the same man and woman.

"This is his brother?" She pointed at the man.

The young investigator nodded.

"Who's the woman?"

The man's face paled. He swallowed and pink blemishes blotted his neck. Eliza turned her attention back to the photos. On the backs were dates – months and years – starting way back in 1919 and finishing this summer just gone. With every year that passed in each picture, the woman aged. Roman's brother, however, did not. A baby joined the photographs in March 1924. A girl who, like the woman, grew up throughout the pictures. In 1963, the woman, now looking aged and frail, disappeared. Then it was just Roman's brother and the girl, or woman as she was then – until 1987.

"What happened to them?" Eliza asked.

The man shrugged. "They got old and died. It's all in the file. I think cancer finally took the girl."

"Who were they?"

"His wife and child."

Eliza looked at the pictures again. So, Roman's brother had found a family to love. He also didn't age. Did that mean Roman didn't age either? It would make sense, seeing how old he was supposed to be.

"Did Roman ever visit his brother?"

Again, the man shrugged. "I have no idea. I don't care either. He'd just barge in here every six months or so and ask for an update. Never wanted to take the photos or the file. Would just glance at them once then tell me to burn them."

"But you didn't, obviously."

"My dad always told me to keep them. I guess he thought he might need them one day." He paused. "You can see the guy in the photo isn't aging, can't you? This Roman bloke was the same, you know. He didn't age either."

"Yeah, well, there's a lot to be said about moisturising." Eliza paused on a photo from 2013. It showed a building – The Rectory Farm Tea Rooms. "What's this?"

The man leaned close. He pointed at the photo. "Not the tea room. See the church just beyond? That's where you'll find the brother."

"Where is it?"

"It's the Church of St Morwenna and John the Baptist. Morwenstow."

CHAPTER ELEVEN

The Sheriff marched straight up to the gates.

An officer stood guard. He straightened as the Sheriff passed but didn't question his reason for being there. Why would he? The Sheriff was one of them again, his dirty, black hair now copying Billy's cut, and his long overcoat replaced with an identical police uniform. The Sheriff cast a sideways glance at the gates – still broken from where Eliza and Roman had smashed their way through a couple of days earlier. He clenched his fists. He'd had both Roman and Jacob in the palm of his hand and still they had managed to escape. The first of many mistakes on his part, mistakes he swore he would not be making again.

He looked at the officer. He was young, no older than twenty, and a thought occurred to him – maybe the officer knew of Eliza's whereabouts. It could certainly save the Sheriff some time.

"I'm looking for Eliza," he said.

"You and everyone else."

"She's been here?"

"Been and gone." The officer nodded up towards the house. "They're trying to track the cab now."

The Sheriff turned and looked at the mansion. It was evident he needed somebody more senior. Somebody who knew what was going on.

The winding driveway seemed longer than he remembered. Four police cars curved around the fountain outside, two of them labelled with forensic stickers. It meant more people inside. Certainly not ideal, but he pushed the door open and entered anyway.

There were no officers in the foyer and none on the stairs. The Sheriff listened for people. He heard a little movement upstairs, but it was the murmur of voices that caught his attention. He looked to his left. The library door was open and light flooded through into the hallway.

"Hey," a voice called from behind.

The Sheriff turned.

"Billy?" An officer half walked half trotted down the stairs.

The officer's epaulette number read 7865. The stripes made him a constable. No name, though.

"What the hell is going on?" the officer said.

"What do you mean?"

"What do I mean? Christ." The officer ran a hand through his hair. He took the Sheriff by the shoulder and moved him across the corridor and into the billiards room. He closed the door behind him. "Your dad's butler has been found dead."

"So? He was old."

The officer frowned. He watched the Sheriff for a moment. "He was found dead in a hidden tunnel behind some secret bookcase doorway in the library."

The Sheriff wasn't concerned by this news. "Has the girl returned yet?"

"Girl? You mean your sister?"

"Yes, Eliza. My sister."

Again, the officer frowned. "Billy, two bodies have been found in your flat." He paused. "One was Eddie. Two others were found mutilated outside."

The Sheriff allowed himself a small smile. Not his finest work, but inventive considering the lack of time he'd had.

"Billy, are you okay?"

The Sheriff looked at him. "I'm fine. I'm just looking for Eliza. My sister."

"She was here. Earlier. Grimes had her, but she ran. That's when your father's butler was discovered."

"Where is Eliza now?"

"Drove off in some cab."

The Sheriff waited. "And? Where did she go?"

"PNC came back with the cabbie's address."

"What is it?"

The officer shrugged. "Grimes is heading over there now."

"I need it."

"Billy, you're wanted for questioning. You have to come to the station."

"Why?"

"Why? What do you mean *why*? For everything I've just told you."

The Sheriff sighed. It seemed Billy's persona was becoming a hindrance. "What is your name?"

"What?" Again, the frown. "Brian. You know that."

The Sheriff grabbed the man by the throat. "Brian what?"

The man tried to scream, but the Sheriff squeezed tighter. "Answer me, or I will pop your eyeballs out."

The officer struggled to speak. "Ro...Rob...Roberts."

"Thank you."

The Sheriff reached into the officer's mouth, pinched hold of his tongue, and ripped it clean out of his mouth. The man began to choke, drowning in his own blood. The Sheriff released him and the officer ran for the door. The Sheriff put out his foot. The man tripped, his face smashing against the floor. The Sheriff stood over him. The officer rolled onto his back and stared up at him, eyes wide. He tried to scream, but only a hoarse whisper left his throat. Certainly nothing loud enough to alert anyone as to what was happening.

The Sheriff relaxed and inhaled. Billy's bones cracked and realigned. His body stretched a good foot taller. His muscles inflated and expanded. Billy's slim stomach enlarged into a paunch. The fat tissue swelled.

The officer below him tried calling for help again, still only emanating the same husky whisper. When the Sheriff felt his transformation was complete, he lifted his foot and stamped down onto the officer's head. Only when he felt the carpet below did he remove his foot. He crossed the room to the curtains and wiped the pieces of brain from his shoe. Then he reached for his radio.

"This is Officer Roberts. I need the address of the cab driver."

CHAPTER TWELVE

Two long hours.

That was how long Eliza had endured Dave the cabbie belly-aching on about how he should be at home sleeping instead of driving her around the Cornish countryside. But it had all been worthwhile.

They left the smoothness of the tarmacked road and bounced haphazardly in their seats while the car navigated dried, churned-up mud. Just beyond a small, country pub, she saw The Rectory Farm Tea Rooms – looking just as it had in the photograph.

Dave stopped the cab and pulled up the handbrake. "Right, there's your church. Now where's my money?"

Eliza looked out the window. Other than the tea rooms and a small, stone building opposite, there was nothing but fields and trees. "I don't see the church."

Dave pointed towards a single-track lane, not big enough to take a vehicle. "You walk from here."

Eliza sighed. She reached into the envelope, counted out ten more twenty-pound notes, and handed the cash to the driver.

Dave took the money. "I'm not waiting for you anymore."

"Let me just make sure—"

"No. I'm going home."

Eliza thought about offering him more money to stay but, honestly, she couldn't take another minute of him. She opened the door and, without thanking him, set off for the church. When she checked over her shoulder, Dave had beached the cab in a pile of mud while attempting to turn around.

Eliza smiled and continued walking.

Just as he'd promised, the tree-tunnelled dirt-track led Eliza straight to the Church of St Morwenna and John the Baptist – and seemed to be the only way in and out. In fact, the church was set so far off the beaten track, Eliza wondered if it was still in service. She followed the path through an overgrown graveyard where the ground swallowed collapsing tombs, and moss covered lopsided and crumbling gravestones. Beyond them, there was nothing but velvet, green fields with views as far as the eye could see.

The church itself was a beautiful, stone building, complete with a slate roof, tower, and a hundred other original features. The picturesque scene was in total contrast to where Roman resided. Eliza approached the entrance, where stone arches framed two wooden doors. She wasn't sure whether to knock or just let herself in.

She went with a knock.

The thickness of the wood drowned out the tiny rap of her knuckles, so she twisted the wrought-iron handle and let herself in.

Her footsteps, although careful, echoed around the nave. She stopped when she reached the first of the pews. The aisle between them led down to a beautifully carved pulpit. Behind that, the chancel sat beneath a beautiful picture-window showing Jesus Christ hanging from the True Cross. Eliza walked down the aisle. She wasn't a religious person by anyone's standards. But there was something about the way the sunlight caught the colours in the stained glass...something about the way the pieces glistened across her apparent ancestor. It was mesmerising. Maybe it was all the more striking because, like Jesus before her, she'd been hanging from the same cross less than a week before.

"I know exactly how you feel," she muttered.

"Hello? Can I help you?"

The voice, male, jolted her from her thoughts. She turned to see a familiar looking man walking down the aisle towards her. At first, she thought it was Roman. That he'd escaped and somehow found a way back. Her first instinct was to run to him and she nearly did. But as the man neared, she registered the minor differences. Roman was slightly taller, and a little leaner. This man didn't have a scar curving his lips or a cocky swagger in his walk.

"Nathaniel?"

The man slowed his pace. He eyed her warily. "I'm sorry. You must be mistaken—"

Excitement fluttered inside Eliza's stomach and she opened the file. "This is you."

She offered over the pictures.

The man glanced at the file. He reached for a photo – one with his wife and daughter. "Where did you get these? Who are you?"

"I'm a friend of your brother's."

The man stifled a cough. He handed back the photos. "I don't have a brother. I am sorry if I have wasted your time." He turned to leave.

"Nathaniel."

The man paused. He turned, slowly, to face her again. "I told you, I—"

"He said you used to be best friends." Eliza made up the space between them. She started up at the man. His eyes were softer than Roman's and lured her in. She reached for his hand, her intention to beg for help, but no words came.

The man gazed back and, for a moment, neither of them moved. Excitement fluttered inside Eliza's stomach once more.

Nathaniel. She blinked and released his hand.

The man looked taken aback. A light frown creased his brow and he cleared his throat. "You have the wrong person. I am sorry, but I cannot help you."

"If you don't help me, we are both going to lose a brother. Maybe you can live with that, but I can't."

"And I told you, I don't have a brother."

"You may not like your brother, but you cannot deny that you have one."

The man sighed. He closed his eyes and muttered something under his breath. When he opened them again, they were clouded with sadness. "How did you find me?"

"So, you are Nathaniel?"

"I haven't gone by that name for many, many years. It's just Nate, now." He reached for the file and started to look through the pictures. "Where did you get these?"

"Your brother had them. He told me to find you."

"My brother would not ask that of anyone, no matter what trouble he was in."

"Yeah, well, it isn't just him who's in trouble. Others are too."

"What a surprise," Nate scoffed. He glanced up from the folder. "You don't know my brother very well, do you?"

"Meaning?"

"Meaning, my brother does not care for anyone other than himself."

Eliza sighed. "You're right, I haven't known him for very long. Less than a week, in fact."

Nate laughed and shook his head like she was a love-struck child.

"And," Eliza swallowed the building resentment, "he is one massive arsehole—"

"I stand corrected. It appears you do know my brother."

She continued. "Who sacrificed his own life to save mine."

"Let me guess. You had an affair with him? It ended and he gave you the *it's-me-not-you* speech?"

"You couldn't be further from the truth."

Nate scoffed. Again, he shook his head in a belittling manner. "Look, you seem like a nice, young lady."

She felt her cheeks redden. "Wow, you're a condescending dickhead, just like he is."

Nate dropped the smile. "I didn't mean—"

"Look, I am not stupid. My eyes are wide open where your brother is concerned. Your brother is a selfish, arrogant, male chauvinist pig. First time I met him, he shoved me into the boot of his Aston."

"That sounds like Roman."

Eliza took a deep breath. "But he needs your help. I need your help."

Nate looked at the photos before him. He traced the outline of his wife's face. Sadness clouded his eyes. Then he slammed the file shut.

"No. I will not get drawn back into Roman's world, and if you have any sense, you won't either. Now you must leave." He thrust the folder towards Eliza.

She half caught it, and a handful of photos and papers fell across the floor. She watched Nate storm up the aisle away from her.

"I'd expect this arrogance from Roman," she threw the folder to the floor and the noise reverberated around the Church, "but you're supposed to be a man of the cloth. It's your job to help people in need."

"My brother is poison. My job is to keep that evil out of this house."

Eliza raced up the aisle. She passed Nate and blocked his path. "Are you listening to anything I'm saying? Roman is with my brother. They will both die if you don't help me."

Nate laughed, but it was half-hearted, more of a reflex. "I'm sure Roman is where he should be."

"And my brother? Should he be there too?"

"Why not? If he's an associate of Roman's—"

"He isn't. He was a police officer...is still a police officer."

Nate didn't respond. He studied her for a moment, his eyes flitting across her face, her hair, her neckline. His gaze met hers, but he immediately broke eye contact. He turned from her and began to gather the photos from the floor. Eliza remained quiet, giving him the time to think, hoping he would see reason.

Nate closed the file and stood to face her. "Here."

He handed her the file, but Eliza declined to take it. "You really shouldn't waste your time on my brother."

"He is in this mess because of me."

"He strung you that line, did he?"

Back to square one. Eliza took the file. "Please, you have to help me."

Nate stared at her for a good thirty seconds before he blinked. "I really need you to go."

"Your brother is in trouble."

"So you keep saying. But let me tell you something about Roman." Nate spun her towards the door, his hands lingering on her shoulders. "He is always in trouble."

"How can you be so cold?"

Nate urged her forward.

Eliza dug her heels in but couldn't stop Nate from guiding her to the church entrance. "Would God approve of what you're doing?"

"I'm sure God hates him as much as I do."

"What kind of clergyman are you?" Eliza reached the door. It was open from when she'd entered. A cool breeze hit her face and she began to realise that her one chance to save Roman and her brother was slipping away. "I thought Roman was supposed to be the bastard brother. I stand corrected."

"Your anger is not your fault, I know that. My brother manipulates people. Women mostly. He messes with their minds and twists things around, but he cares for nobody other than himself. Trust me."

Eliza shrugged away from him. "He mourned you after you died. Did he ever tell you that? He drank himself into oblivion."

Again, sadness touched Nate's eyes. "I cannot expect you to understand."

"What? That you sent him to Purgatory?"

Nate's eyes narrowed.

"Because that's where he is right now. With my brother. That's where he would be sent, right? Being a reaper and all." She let that revelation sink in. "Trust me. I understand everything perfectly."

Nate stiffened. "How do you know all that?"

"Roman told me."

"That he went to Purgatory?"

"Yes. Maybe you sent him there out of revenge because he had an affair with your wife."

Nate glared at her and Eliza immediately regretted bringing his wife into this whole mess.

Nate stepped away from the door and walked back to the pew. He leant against it and crossed his arms. "Is that what your files say?"

"No."

"There is no way Roman told you all that."

Eliza shrugged. She finally had his attention.

Nate stared at the file. Eliza thought about handing it over and letting him see for himself that it didn't contain anything about his previous life.

"When you say my brother sacrificed himself to save you, what do you mean?"

"I'm a mind mover."

Nate's eyes widened. "Jesus Christ. Now his involvement with you makes sense."

He stood and paced the floor. Eliza hadn't expected the revelation to make him so angry.

"You know, you almost had me believing." Nate didn't stop pacing. He ran his hands through his hair, exactly the same way Roman did. "But he hasn't changed one bit." He stopped abruptly and turned to her. "Did my beloved brother not confide in you the reason he was condemned to Purgatory in the first place?"

Eliza thought back to the forest and how Roman had vowed never to speak of it. She shook her head. "All I know is that he didn't blame you."

Nate laughed. "Well, that's big of him."

Eliza remained silent. Somehow, she'd managed to turn this gentle vicar into an angry, irritated, short-tempered man. Christ, she'd turned him into Roman.

"My brother tried to kill a mind mover so he could get into Heaven. It was me who stopped him and, as you know, it was me who sent him to Purgatory. If he is back there, by whatever means, it was meant to be."

"He's changed."

"He makes you believe what he wants you to believe. That's his gift. I know this better than anyone; I've given him more chances than most. He is incapable of change."

"You're wrong," Eliza said firmly. "My father sacrificed me on the True Cross. I died and the gateway opened. Roman had the one thing he's always wanted right in front of him. But when push came to shove, he gave it all up to save me."

"If you were dead, how do you know he meant to give it up? Maybe it was unintentional."

"He tainted my blood with his own. Sent my father to Purgatory instead and closed the gateway. Could that have been unintentional?"

Nate took up his former position against the pew. He folded his arms defensively, but bitterness no longer hardened his features.

Eliza watched him for a moment. He and Roman shared so many similarities: the way they crossed their arms, the way they tutted, the condescending way they corrected her. But Nate was different. Aggression and hatred didn't rule him like they did Roman. There was a tenderness to his demeanour, even when he was cross.

"May I?" She pointed at the pew beside him.

Nate nodded and Eliza sat down. "I think, if you don't help me, you'll live to regret it."

"I usually do where Roman is concerned."

"You've spent your life helping others. Seeing the best in people. Isn't it about time you did the same for your own brother? Maybe he'll surprise you."

"Maybe." Nate looked at her. "But I won't hold my breath."

"Does that mean you'll help me? I'm going after him, either way. But I stand a better chance of surviving if you help."

Nate pursed his lips. His body tightened and Eliza worried she might have lost him again.

"I need time to think."

"I don't have time to wait."

Nate stood, but his arms remained crossed. "You'll have to. Go to the pub and wait for me. I'll come and find you."

Eliza watched him walk down the aisle to the front of the church. He crossed the chancel and disappeared through a tiny, wooden door. Eliza waited, not knowing what to do. Nate was not how she'd imagined him to be. He was more like Roman than Roman had given him credit for. Did that mean he would be just as stubborn? Was Nate heading out through a back door and running for the hills while she sat waiting like an idiot? That's what Roman would do.

Eliza stood and thought about chasing after him. Instead, she walked to the church door, stepped out into the morning air, and headed for the pub. She had to believe Nate was the honest man Roman had made him out to be.

CHAPTER THIRTEEN

Roman lay suspended on the rack.

The pain in his arms and legs had faded hours ago, or was it only minutes? Time stood still down here in the torture room. So much so, Roman thought death had already taken him. But he hadn't healed and the blurred flicker of the torch's flame in his left eye confirmed he wasn't lucky enough to be dead. Yet.

"Roman, Roman, Roman." Thomas leaned over and blocked the glow of the room from his limited view. "I'm beginning to think you like all this pain."

Roman tried to respond with a sarcastic comment, but it lodged in his throat. He'd lost the ability to talk hours ago, or maybe that had only been minutes as well. His verbal failure also prevented him from revealing how he'd escaped the torture room – information the Sheriff craved. And Thomas knew it. Any torture Roman endured while tied to the rack now was purely for his torturer's pleasure.

Thomas turned the crank. A new pain exploded across Roman's shoulders. His femur dislocated from his hip joint and his stomach cramped. A groan whimpered past his lips.

Thomas smiled. He released the crank and turned to where Billy hung from his shackles. "Maybe he knows how you escaped."

Roman shook his head. He'd promised Eliza he'd never hurt her. He didn't want to be forced to watch her brother suffer further pain because of his own refusal to play ball. He struggled against his binds and tried to communicate Billy's innocence in this whole affair – after all, Billy knew nothing about Roman. It was a mistake that Billy was even here. His frustration erupted at his inability to communicate and his threats rolled out as nothing more than grunts and snorts.

Thomas walked over to Billy. He seized his jaw and lifted his head. Billy was dead and Roman exhaled his relief. Billy was safe, for now. Later was a different kettle of fish. But Roman didn't intend on them still being here later.

Thomas cocked his head back Roman's way. "Shame. I was going to introduce him to the Judas Cradle."

A sour taste hit Roman's mouth. Thomas stared at him and Roman tried to shrink away and increase the distance between them. He'd only endured the Judas Cradle once before. Prisoners referred to it as the pyramid of horror. Roman thought the description did not do it justice. Thoughts of how to escape raced through his mind. He could see what Thomas was thinking – Roman was next for the pyramid. The guards would have to untie him first. He would be free to fight. Kill, if need be. Anything he had to do to get the hell out of there.

"Strip him," Thomas ordered his men.

Six guards crowded Roman. They grabbed his ankles and wrists and severed the rope restraints with the single slice of a knife. Roman sunk through the frame but didn't fall while they still held him. His attack upon them would have to come soon. And then his freedom. The guards lifted him out over the frame. The previous torture crippled his body and hollers of pain were wretched from him without limitation. He felt his trousers ripped from his being and tossed to the floor. He wanted to fight – tried, even – but his limbs wouldn't perform, his torn muscles and dislocated limbs no use to him.

The guards carried Roman's naked body through the chamber. Prisoners – the ones still alive, watched from their shackles. Relief flooded their eyes that it was not them heading towards the Cradle, but also a sadness that anyone, even Roman – the man who'd fled and left them behind to rot – had to endure it.

Roman was not an easy bastard to break, as Thomas was all too well aware. Roman knew the torture on the rack had just been part of Thomas's foreplay. It wasn't gruesome enough to make Roman want to sing – none of the implements in here were. But the Cradle was different. The Cradle was pure, undignified evil. And whether Thomas's original plan had been to sit Billy on top of it, or whether he'd always intended the humiliation to belong to Roman, it no longer mattered.

The Judas Cradle appeared before Roman like an Egyptian pyramid. Ropes hung from the ceiling on winches. Roman struggled and tears welled in his eyes.

Maybe it was just as well he couldn't speak. With this device in play, he didn't trust himself not to blab his secrets like a small child. Tremors shook his body and his breaths quickened until he was close to hyperventilating. He ignored the sweat that dripped from his body and tried to pull his knees to his chest.

Thomas greeted Roman with an ear-to-ear smile. He reached for his face and stroked his cheek. "Ready?"

Roman flinched and turned his head. The guards stood Roman upright, but without the use of his legs, he collapsed to the floor.

Thomas laughed. "You are making this too easy, Roman."

The guards pulled Roman's arms behind him, quickly securing them tight with more rope. They yanked him back to his feet and secured several ends of rope that hung from the winches around his ankles and biceps.

A couple of guards walked to a pulley. They yanked on the rope and Roman's legs swung out from under him. He hovered mid-air, swinging like a pendulum. The guards pulled again and Roman was lifted higher into the air. More guards waited at the top of ladders. They hauled Roman across to the middle of the cradle. Old blood and dried shit dirtied its point. They positioned Roman above it and lowered him down until Roman felt the tip impale his orifice.

His body stiffened and as much as he tried, he couldn't stop a wail escaping. He wouldn't last up here. He'd crack. He'd maybe endure a day. Three at the very most. Hopefully, he would die quickly.

The guards tightened the ropes and Roman was shoved down further onto the tip of the cradle. The spike forced itself further inside him, and a second scream bounced off the chamber walls.

Delight twinkled in Thomas's eyes. The Judas Cradle was made for long-term torture and Roman prayed he wouldn't be driven down any further. Not for a few hours, at least. He needed time to think. He needed time to die.

Thomas turned. He headed towards the exit, the guards shadowing his every move. They disappeared from sight, the main door closing behind them. Only when the echoes faded did Roman allow his tears to flow.

CHAPTER FOURTEEN

Sat Nav was a wonderful thing.

Using a borrowed police car, the Sheriff reached the cab driver's address in next to no time at all. He walked past the other police vehicle, which was parked across the drive, and pressed the front doorbell. It chimed a distorted version of *Greensleeves* and the Sheriff immediately thought of Jacob Witenie. Anger tensed his shoulders and he clenched his fists. Thinking of Jacob made him think of Roman, and thinking of Roman brought with it the urge to kill anything that crossed his path.

He heard footsteps – female – approach and the door opened.

A middle-aged woman frowned at him. "Hello?"

The Sheriff straightened, fighting the urge to run his fist through her abdomen. "I am looking for my colleague."

"Of course, come in." She walked off down the hallway, leaving the Sheriff to close the door behind him.

He caught up with her in the living room. A man sat in a chair and, opposite, a police officer sat on the edge of a sofa. PC Grimes, the Sheriff assumed.

Grimes stood as soon as he saw the Sheriff. "Brian? Is everything okay?"

"Have you located the girl yet?"

Grimes frowned. He parted his lips as if about to say something then cleared his throat.

He turned to the man in the chair. "Mr Smith, this is PC Roberts."

The Sheriff stared down at the man. "Where is the girl?"

The man shrunk into the chair. "I've told this officer all I know."

"And what would that be?"

Sweat glistened across the man's face. He swallowed and glanced between the two officers before settling his gaze back on the Sheriff. "That a young woman paid me to drive her all over Cornwall."

"Where is she now?"

"At a church in Morwenstow."

"Name?"

"Baptist of Morwenna or Rowenna. Something like that."

"Okay." Grimes closed the small, black notebook he held and slid it into his jacket pocket. "I think we have everything we need."

The Sheriff pursed his lips. His whole body tightened. Grimes's interference was costing him time. He reached for him, his fingers eager to tear the flesh from his meddlesome bones.

"Er, she was looking for a man," the cab driver added.

The lure of death and mutilation quickly evaporated from the Sheriff's thoughts.

He pushed past Grimes, hardening his glare as he stood over the cab driver. "What man?"

"I don't know."

Grimes gently pulled the Sheriff back. "Why didn't you mention this before, Mr Smith?" Grimes reclaimed the notebook and opened it.

"Because I never saw him."

The Sheriff turned for the door. He had what he wanted. He heard Grimes thanking the driver for his cooperation and then the Sheriff's boots hit the gravel driveway and drowned out anything else. He stormed back to the police car, opened the door and got in.

PC Grimes was at his side before the Sheriff had a chance to start the engine. "Jesus, Brian. What the hell was that all about back there?"

The Sheriff ignored him. He punched Morwenna Church into the car's navigational system. The location popped up and he tried to close the door.

Grimes stopped him. "I'm waiting for an answer. I've never seen you like that before. You were totally unprofessional in there."

The Sheriff stretched his arms and flexed his fingers. He cracked his neck and, without looking, seized Grimes by his throat and pulled him into the car. Grimes kicked and struggled, but the Sheriff effortlessly dragged him across his lap to the passenger seat. He squeezed his fingers around Grimes's throat. Grimes's struggle intensified. He clawed at the Sheriff's hand, struggling for air. The Sheriff smiled.

His fingernails lengthened and pierced the copper's flesh. Grimes thrashed harder. His back arched and his flailing legs kicked the air outside the car.

The Sheriff watched as death arrived and slowly began to suck the life from his victim. He yanked Grimes's head upwards, stretching his neck tight. Grimes's eyes widened and he struggled harder.

The Sheriff yanked again and the officer's spine severed free from his skull.

Dropping Grimes's head into the footwell, the Sheriff pushed his decapitated body out of the car. He closed the door and, with blood dripping from his fingers, pressed start on the Sat Nav.

CHAPTER FIFTEEN

The wooden chair was uncomfortable.

Eliza glanced around the empty pub, void of any other patrons. Even the elderly gentleman who'd served her drink, and whom she'd assumed to be the manager, had disappeared from behind the bar. She went to check her watch, remembered she didn't wear one, and looked for a clock. It seemed an age since she'd first sat down. And there still wasn't any sign of Roman's brother.

She went back to looking out of the window, something she'd done continuously since she'd sat down. She knew every bush outside and every blade of grass off by heart. The cab was long gone and the small lane she'd arrived on was empty. So was the tree tunnel that led down to the church. So far, Nate was a no show. Eliza's stomach tightened. Had he duped her? Probably. He was a Holbrook after all. Odds on, she'd return to the church to find the door locked and Nate long gone.

She exhaled, heavy and long. It failed to extinguish the apprehension that bubbled away inside her stomach. Her drink sat on a beer mat in the centre of the small, round table. Diet Coke filled half the glass and a mountain of ice pushed it to the brim. Eliza hadn't taken a sip. Not yet. She wasn't thirsty. And other than the overpriced biscuit at Kings Cross, she couldn't remember the last time she'd eaten. But she wasn't hungry either. In fact, the thought of eating made her nauseous. Being played for a fool clearly killed a person's appetite. She wrapped her fingers around the glass and let the icy condensation soak her skin. Why on earth had she ordered a Coke anyway? She didn't even like Coke.

She glanced out of the window again. Still no Nate.

He was no better than Roman. His holier-than-thou facade had tricked her and she'd fallen for it hook, line, and bloody sinker. She stood up, knocking the table. It wobbled and Coke spilt across the surface. Eliza tutted. Not that it mattered. It was a spilt drink – nothing more, nothing less. What *did* matter was saving her brother and Roman.

"I'll get a cloth."

Eliza turned. Nate was already reaching over the bar.

When he turned to face her, he had a blue dishcloth in hand. "Every table in here is wonky."

Eliza stared at him. "How did you get in here? I've been staring out of that window since I got here."

"Shortcut across the fields. I came around back."

"You mean there's a route shorter than the thirty-second tree tunnel?"

Nate wiped up the spillage and returned to the bar. This time he walked behind it and pulled himself a pint. Heineken.

He glanced up. "You need a refill?"

Eliza shook her head.

He came back around the bar, grabbed a bag of peanuts from the cardboard hanger as he passed, and pulled out the chair opposite her.

Eliza watched him sit. He took a long gulp of beer and opened the bag of nuts.

"What kind of vicar are you?" she asked.

"Who said I was a vicar?"

"You work in a church."

Nate shook a handful of nuts from the bag. "Doesn't make me a vicar." He threw the peanuts in his mouth.

"So, you're not a vicar?"

"No, I am."

This guy was turning out to be more infuriating than Roman. "But you drink. You swear. I mean, Christ, it could be Roman sitting opposite me right now."

"I am nothing like my brother."

"At this moment in time, I beg to differ."

Nate put down the bag of nuts. "I thought about what you said, back in the church."

The flutter of excitement returned. "And? Are you going to help me?"

Nate looked at her. "I want to know more about you first."

"Me?"

"Yeah. Who am I helping?"

"I thought we did our meet and greet in the church."

"I guess there's no reason for me to stay, then." Nate started to rise from his chair.

The table wobbled and Eliza grabbed her drink. "Fine. I'm a nurse."

"And a mind mover."

"Yes."

Nate slowly sat again. "And my brother knew this?"

"Yes. Look, like I already said, he saved me after my father tried to sacrifice me. He had a chance to enter Heaven. Instead, he altered the path to Purgatory and brought me back to life."

"He can still do it, you know. Use you to get into Heaven."

Eliza stared at Nate. For the first time, she saw his eyes were just a blue as Roman's. "The Cross is gone."

"The Cross is never gone. Trust me, it's just hidden again." Nate shifted position. "I assume it was Purgatory who came looking for him?"

"Yes."

"Well, saving someone's life when you weren't ordered to will have that effect."

"You included?"

"No. But I am not an escapee on the run." He scooped up a couple of nuts and threw them into his mouth. "Plus, my brother is a reaper who has had his powers revoked. Using his powers to save you was like turning on his GPS tracking."

"What do you mean?"

"He messed with the waiting room's numbers. There is no way that unbalance would have gone unnoticed. And it wouldn't have taken too much digging to find out the culprit was Roman."

"But they didn't come looking for Roman. He killed someone else to take my place before I was registered, or whatever."

"He killed someone—"

"What I'm trying to say is it was me the Sheriff tracked."

Nate sat up. "The Sheriff came for you? You must have that wrong."

"A soul hitched a ride back with me."

"And Roman knew this?"

"Yes. Well, not at first. But afterwards. Yes, he knew."

"And he stayed with you anyway?"

"Yes."

Nate raised a brow.

"Why does that surprise you?"

"Because Roman never willingly puts himself in harm's way for anybody."

Eliza remained quiet for a moment. She gave the building atmosphere between them time to settle. "He has changed."

Nate scoffed.

Eliza spoke softly, not wanting to add any further tension between them. "I didn't know Roman back when you two were brothers. And I didn't know him as a reaper. God knows I understand that his behaviour towards you in the past was unforgivable. But that is what I am asking you to do – forgive him. The Roman I know has gone from kidnapping me to saving me – risking himself many times over. None of that was so he could get into Heaven, nor because he was gaining something out of it. He did it because it was the right thing to do."

Nate looked at her for a second or two then turned to the window. He gazed out at the same view she'd stared at while waiting for him and sighed. "So, how did you and my brother meet?"

"This Shadow thing was trying to kill me one night – you know, to stop the gateway being opened, etcetera, etcetera. Roman showed up out of nowhere and turned the thing to dust."

"Because he needed you alive himself." Nate shook his head. "He's always playing an angle. You need to remember that."

"I didn't say he wasn't out for his own gain in the beginning."

"And you reckon he's had a complete personality change in less than a week? You're deluded."

Eliza wanted to argue. Instead, she let the subject lie. She looked at the glass of Coke. The ice had already melted, which meant the drink would taste more of water than anything else.

She took a sip anyway. "What exactly is a mind mover?"

Nate raised his eyes and looked at her. "You don't know?"

"Oh, I know I'm a descendant of Jesus, and all that blood stuff. But I don't understand the powers. Did I inherit them?"

"Yes, from your mother. Did she not tell you? Teach you?"

Eliza thought back to what Roman had told her. "I don't know my real mother."

"And you never felt you were different?"

Eliza shook her head. "So, what is the point of them? Of me? I mean, I can't even control these so-called powers. When I make things move, I don't even know *how* I'm doing it."

"How long have you known you're a mind mover?"

"Just over a week. Since my birthday."

Nate nearly spat out his beer. "A week?" He wiped his mouth. "Jesus. Pretty much every mind mover I have ever met knew their heritage from the moment they could string two words together. They spend years practising their gift."

"Could you teach me to control it?"

"Yeah, of course I could."

A flash of joy swept through Eliza.

"If I had a spare decade or two."

And the joy was snatched away as quickly as it had arrived. "What?"

"I just told you, mind movers are taught from an early age. A crash course on the basics would take six months, minimum." Nate flicked another couple of peanuts into his mouth. "You'd be better off forgetting the power."

This was going nowhere. Eliza pushed the glass of Coke across the table and stood up. "Are you going to help me save our respective brothers or not?"

"There is no way to save them."

"Fine. Then tell me how to get to Purgatory and I'll save them myself."

"You're mad."

"Do you know how to get into Purgatory or not?"

Nate looked up at her. "You enter that place, you will never leave."

"Roman did once. We will again, together."

"And how'd he manage that?"

"The same way the soul did with me. He hitched a ride."

Nate smiled. "To do that, you need to know who's destined to be returned. How are you going to know?"

"Roman did it before."

"A fluke. Trust me."

"And the guy that hitched back with me? Was that another fluke?"

"Had to be. There is no way for anyone imprisoned in Purgatory to know."

Eliza felt her cheeks flush. "Look, I have no idea how he knew, but he did. That's enough for me to believe he can do it again."

"And that's your plan? To hope he knows?

"It's all I have."

Nate reached for his beer but didn't drink any. "If you're caught and then somehow miraculously escape, you will be hunted by Purgatory, just like the Sheriff hunted the soul inside you."

"He could only track Jacob when he showed himself."

"So, you're going to hide inside someone forever? Is that how Roman survived?"

"Roman left his vessel straight away."

"Another lie he told you."

"I believe him."

Nate laughed and gulped down a mouthful of beer. He wiped the froth from his lips. "Even if you got him out, Roman would have to keep one step in front of the Sheriff for the best part of a century for his scent to wane and become undetectable. Not even Roman is that good."

"I think you've forgotten – he's done it once already." Eliza turned her back on Nate. He wasn't going to help her and she was wasting time here trying to convince him. "Thank you for your time. I'll find another reaper to help me." She walked to the door and left.

Light rain hit her face. Great. She had nowhere to go and she was going to get drenched.

"Hey," Nate called out.

Eliza stopped but didn't turn. She heard him jog up to her and only spun to face him when she felt him behind her.

He looked at the ground and kicked a loose stone from the slab path. "Okay."

"Okay?"

He looked up. In this light, his eyes were a brighter shade of blue than Roman's.

"I'll help you."

Eliza's heartbeat quickened. She wanted to scream in delight. She wanted to fling her arms around this wonderful man and thank him over and over. Instead, she held her hand out.

Nate shook it, his grip soft and tender.

"Can we go there right now?"

Nate released her hand and stuck his hands in his pockets. "Everything in good time. First, you have to tell me something."

Eliza waited.

He smiled disarmingly. "What's your name?"

CHAPTER SIXTEEN

The boiling kettle whistled through the house.

Nate entered the kitchen. He rubbed the cramp from his stomach and grabbed two mugs from the cupboard. Unease gnawed his insides. He was in over his head. The voice of reason that lived deep inside him screamed at him not to get involved with her. Behind him, the kettle continued to screech for attention and he lifted it from the gas. Immediately, the noise stopped. He filled the mugs with water, silently cursing for forgetting the tea. Putting the kettle down, he grabbed a couple of teabags from the ceramic caddy. He couldn't think straight. Roman had to have an angle, but what was it?

He heard Eliza enter and glanced over his shoulder. She was standing in the doorway. Her newly washed hair freshened her face, but the tiredness remained in bags beneath her eyes. He felt an overwhelming urge to pull out a chair and sit her at the table, but he resisted.

"Can you pass the milk?" he asked.

He'd laid out one of his check shirts and a pair of joggers while she'd showered. The shirt swamped her tiny frame. And the trousers? As he watched her walk to the fridge, he wondered how they managed to stay around her waist. Nevertheless, they were clean and dry, and a hundred times better than the outfit she'd arrived in.

"How're the clothes?" he said.

Eliza ran her palm down the cotton shirt. "They're warm."

"Sorry I didn't have anything more suitable. It was either those or a cassock."

Eliza passed him the milk. She seemed to want to say something, but held back and smiled.

"You're still hell-bent on going to Purgatory?"

"Yes."

"It is a one-hundred-per-cent certainty you will not return."

"Funny. Your brother had the same lack of faith in me."

Nate turned back to the tea. He poured the milk and hoped she liked it milky. He stirred, squeezed the teabag, and passed her a mug. She took it, blew some cool air across the top, and sipped. Her nose wrinkled and she sipped again. She was extremely beautiful and seemed smart as hell. Nothing like the girls his brother usually hung out with.

Nate picked up his own mug and leant against the counter. "Why are you so happy to die for my brother?"

"For *my* brother," she corrected.

Nate smiled. He knew avoidance when he saw it. "Then tell me. What's the deal with you and Roman?"

Eliza's smile faded. She put down her tea. "Look, I don't mean to be rude, but there isn't time for a heart to heart right now. You promised to show me how to use my powers and get me into Purgatory. As much as I'm enjoying our tea and chat, do you think we could get started?"

She was feisty too. Nate's respect for her grew with every passing minute. "You're asking me to send you to your death for my untrustworthy brother—"

"Remember we're talking about my brother too."

"—my brother who is, quite frankly, not worth saving." Nate reached for her tea and placed the mug back into her hands. He reluctantly returned to his position against the counter. "If I am to do all of this, as you're asking, I need to be certain I am doing it for the right reasons."

"Saving my brother isn't a good enough reason?"

"I have never met your brother. You, on the other hand, I am now acquainted with. And, so far, I cannot condone you giving your life for anyone else's."

"So, you're not going to help me?"

"I didn't say that."

"Then what are you saying? You're confusing the hell out of me with your *no I won't do it – yes I will – oh, wait a minute, no I won't* attitude."

Nate grinned. "Are you like this with Roman?"

"Like what?"

"This argumentative?"

"I don't know. I suppose so. He aggravates the crap out of me as well." Eliza frowned. "Look, what does my bickering with Roman have to do with anything?"

"I'm trying to work him out."

"There's nothing *to* work out." Eliza sighed. She slammed the mug down on the counter. "He surrendered to the Sheriff and went to Purgatory so I didn't have to."

"Uh-huh."

"What would you know, anyway? You keep making the point that I haven't known him very long, but when was the last time you saw him? Spoke to him, even?"

Nate didn't answer. She already knew it had been centuries since he'd spoken to his brother.

"You're so hell-bent on living in the past, how can you be so sure he *hasn't* changed, eh?"

She was right, of course. Not about Roman changing. Nate honestly believed his brother would never change his spots. But his belief was not enough – or at least not enough to satisfy Eliza. He walked to the sink and poured his drink out. The liquid browned the white porcelain before swirling around the plughole and draining. What he was about to do didn't sit right with him. He was a man of the cloth – had been for more years than he could count. He had taken an oath to protect life, not hand it over on a silver platter to the devil himself.

Nate straightened but couldn't bring himself to look at Eliza. Helping her enter Purgatory was bad enough. Staring her in the eye while he did it was something else.

He glanced out the window at the Cornish landscape. "Show me what you can do with your powers."

"I can't. I don't know how I do it."

He knew she didn't stand a chance of learning how to use her powers in the couple of hours he was going to give her. Nevertheless, the time might be enough to convince her to forget about helping Roman.

"Take a deep breath. Calm down. And try anyway."

He waited. Outside, a few sheep grazed in the field just beyond the churchyard. Blue dye marked their wool and, next year, more blue dye would mark a whole new replacement flock.

"I'm still waiting," he said, still not looking at her.

"I'm trying. I told you, I don't know how to do it."

"Then you are not concentrating hard enough."

"I am concentrating."

"Not hard enough."

"God damn it. What do you want me to do?"

"I don't know. What is it you are trying to do?"

He heard Eliza curse under her breath.

"Swearing won't help you."

"I'm not swearing."

The door slammed shut.

For a moment, Nate wondered if she'd stormed out and physically closed it, rather than doing it with her mind. He turned, happy when he saw it was the latter.

Eliza stood rigid, watching him. "I was trying to close the door."

"Well done. You succeeded." Nate walked to the door and reopened it. The gift was clearly within her. "Close it again."

"But I don't know how."

"Use your emotion."

Eliza's stared at him. Her blank expression said it all. She really didn't have a clue.

Nate took her by the shoulders. She was stiff as a board. "You need to relax for starters." He rolled her shoulders until he felt a little movement in them. "Now." He stepped back. "Tell me what you felt just before that door closed."

"It's like a movie reel playing inside my head. I see things happen and then they happen for real."

"Okay, just before the movie reel. What do you *feel*?"

Eliza inhaled. She held the breath for a second then exhaled. "Anger."

"Okay. That's good. Now you need to learn how to take that anger and control it."

Eliza laughed. "In a couple of hours?"

Nate shrugged. "It's a power that takes years of practice to learn to control. I told you that. There are no shortcuts."

"Then why are we even bothering?"

"Because you're going to need all the help you can get." He placed his hands on her stomach, aware of how slender she felt. He pushed the thought from his head. "The energy is here, in the pit of your stomach. It feeds off your emotions."

"You mean anger?"

"Anger. Sadness. Happiness. Love. Any emotion can trigger it." Nate removed his hands and stepped behind her. He couldn't believe he was going to use this example. "Close your eyes." He gave her a moment. "Now concentrate on my brother. I want you to think of a single moment with him. A time that shines out above all the rest. You got it?"

Eliza nodded.

Nate lightly placed his hands on her shoulders. "Okay. An emotion will accompany that memory. You feel it?"

Eliza nodded.

"All right. Hold that feeling. Now imagine the door closing. Imagine pushing it with your hand. Don't let go of that emotion. Use it. It's in your hand and you can just flick that door shut."

He felt Eliza's shoulders tense. Her hand lifted. With a flick of her wrist, the door banged shut. Nate stepped back, momentarily stunned. He hadn't expected her to actually close the door. Truth be told, he hadn't even expected her to move it – not even a little. Yeah. This power was just itching to get out of her.

Eliza spun around. Joy brightened her face. "I did it."

"You did. Can you open it again?"

The happiness in her eyes dulled slightly. "You mean pull the handle down and open it?"

Nate nodded. "It's the same principle. You think it and then you do it." He turned Eliza back to the door, wanting to see if she was a one-trick-pony. "Just think of that same memory of my brother. Do exactly what you did before."

It was obvious, after a minute of nothing happening, that the miracle wasn't to be repeated. More practice was needed. Nate sighed with relief, thankful he still had a couple of hours to change her mind. He left her staring at the door and put the kettle back on the stove. When he glanced back at her, he could see she'd lost her concentration.

"So, how is my brother?"

Eliza turned to face him. She looked genuinely surprised by his enquiry. "It's hard to tell most of the time. He's not one for sharing."

Nate smiled. "He told you things, though."

Eliza took his mug from the sink. She washed it out then reached for hers and did the same. "Do you think you can ever forgive him?"

"Forgiving him is not the problem. I did that years ago," he lied. "Trust is the problem. I don't trust him."

"Trust can be earned back."

"You have good intentions, Eliza, but you have much to learn about people."

"That's a little condescending."

"You're right. I apologise." Nate took the mugs. "The simple fact is, too much time has passed between us."

"But if you help me get Roman out of Purgatory, the two of you can patch things up."

"I cannot get too involved in helping you. I am risking everything just by showing you how to get in."

"What do you mean? What do you stand to lose?"

"My status as a reaper." Nate refilled the cups with boiling water. This time he remembered the tea bags. "Roman ruined my marriage and I lost my wife and son. Being a reaper is all I have. I love it. I will not let Roman take that from me as well."

He squeezed the teabags then stopped. Eliza was right. There wasn't time for tea. He pushed the mugs away and grabbed two coats from the hallway.

"Are we going out?"

"We are." Nate handed Eliza a red anorak. "Tomorrow there's going to be a car accident. A big one. I need to show you the people I'm going to resurrect. Those are the ones you'll be using to hitch a ride back with – if you make it that far."

CHAPTER SEVENTEEN

Water hit Roman's face. Warm and reeking of ammonia.

It was piss.

He spat out what reached his mouth and blinked away what stung his eyes. When he opened them, the glow of torchlight flickered in both pupils. So, death had found him first. He'd be fully healed now. Thank God for small mercies. He tried to move. Pain ripped through his arse. He bit back his pain and fucking cursed everyone and their sister until the pain subsided. He inhaled and waited for his vision to focus. Shit. He was still impaled on the cradle.

He hadn't noticed the two guards standing beside him until one of them cleared their throat. Roman cast a glance to his left. One of the men climbed down the ladder and hurried out of sight. No doubt to inform Thomas he'd woken. The other guard remained watching Roman's every move.

Unbothered by his audience of one, Roman pulled against his restraints. A sharp intake of breath momentarily paralysed him. The movement made the tip of the pyramid feel like a red-hot poker being shoved up his backside. If it was the last thing he ever did, he was going to fucking kill Thomas. The pain slowly dulled and he didn't bother with a second attempt. He needed a moment.

A man's voice cried out in agony from somewhere at the other end of the chamber. Roman couldn't see who it was or what device was being used on him. Poor bastard. Then came the crack of a whip and another person – much, much younger – screamed. Roman had clearly stirred up some old desires if Thomas was torturing two prisoners simultaneously. Their screams continued for a little longer and then died.

Moments later, Thomas bounded into view. Zeal filled his every step. "Ready for more anal prodding?"

The thought made Roman want to puke. But, then, so did caving in and telling Thomas what the Sheriff wanted to know – how he had previously escaped the chamber.

Two guards stood either side of Thomas. Under his orders, they took to the pulley. Roman braced himself. He'd rather die – again – than give Thomas the satisfaction of breaking him. But he also needed to get off this thing and heal if he was to stand a chance of escape.

The guards untied the rope from the pulley. They released a little of the tension and lowered Roman further onto the pyramid's point.

"Okay, okay," Roman hailed. "I'll tell you what you want to know."

The guards didn't stop lowering him.

"I fucking said I'll play ball." Roman screamed, holding nothing back.

The guards stopped and took the weight. They looked to Thomas for direction.

"Tell me now," Thomas said to Roman.

Sweat ran into Roman's eyes. Pain burned into his stomach. "Get me off this thing first."

Thomas rubbed his chin. A flicker of contemplation filled his eyes. "If you try to escape, I will stick your friend up there. If your answer fails to satisfy me, I will put your friend up there. If you give me just one wisecrack, I will put your friend up there. Do we understand each other?"

Roman tried to reposition himself. He couldn't do it and swallowed back the excruciating agony that crippled his body. "Okay, okay. Just get me down."

"Say please."

Roman took a breath – as slow and as measured as he could. Tremors shook his body. Pain seized every bone, every muscle, every ounce of his sanity.

"Please," he whispered.

Thomas sneered. "Get him down. Don't redress him."

Roman grit his teeth. He promised himself he was going to kill this fucker. The guards pulled the rope and Roman was lifted from the pyramid. He bit back what he could of the pain. The rest blubbered out. Agony and humiliation wrapped themselves around him like a blanket. He fought to hold back his snivelling but, truth was, he cried more from relief than the pain in his rectum.

The guards swung him away from the Judas Cradle and he glanced at the point. He couldn't help himself.

Fresh blood and other bodily waste. As if his humiliation couldn't get any worse. The guards lowered him to the floor and cut the ropes binding him. Roman immediately clasped his arse to ease his pain, but the guards stopped him. They dragged him across the floor, not allowing him the time to stand. When they reached the shackles, they hoisted him up and secured his wrists.

Roman was powerless to stop them. He hung there while they secured his feet. His head drooped and he stared at the dirty floor, darkened by old blood and faeces. It wasn't just around his feet, but everywhere. There wasn't an area in the whole chamber where blood hadn't been spilt.

Thomas approached him. He held an iron bar and prodded it beneath Roman's chin.

"So," he said, lifting Roman's head until he stared him in the eye. Satisfaction and excitement oozed from him. "How did you escape?"

Roman turned his face away. He spat out a gobful of bile and watched it land centimetres from Thomas's shoe – the same brown moccasins the fucker had worn centuries earlier. Roman slowly raised his eyes. He might be strung up, naked, and with an arsehole the size of a volcanic crater, but he still had some defiance left in him.

"You should look closer to home."

Thomas frowned.

"Your men. They're not as loyal as you think."

The frown faded a little and Thomas narrowed his eyes. "You're lying."

"Am I?"

"Then why haven't more prisoners escaped?"

Roman tried to shrug. It was almost impossible while strung up. "Maybe I just offered something worth bargaining for."

Thomas continued to observe him, scrutinizing every beat that pulsed blood through his veins. He only needed one tiny imperfection to betray that Roman wasn't telling the truth. But Roman had walked this land for an eternity. During that time, he had met many different personalities – good, bad, and just plain crazy. He knew how to play this game – better than Thomas, he'd wager. Roman knew all the tell-tale signs when someone was lying, just as he knew if they were telling the truth. Everyone, that was, but Eliza. He could never tell what the hell she was thinking. Her body language was all over the place. One moment she seemed to hate him and the next she was holding his hand and kissing him. It had driven him completely nuts. And he cherished every memory of it.

Thomas continued to stare at him. "Who is it that you think betrayed me?"

"I said I'd tell you how I escaped. That's all."

Thomas's face hardened. He stepped forward and grabbed Roman's throat. "Tell me. Now."

Roman held his stare. He couldn't give up his lie too easily. He waited for Thomas to believe he wasn't going to talk. Waited. Waited.

Thomas blinked. "Put him back up on the Cradle."

There it was. Roman's cue. "No. Okay. There was a guard back then. Scrawny looking. Glass eye."

"I know of whom you speak."

Roman kept staring. His arms ached. His legs could hardly hold his weight. If it weren't for the shackles around his wrists, he'd have collapsed by now. He waited for Thomas to realise no more information was going to be forthcoming.

"Why?" Thomas eventually said.

"Why what?"

"Why would he let you leave?"

"As I said. Maybe I had something he wanted."

Without warning, Thomas turned on his heel. He stormed off through the chamber, the tail of his robe flapping behind him, trying to keep up.

Roman heard the torture room door open and, moments later, slam shut again. He glanced towards Billy. The cop's head drooped to the side and rested on his shoulder. All signs of previous torture had vanished, but he remained deceased. Better for him if he stayed that way, for now.

The torture room door opened again. This time Roman didn't hear it close. Thomas marched into view, shunting a hooded guard before him.

He stopped in front of Roman and yanked back the guard's hood. "This is the man?"

Roman stared at the guard. He hadn't aged at all over the few hundred years since Roman had last seen him. The guard looked up at him. Without a doubt, the recognition was there. So was the fear. The guard's eyes widened, almost to the point where Roman thought they stood a good chance of popping out. It was evident that he had no idea what was going on or why he'd been forced in here. Roman should feel guilty. The man would surely die the moment Roman confirmed his involvement in his escape, something he'd completely made up. The guard had nothing to do with Roman absconding. If memory served, Roman couldn't even remember him being on duty that night. But Roman didn't feel guilty. The guard before him, under direct orders from the Sheriff, had inflicted reams of torture on him – and had looked to enjoy every minute.

Roman grinned. Payback was a bitch. "That's him."

The guard turned to Thomas and began to protest his innocence. Hanging beside Roman was the heretic's fork. Thomas took it and swiped its end across the guard's neck. The guard's throat gaped open and blood jetted across the immediate area. He clasped his wound. It did little to stem the blood loss and he dropped to the floor.

"Let him die," Thomas said to the other guards. "When he awakens, I will torture him myself."

Thomas turned back to Roman. He stepped over the choking guard until he was inches from Roman. "The Sheriff will soon return with your lady friend. I wonder how she will fair on the Cradle."

"You lay one finger on her, I'll fucking kill you."

Roman pulled on the shackles. It was his anger being valiant. It was also a waste of energy – energy he didn't have spare.

Thomas turned to leave. When the guards didn't follow, he stopped and looked back at them. "He can be left alone now we have our answers."

The guards nodded and followed him to the door. The dying guard remained on the floor, swimming in his own blood.

Roman stared at him. The guard's blood formed a perfect circle – not including the splatter caused by the initial slice. The blood swelled in size around the guard, maintaining its uniform circumference. It reached Roman's feet and wet the tips of his toes. For a split second, he wished he could go back ten minutes. Maybe tell a different lie. Maybe spare the guard's life.

He felt his throat thicken and he swallowed the growing ache away. Was this him feeling guilty? Again? How the fuck could he feel guilty over this prick? Shit, he'd changed since meeting Eliza.

Billy groaned and murmured something about bacon.

Roman turned to him and spoke without giving him time to adjust to his newfound life. "Billy, you awake?"

Billy raised his head. His eyes remained shut. It was normal to be disorientated for a while after coming back to life.

Unfortunately, Roman didn't have the time to wait. "Hey, open your eyes and look at me."

Slowly, Billy opened his eyes. He squinted at the chamber like he was seeing it for the first time.

"Look at me," Roman said again. "We need to get the fuck outta here."

Billy turned to him, briefly casting an eye over his nakedness. He didn't ask what had happened. "How?"

"I'll untie you."

Billy looked up at Roman's shackles. "You're chained same as me."

Roman dislocated his thumb. The lack of pain it caused surprised him.

Billy's eyes widened. "What the hell are you doing?"

"Getting out of here."

"You're breaking your own hands."

"Do you have a better idea? Besides, it worked for me first time around."

Roman pulled his hand through the shackle and reached for his other hand. His legs shook under his weight and he prayed they'd hold him long enough to dislocate his other thumb.

Billy winced and turned his head.

Roman slid his other hand free. He fell to the floor – landing in the blood. Pain erupted inside his arse and he bit back his lip. How could he fight in this condition? He looked at his feet. They hadn't been shackled the last time he escaped and no amount of dislocating would get them free of the shackles. *Fuck*.

The dead guard lay in front of him. Roman rolled the man over, heard a jangle, and saw a set of long, iron keys secured to his robes. He grinned and unhooked them. Twenty or so keys hung from the ring. He took the first and tried it in the shackle around his ankle. It fit the lock but didn't turn. Roman released it. He took the second key on the ring, and tried again. The second key didn't work either. It was the same with the third, fourth, fifth…heck, he lost count.

Then, with two keys to go, one turned, and the shackle sprang open. Roman quickly unlocked the second clamp, finally free. He stood, unsteady, mustering every ounce of strength he had left to get him through the next couple of minutes.

Hope shone in Billy's eyes. Roman saw it. He felt it in his own heart. He reached for Billy's left shackle and repeated the odious task of finding the right key. He found it quicker than he had his own.

The shackle opened and he handed Billy the key. "Unlock the rest."

Roman eyed the dead guard's shoes. They looked a little large for Roman, but bigger was better than smaller. He removed them and slipped them on his own feet. Then he stripped the robe from guard's body. It was bloodstained, but anything had to be better than running through the passageways in his birthday suit. He pulled the brown fabric over his head, threaded his arms through the sleeves, and tied the belt. Now he searched the chamber.

"What're you after?" Billy said. He'd managed to free his other hand and now frantically worked on his feet.

"Weapons. We're going to need them."

Roman limped across the chamber. On the walls, between prisoners and torture devices, hung weapons. Hundreds of them. Swords, daggers, spears, flails, battle-axes. Another wall held a flock of maces. Roman didn't waste time, grabbing a selection.

"Grab what you can," he told Billy when he joined him.

Roman took the keys from him and approached the prisoner who hung opposite him – the one he'd left behind to suffer the first time. He pressed the key ring into his hand. "Get yourself free and then release everybody else."

The man clasped the keys. He looked at Roman, grateful to be given the chance to survive this time. He nodded his thanks and immediately set the keys to work in the lock.

Roman had done his bit. He raced to the door.

Seeing his trousers in a heap on the floor by the rack, he grabbed them and glanced at Billy. "Let's get the hell out of here."

CHAPTER EIGHTEEN

Eliza stepped out into the rain.

It wasn't heavy rain, but that fine rain that drenched you regardless. She pulled on the mac Nate had given her and looked out across the fields. She hadn't noticed it before, but the coastline was less than a quarter of a mile away. How nice it would be to head down to the cliffs and watch the day roll past. Maybe in another lifetime.

Nate closed the kitchen door behind him and joined her. "The car's parked over in the garage."

Eliza hadn't noticed a garage when she'd first arrived. Then again, she hadn't been looking for one. Even now, after scanning the grounds, she couldn't see a building that matched that description. Nate walked around the church and Eliza followed. Sure enough, there was the garage. Battered, wooden doors hung on hinges too old to be fully functional anymore.

Nate pulled one of the doors open. The other he raised half a foot off the ground before sweeping it aside. Inside was a white Ford Fiesta van. Eliza smiled. It was the first time she'd noticed an obvious difference between Nate and his gearhead brother.

Nate looked embarrassed. "It's not my car."

Eliza killed her grin. She shook her head, wanting to tell him she didn't mean any disrespect, but the words never came.

And, Nate didn't wait for them. "I'm betting Roman's car is something of a smoother ride." He pushed a button on the key fob and Eliza heard the doors unlock.

She didn't mention the Aston. *Best not.*

Nate opened the driver's door but didn't get in. He leant on the roof, the key held between both hands. "Are you sure you want to do this?"

Eliza looked at him. Worry etched his face. She opened the passenger door and got in – his question answered as far as she was concerned.

Nate got in the car and settled beside her. He fiddled with the keys.

"Nate, this is the right thing to do."

Nate glanced at her. "I think you're making a huge mistake and I'm doing nothing to stop you."

"That's your head talking. Listen to your heart. What does that tell you?"

"The exact same thing. That this is wrong."

From this angle, he looked just like Roman. The chiselled features – although not quite as defined as Roman's – were there, along with the famous Holbrook scowl his brother had thrown her way more times than she could count.

"Stay here." He turned to her, his eyes pleading. "Getting involved with my brother is going to get you killed."

"I have to help."

"I could stop you, you know."

"I know."

Eliza rested her hand upon his. It felt nice to touch him. She almost felt safe. She remembered the last time she'd rested her hand upon Roman's, back in the motel. She felt her face warm. Roman's moment of vulnerability had led to an eruption of passion between them. That was the emotion she'd thought of back in Nate's kitchen. She removed her hand. Lustful memories dampened her neck and she lifted the collar of her shirt.

"I take it he's here for you?" Nate had turned back to the windscreen.

Eliza followed his gaze. The rain was falling heavier, blurring the images outside. She squinted and saw movement over by the church. A person? No. It was a police officer, walking the perimeter of the church. Eliza ducked down in the seat.

Her mouth dried and she struggled to swallow. "He must have traced the cab."

"What cab?"

"The one I fled in when the police chased me from my father's house. I paid the driver. The police must have traced the number and tracked me, or something. Damn it. If they find me, they'll arrest me."

Nate's face hardened. He pursed his lips. "Eliza. Look more closely."

Eliza did. The officer stopped and peered through the church window then walked on. At first, Eliza didn't notice the subtle differences. Like, the guy's arms hung just a little too long for a human. And when he walked, there was the faintest hunch in his shoulders. All very easily missed, if you weren't looking for it.

She inhaled sharply and her heart began to race. "The Sheriff."

He'd kept his promise to find her. She'd be damned if she was going to let him take her back, though. She wanted to go to Purgatory, yes. But she'd get there her way, not his. She reached for the door handle, ready to flee.

Nate held her still. "You're in deeper than I thought."

"We can still get out of here."

"It's too late."

"Can you stop him?"

"Yes, but I cannot kill him." Nate cursed. "I need to send you now."

"But you need to show me the people. If we drive fast, the Sheriff won't catch us."

"Our field trip is over. I'll describe the people to you."

"What? Are you crazy?"

"It's all I can do. Think about it. He hasn't seen you. He doesn't know you're here."

"You don't understand. He's strong. He'll kill you."

"Let me worry about the Sheriff. Now listen. The people destined to return from the waiting room are as follows – in this order. First is a woman – black, dark hair, brown eyes."

"Oh my God. That could be a million women. How am I supposed to know her when I see her?"

The Sheriff rounded the corner of the church. For a while, at least, he was out of sight. Normally, his absence was something Eliza wished for. At this very moment, though, she wanted him right where she could see him.

"She has a tattoo of a heart on her wrist," Nate said. "A little, red one right here." He touched Eliza's wrist just below her palm. "Second person is a man. Bushy beard. Thickset."

"Jesus. Really? I need more to go on. How about height? Hair colour?"

"Six foot. Dirty blond. He'll be wearing a blue jumper."

"That helps."

Sarcasm oozed out of her. She glanced back at the church. Still no sign of the Sheriff.

"Third one is tricky."

"You mean trickier, right?"

"It's a little boy. Five years old. Blond hair." Nate checked out the window then looked back at her. "He's a twin."

"Please tell me they don't both die."

Nate nodded. "Only one comes back."

Eliza quietened. She choked back her sadness. "But they're just children."

Nate looked away from her again and scanned the church. "There's going to be a lot of kids there. A school bus takes the brunt of the impact."

"Dear God." Eliza closed her eyes and wrapped her arms around her stomach. She felt terrible asking her next question but couldn't see any way around it. She opened her eyes. Nate's attention was still on the church. "How do I know which twin?"

Nate shrugged. Not in a careless way – more defeated. "Pure guess work." He checked his watch. "You will have exactly fourteen hours and twenty-three minutes. It may seem like a long time, but Purgatory messes with time. What you'll actually have is thirty-three minutes to find Roman and your brother, get to the waiting room, and hook onto the souls that are to return."

"What if I'm late?"

"Then you don't come back."

"Won't you come with me?"

"I can't. I need to be at the accident site to bring back the dead." He reached across her and took a pen from the glove box. He turned her hand palm up and started to draw a succession of lines. "This is the torture chamber. This is where you will find your brother and Roman. Follow this line. It will lead you all the way to the waiting room. These crosses mark where you have to go up a level." His index finger lightly traced the line. "Here, where there are two crosses – go up two levels."

He paused. "Because I have no idea where you're going to land in the tunnels, I cannot tell you how to find to the torture chamber. Search for the stalagmites and stalactites. They surround the chamber. You'll hear the screams the nearer you get. If you can, try and get a cloak from a guard. Disguise yourself. But only if the opportunity presents itself. Do not take any unnecessary chances. You hear me?"

He closed her hand, held it for a moment. "Are you sure you want to do this?"

Finally, this was it. Eliza was going to Purgatory. She nodded, not as convincingly as she'd have liked.

"If you manage to pull this off—"

"When I pull this off."

"When you arrive back here, the Sheriff won't be able to track you as you won't have been logged in the waiting room. However, he will be able to track Roman the moment he leaves his vessel. Your brother too, if he was caught."

"I know how it works. One problem at a time though, eh? Let's just work on not getting caught and making it back."

Nate removed his watch. He set the timer to thirty-three minutes and pressed the stop-watch.

"Count-down has just started." He fastened the strap around Eliza's wrist.

"What about you?"

"What do you mean?"

"The Sheriff."

"I told you – I'll deal with him." Nate smiled. "Right. Are you ready?"

"Does it hurt?"

"No. Just remember you are entering as a whole being. You will be sensed within sixty seconds of arrival – Purgatory time."

Eliza nodded. Her body wanted to shake. The tremors were there, simmering beneath her skin. But, fact was, she was too damn scared to shake.

"If you find Roman and your brother dead, don't wait for them to revive. You get back to the waiting room and let me bring you back. Got it?" Nate glanced back at the Church.

Eliza nodded again. She hadn't thought about what she would do if she found either Roman or Billy dead. She'd just assumed they'd be alive and fit enough to escape. If they were dead, could she really turn her back and leave them behind?

She didn't have time to think about it.

"Christ." Nate turned to her. "Sheriff's heading this way. Remember what I said."

He plunged his palm into her chest.

Eliza felt his hand push through her skin. His fingers clasped her heart and she stiffened. She was about to release the scream building inside her when Nate's hand tightened and daylight slipped from her vision.

Darkness engulfed her until only a speck of the Cornish morning remained. She reached for it, wanting to return, but the darkness dragged her further in.

Nate's hand released her and, slowly, the church, the garage, and Nate slipped from her grasp. Eliza was all alone.

Nate's final words rattled through the darkness after her. "Look for blue laces."

CHAPTER NINETEEN

Nate lifted the Ford's bonnet and leaned over the engine.

He wasn't a car person. Couldn't really tell the difference between a spark plug and a dipstick, if he was totally honest. But, regardless of his lack of knowledge, he tinkered with what he assumed was the cap for the washer fluid and tried to give off the illusion that he knew what he was doing.

The Sheriff reached him. "Nathaniel."

Nate straightened. "You're a little out of your way, aren't you?"

"You know why I'm here. Where is she?"

Nate slammed the bonnet shut and turned. The Sheriff stood at the centre of the garage opening. Rain trickled through his hair and dripped from his chin. Nate wiped his hands on the corner of his shirt, something he'd seen James Dean or Steve McQueen do in a film that he forgotten the name of. Either way, it had convinced him the actors knew a bit about cars. Hopefully, it'd have the same effect on the Sheriff.

Nate walked out into the open. He passed the Sheriff and closed one of the garage doors – the working one. "Fugitives aren't my area."

He walked across the way and lifted the broken door. He started to close it but paused when he reached the Sheriff. He motioned for his unwelcome visitor to move.

"She was here, Nathaniel. I sense it."

"If that's the case then why are you asking me? Get that nose of yours to hunt her down." Again, Nate motioned for the Sheriff to move.

The Sheriff reluctantly stepped back. "You know the penalty you will pay if you've helped her."

With both doors secured, Nate started back for the church.

The Sheriff grabbed his arm as he passed. He leaned in – way too close for Nate's liking. "This is me asking nicely, boy."

Nate twisted free, spun one-eighty, and back-kicked. His foot plunged into the Sheriff's stomach and the Sheriff catapulted backwards and crashed into the garage. The broken door rattled on its hinges and splintered free. The Sheriff straightened, his face contorted with rage. He sprang towards Nate, hands out, fingers curled, his claws pushing through the cop's fingertips. Nate stood his ground. He raised his hand.

The Sheriff froze, mid-flight.

Nate stared at the police officer suspended a meter, maybe a little higher, above the ground. Paralysis held him there. He couldn't move. He couldn't continue his attack. He couldn't even speak.

Nate, however, could. "You may have power over my brother now he no longer has reaper status, but don't you dare make the mistake of thinking you have power over me."

Nate lowered his hand. The Sheriff lowered with it.

Nate waited for the Sheriff to reach good old terra firma before stepping up to him. "I said the girl has not been here. And, now, I want you to leave."

"She is the key to destroying your brother."

"Are you asking me to sacrifice an innocent girl just to feed your twisted vengeance against my brother?"

"You hate him."

"More than most, yes. But I will deal with my brother in a way that doesn't involve innocent parties."

Nate turned for the church. If the Sheriff had any sense, he would take that warning and leave. But the Sheriff was a power-hungry, old fool. Nate knew that. He also knew the Sheriff would not leave without a fight. Sure enough, Nate heard the Sheriff storm up behind him. Without looking back, Nate flicked his wrist. No big wave of the arm. No obvious motion of the hand. Just a little flick that the Sheriff probably hadn't even witnessed. That little flick sent the Sheriff hurtling back against the garage. This time, both doors smashed inwards and crashed into his Ford.

Nate clenched his fist. He'd half lied to Eliza when he'd spoken about the vehicle. The car wasn't his, but he loved it – dearly. Hearing the garage door land against it annoyed him. It was unnecessary. And Nate felt the need to vent his anger on the Sheriff for causing the confrontation in the first place. He inhaled, deeply, and forced himself to continue his walk towards the church. The Sheriff was not a stupid man.

He would stick close to Nate because Nate was his link to finding Eliza. The last thing Nate wanted was the Sheriff close by tomorrow at the accident site.

No. Nate had to ditch the Sheriff. And quick.

CHAPTER TWENTY

Holy fuck, Roman's arse hurt like hell.

The Sheriff may as well have just fucked him six ways from Sunday and been done with it. On the plus side, he felt better wearing his trousers again.

"Do you know where you're going?" Billy called from behind.

Roman didn't dignify his question with an answer. Of course he knew where he was bloody well going. Did Billy think his light sprint through the tunnels was just part of a fitness regime or something? He cast a quick eye around the tunnel again, sure that it looked a little familiar, at least.

Christ, now he was doubting himself.

He neared a corner and slowed, motioning for Billy to do the same. "I can hear someone."

Billy leaned over and tried to peer around him.

Roman pushed him back. "They'll see you."

"Well, is there another way around?"

Roman shook his head. He glanced up at the rocks. "How are you at climbing?"

"Is that a joke?"

"No. Why would I joke?"

Billy glanced up. He started to nibble the skin on his left index finger. "You sure there's no other way?"

"You frightened of heights or something?"

"Only when they're above big, pointy stalagmites."

Roman had no idea what he meant. He reached up and felt for a jut. Pain burned through his abdomen, but he gripped the rock and hauled himself up.

It was too late. A guard rounded the corner. Roman halted, his boots shoulder-height with the guard. He closed his eyes and prayed the dim light was enough to conceal him. Who was he kidding? His luck had walked out on him the moment he'd stepped in to save Eliza at the railway station. The guard's yells for help echoed down the corridor. Roman opened his eyes. The pain crippling his lower back was stopping him from thinking straight.

The yelling abruptly halted and Roman refocused in time to see Billy kick the guard's forehead. It was enough to send the guard sprawling to the ground. Billy jumped off the wall and immediately started stripping the unconscious man of his robe.

Roman lowered himself back down to the ground, jumping the last foot. The impact from the landing penetrated his backside and his knees weakened. He reached for the wall, hiding his discomfort from Billy.

He needed a moment to recover. "You're wasting your time if you think a disguise is going to help you. The guy had a pair of lungs on him bigger than hot air balloons."

"Maybe, but I'm bloody freezing." Billy threw the robe over his shoulders. "Come on. This way's clear now."

Roman nodded. He wiped the building sweat from his brow, inhaled until his lungs felt like they would burst, and straightened. Pain burned his insides and he reached for the wall again. His trousers felt damp – with blood, not piss. He was going to fucking mutilate Thomas for this violation.

Billy must have noticed him struggling. He wrapped an arm around Roman's waist and urged him on. Every step hurt, but Roman had to numb his mind to it. He needed to concentrate on finding the way out of here. They turned the corner. Fuck. Every passageway looked the goddamn same. Roman wriggled free from Billy's hold and retook the lead. He quickened his pace. His whole body screamed at him to stop, but his response was to run faster. He would not become a victim. He was way too strong for that. Billy kept up with him easily, which made Roman question whether he was running as fast as he thought he was.

He heard guards coming up behind them. Billy clearly heard them too. He pushed Roman forward, forcing him to accelerate into a sprint. Roman responded – for as long as he could. But the pain was taking its toll. Roman slowed, his groin no longer capable of maintaining the demanding movement.

Billy stopped alongside him. "Okay, mate. We'll go up. Let them pass."

Roman nodded. He stretched for the rock, biting back the pain as he climbed. Billy stayed with him the whole time. The guy was braver than he'd given him credit for.

He'd thank him later – if he got the chance.

CHAPTER TWENTY-ONE

Eliza opened her eyes.

Near darkness surrounded her. Cave walls fenced her in and, for the briefest of moments, she thought she was back in her father's secret room. She bolted upright and reached for the shackles she assumed were locked around her ankles. But they weren't there. She looked for Mr McKenzie, but he wasn't there either. Sweat dampened her skin and she shook the confusion from her muddled mind. Previous horrors charged through her thoughts: the cross, Jacob, the Sheriff. She took a harder look at her surroundings. Cave walls, but not the room at her father's. Not any room. She was lying in a passageway.

She glanced back at her feet, feeling the fabric of the jogging bottoms, baggy around her ankles. She caught a glimpse of the watch Nate had strapped around her wrist and, in a flash, she remembered. Purgatory. The clock's countdown had already commenced, the digital display urgently reminding her of the thirty minutes remaining to find her brother and Roman. Hell, she'd been unconscious for just under two minutes. That was two minutes too long down here. She got to her feet, remembering Nate's instructions to locate the stalagmites and stalactites. If she found them, she'd find the torture chamber.

Darkness loomed all around her, making it almost impossible to see any further than a couple of feet. Above her was no different – black gloominess and not much else. There certainly weren't any of the stalactites she needed to find. She checked her watch again, the red illumination the only light available to her. Twenty-nine and a half minutes remained. Crap. She really needed to get her arse in gear.

Both ends of the passage disappeared under a cloak of darkness, making it impossible to decide the best way to proceed. It was gut instinct alone that enticed her to go right. She felt for the wall as she ran, trying to keep her balance. Seconds ticked down and still no stalactites materialised overhead. She continued to run, her fingers lightly brushing the walls, her need to save the two men in her life forcing every step out of her.

The countdown on her wrist reached twenty-seven minutes. She glanced up. Still no stalactites. It was hard to fight when you were losing so spectacularly.

Determination screamed at her to keep moving and she quickened her pace. She could do this. She'd managed to break into Purgatory; she sure as hell wasn't leaving without the two men she'd come for. She reached a crossroads and slowed. Nate had inked this crossroads on her palm. It aided her if she was running from the torture chamber. However, right now, she had no idea which way that was.

Again, gut instinct told her to run forward and she had no reason not to listen; it had served her well so far. So forward she ran, along the darkened corridor, praying that a stalagmite would soon block her path.

Somewhere along the passageway, a voice hollered.

Eliza slowed her footsteps until she could barely hear them herself. Had someone seen her? Heard her? More shouting bellowed through the tunnel. Different voices – another two or three people – maybe more. They weren't calling after her, but shouting at each other. She halted and backed up against the wall, trying to blend in with the protruding rock. The voices sounded to be some distance ahead. But whether they were a little way in front of her or a long way in front of her, moving forward no longer seemed like a viable option.

She squinted and searched the darkened tunnel. This passageway was like a rat run. There had to be another opening, another tunnel – anything so she wouldn't have to retrace her steps. She checked her watch. It looked like the countdown had reached twenty minutes, but the gloomy light made it almost impossible to see properly. Rocks pressed into her back. Time was ticking down regardless of whether she could see or not. Waiting here was as bad as going forward.

She closed her eyes and summoned some of that Roman-calibre courage she'd discovered over the last week. After everything she had survived – the Shadow, her father, the Sheriff, Jacob – running through these tunnels should feel like a walk in the park. One thing she was sure of: Returning without Roman and Billy was not an option.

Eliza pushed away from the wall and continued onwards, letting the wall guide her until she reached the end of the passage.

Now she had to choose left or right.

The shouting grew louder, echoing around her and making it impossible to tell from which direction the voices came. Again, she contemplated retreating. She glanced at the watch but couldn't really see it. Crap. She took a deep breath, edged her way to the corner of the right-hand passage, and slowly poked her head around it.

Somebody smacked straight into her.

CHAPTER TWENTY-TWO

Eliza tumbled backwards and hit the ground with a thud.

She clawed at the dirt and scrambled away from the threat. In the darkness, she just about made out the outline of a person. This was it. The guards had found her. Her mouth dried. Thoughts of Nate and his advice pushed through. A hunched figure moved towards her and Eliza squeezed her eyes shut. She forced her mind to ignore the thoughts of torture that most likely awaited her. She needed to find the security of the motel room. To feel Roman's embrace. To let the emotion of being held in his arms start the movie reel, like it had in Nate's kitchen. Only this time, instead of closing a door, it had to stop the guards from taking her prisoner.

Roman's kiss found her and the movie reel began. "Eliza?"

She felt hands upon her shoulders. Her eyes shot open. Upon her command, the man clasping her catapulted backwards. He struck the wall and dropped to the ground. He didn't move again.

A second figure raced into view. Like the first man, he leaned down and reached for her.

"No," Eliza screamed and hurled him away from her.

But the second man didn't stay down. He jumped to his feet. "Eliza. It's Billy."

Billy? No. The guards were playing with her. Using her brother against her, just like the Sheriff had done. Eliza tried to concentrate again, but Roman's kisses were lost to her. The motel room faded away and the movie reel disbanded. This time when the man came up to her, she was powerless to send him away.

She punched out, but the man secured her wrists. Eliza struggled, but his grip tightened. She fought until she could no longer lift her exhausted arms. She stared at him. His outline, his stance, everything told her it was her brother. But she'd been fooled before, back at her father's when it had really been the Sheriff.

The man leaned forward.

Now she could make out his eyes. They were panicked, not cold. Kindness warmed these eyes.

"Billy?"

"What the hell are you doing here?" Billy's hands released her wrists and within seconds he had her wrapped in his arms.

"I came for you."

"How?" He pulled away, lifting his hands to cup her face. "Are you okay?"

Eliza nodded. She probably didn't look okay. But it didn't matter. Her brother was alive. She'd found him.

She hugged him again. "Where's Roman?"

"He's not in a good way." Billy glanced behind him – at the first man Eliza had sent sprawling back against the rocks.

Eliza went to him and Billy followed. Roman lay on the ground. He looked crippled. Eliza knelt beside him. She rolled him onto his back, felt his neck, and found a pulse.

"What happened to him?" She ran her hands down his sides and felt for broken ribs.

"I don't know how to explain…"

Eliza held his shoulders and lightly shook him.

Roman blinked awake and, in that instant, Eliza wanted to embrace him. Kiss him. Let him know how happy she was to see him.

"I'm so sorry," she said. "I didn't know it was you. Are you okay?"

Roman's blue eyes found her and she waited for that sparkle of recognition.

"What are you doing here?" he demanded.

"You told me to come and get you."

"I told you to find my brother." His voice was weary.

"I did. That's how I got here."

"My brother's here with you?"

Eliza shook her head.

"He sent you alone?" Roman struggled to sit up and Billy quickly supported him.

Eliza reached out to help, but Roman avoided her touch. She had no choice but to let it go and leave helping him to Billy. "It's what you told me to do."

"I told you to find him so *he* could come and get me. Not you." Roman clambered to his feet. He cursed the pain as he stood. "I'm going to fucking kill him."

"You really think I'd come here and not be prepared?" They'd only been reunited for a minute but the argument between them started. "Your brother and I have a plan, you moron. I know who he's pulling out of the waiting room."

Roman straightened, his interest clearly piqued by that pertinent piece of information. "He's told you who's leaving?"

"Yes. More to the point, I know when." Eliza held out her wrist. She had to stare hard, but the watch showed just under fifteen minutes remaining. She flipped her hand over. "Your brother drew this. It leads from the torture chamber to the waiting room."

Roman didn't even look at the map. "He's helping?"

"Yes. He is your brother, after all."

"Hey," Billy butted in. "How about we do the Walton's reunion later." He took Eliza's hand and bent closer to study Nate's map. "We came down here, right? So, we need to head back the way Eliza came."

"We came down from this way," Roman corrected him.

"Will we make it back in time?" Billy asked.

"It's a ten-minute run." Roman started to jog.

Shallow breaths betrayed his fitness. He wasn't up to running.

Eliza turned to Billy, but Billy just shook his head. "Thinks he's bloody Superman. You can't tell him otherwise. Let him have his moment."

Eliza wanted to argue, but now was not the time. The voices she'd heard were almost upon them. They had no choice but to follow Roman and hope they reached the waiting room before their hunters caught up with them. Or before Roman crashed and burned.

Together, they raced through the tunnels. But they weren't moving quickly enough. Roman was slow and holding them up.

Billy pushed Eliza to the front. "You lead us." He wrangled himself under Roman's right shoulder.

Eliza ran. Their remaining time – or lack thereof – was at the forefront of her mind. She wanted to check her watch but didn't want the others to see. There was no point piling further pressure on an already urgent situation. Every ten seconds or so, she glanced over her shoulder to make sure they were keeping up. Billy half carried half dragged Roman along. It helped somewhat, but their pace still lagged. Pain creased Roman's face. Eliza had never seen him so helpless – other than the time she'd found his deceased body slumped over his steering wheel. She couldn't imagine what kind of torture had caused such invalidity this time.

"You two need to go on without me," Roman finally said.

Billy repositioned himself, taking more of Roman's weight. "We leave together or we don't leave at all." He glanced at Eliza. "Keep moving. We'll catch you up."

Eliza slowed and turned to face her brother. "No. We leave together, just like you said."

"Eliza, I can't let them catch you. I couldn't stand to see you in the torture room. I'm not strong enough for that. Roman isn't strong enough for that."

"We'd better get a move on then." Eliza spun to face front and quickened her pace.

A guard sprang out of the darkness and landed in front of her. He crouched, arms open, stopping her from passing. Eliza turned and tried to push Billy and Roman out of harm's way. A second guard descended the rock face and grabbed her by the hair. She tried to run, but he held her back – long enough for the guard behind to yank her into a vice-like grip.

"Duck," Billy yelled.

Eliza didn't stop to think. She tilted her head forward – as low as she possibly could. Billy smacked the guard behind her, knocking him to the ground. Eliza tumbled backwards with him. The guard hit the ground face-up, breaking Eliza's fall. His arms still hugged her and she headbutted backwards twice. The guard cried out and Eliza elbowed him in the ribs. She rolled off him and stood. The second guard descended the rest of the wall and pounced.

Billy shot between them. He grabbed the guard and shoved him against the wall, smashing his head against the rocks. Then he did it again and again and again. At first, the guard yelled out. By the time Billy stopped, he made no sound at all.

The guard on the ground started to get up, his sights set on Billy.

Eliza stepped forward. She kicked the guard between the legs. He cried out, his knees buckled, and he collapsed back into the foetal position, no longer a threat.

"Let's get the hell out of here," Billy said.

Eliza raced to Roman. He clawed at the wall, struggling to stand. She wriggled beneath his right arm and wrapped her arm around his waist. Billy retook his position on Roman's left. Together, they started to move forward again.

Two more guards raced up behind them. One struck Billy in the back of the head and Billy fell to his knees. Roman reached out to help, but a second guard grabbed Eliza around the waist. He lifted her away from Roman and pinned her against the wall.

Roman followed them. He punched the guard in the back and pulled him away from Eliza. But Roman was weaker than Eliza had ever seen him before. The guard turned and, with very little opposition from Roman, struck him – closed fist – across the face. Eliza leapt on the guard, but he shrugged her off. He grinned, turned back to Roman, and punched him again. Roman held on for two further hits before he went down.

Eliza glanced at Billy. Another guard had caught up with them and her brother now faced two attackers. The other guard drove kick after kick into Roman's stomach.

Anger boiled up inside Eliza and she didn't try to stop it. No, she was going to use it. She closed her eyes and embraced the anger that consumed her. The movie reel started to play. She opened her eyes. The guard that straddled Roman lifted into the air, higher and higher until she lost him in the darkness above. The two guards fighting Billy stopped dead – mid-grapple. Simultaneously, their necks cracked inwards, towards each other. In unison, their lifeless bodies dropped to the ground.

Eliza raced to Roman and helped him to his feet.

"We're going to make it," she promised him.

Howling sounded in the distance.

"Hellhounds." Billy hurriedly retook his position on Roman's left. "We need to get out of here right now."

The mutts' snarling moved closer. The hair pricked along Eliza's skin. The sound was everywhere. In front. Behind. Above. Below. The growls vibrated against her body.

Hot breaths warmed her legs. "Where are they? I can't see them."

"Just run," Billy shouted.

Eliza moved quickly. She felt Roman trying to run with them, but he was weak and his feet mostly dragged through the dirt. She desperately wanted to look at Nate's watch. But checking it wouldn't help them get to the waiting room any quicker.

The passage curved around a series of bends, the hellhounds hard on their heels. Eliza tried to think of the motel room. With Roman pressed this close to her, summoning up that emotion should be easy for her. But panic riddled her mind. All she could do was run and hope they reached the waiting room before the dogs caught up with them.

"Look for the light." Roman's order was weak, but she heard.

Jaws snapped at her ankles. Fangs nipped her skin. Eliza quickened her pace and prayed Roman could hold on just a little longer.

"There," Billy shouted.

Eliza saw it. Yellow light a little way ahead. The hellhounds howled louder, as if calling to others for help, and Eliza kicked faster. Roman had become a dead weight and her aching arms screamed for some respite. But it wasn't enough to stop her running.

They reached the source of the light and bounded through the waiting room doorway. The hounds could be heard outside, but they didn't enter. Maybe they couldn't. They didn't scratch or claw or try to get in. Roman fell from Eliza's grip and sprawled onto the floor. He gasped for air. Pain creased his face and he clutched his stomach. Billy knelt beside him, catching his breath.

Feeling returned to Eliza's biceps. She needed the guys back on their feet. They weren't home and dry yet.

She glanced at the watch and her heart stopped.

They were late by forty seconds.

CHAPTER TWENTY-THREE

TUESDAY

Pink and blue police lights lit up the Ford's rear-view mirror.

Nate pressed his foot down on the accelerator and, for a brief moment, pulled away from the pursuing vehicle. But as with his previous attempts to out-run the Sheriff, the police car caught up again. Nate glanced at the clock on the dash. He was still twenty minutes from reaching the accident site. He had to shake the Sheriff loose.

He tried to think of options – better courses of action than those he'd already thought of. But the same two kept springing to mind. The first was to stop his vehicle, drag the Sheriff out of the police car, and physically put a stop to him following. However, the Sheriff sustaining harm of that magnitude would alert the Elders, and Nate didn't need that kind of attention. The second option was to drive fast and lose him – and that's what Nate had been trying to do for best part of thirty minutes.

So far, he'd been unsuccessful, which was making option one look more and more appealing.

About a mile ahead, a sharp chicane curved the road. Nate dropped the car into third gear and accelerated again. He'd travelled these roads for decades and knew them like the back of his hand. The countryside passed by in a blur. Still, the pink and blue lights kept up with him. But that was good. Nate wanted the Sheriff to speed up.

Road signs warning of the bend whizzed by, hopefully going unnoticed by the Sheriff. Up ahead, black and white metal chevrons curved with the road. Nate sped up. The police car sped up. Nate hit the entrance to the bend. He braked and as the car began to skid, he accelerated again. The car coasted around the bend, its back end kicking out but never quite overtaking the front.

Nate exited the bend and straightened up. He checked the rear-view mirror. A succession of blue flashes – no pink – lit up the trees, but the police car didn't materialise. Nate slowed and put the car into reverse. Slowly, he backed up to the bend. A silly move, but he had to be certain he'd stopped the Sheriff, at least for a while. More of the trees came into view, blue lights flashing the darkness away in quick succession. The black and white chevrons had buckled apart and the police car was wrapped around a tree mid-bend.

Nate smiled. Now the Sheriff would have to make his way on foot. That would give Nate the time he needed to bring Eliza and his brother back from the waiting room. He stuck the Ford into first gear and pulled away. That was one problem out of the way. Now he just had to get to the crash site.

The accident had already happened by the time Nate arrived.

He pulled up on the hard shoulder and stopped just short of the police cordon. Police had blocked the road and traffic queued as far as the eye could see. Nate jumped out of the Ford and ran to the forefront of the massacre. He was late by half an hour. Any longer and he'd lose the window to bring Eliza and his brother back.

He scanned the site. Death hung in the air all around him. It was a smell he never got used to. To his left, he heard a woman crying for her deceased husband. Little did she know she would soon be joining him, all thanks to an unidentified blood clot. Beyond her, a survivor helped police pull a young woman from the wreckage of a Peugeot. A motorcyclist lay groaning beside the central reservation, his mangled bike lying on the other side of the road. None of them were the people Nate needed.

The overturned school bus lay in the middle of the two lanes about one hundred metres ahead, but that was the last call on his list. Damn it. He had to move quick. He had one other soul to return before he brought back the three he'd described to Eliza.

He continued to scan the wreckage for the female he was after. Closing off his mind, he let his senses guide him through the misery. He paused and opened his eyes. Two paramedics crouched beside the black woman he'd described to Eliza. One flung open a defibrillator box and pulled out two pads.

Christ. He had just run out of time. He continued to search the wreckage, looking for a red Porsche. If he found the car, he'd find the first soul he needed to return. He spotted it lying on its roof just beyond the school bus.

Nate started to sprint through the mayhem and none of the emergency services thought to stop him. He glanced across at the paramedic pulling the backing off two pads and strategically sticking them to the black woman's chest. Nate's instructions were to bring this woman back from the waiting room on the first shock. If the defibrillator had to shock her a second time, Nate's window would close and the woman would not return – and neither would Eliza.

He passed them and hurried to the Porsche. The woman was still buckled inside, her eyes closed. Nate pulled the door free and dragged her out. He lay her flat on the tarmac. Wasting no time, he punched down through her chest and clasped her heart in his hand. He wasn't rough about it, just less gentle than he would normally be.

He glanced over his shoulder. The paramedic reached for the defibrillator case, ready to push the button.

Nate looked away. His fist tightened around the girl's heart, immediately feeling her warmth flood his body. The trauma that had come before the woman's death hit him – the impact of the crash, the air bag when it punched her in the face, the steering wheel as it crushed her windpipe. For a second, he struggled to breathe then the woman's heart began to race. Nate removed his hand and her eyes shot open. She gasped for air and, for a second, her body convulsed. Then she stilled. She glanced at Nate and her eyes closed again. But she was alive.

Nate turned back to the black woman. The paramedics administered the first shock.

"No." Nate raced back towards them.

The paramedic checked the black woman's reading then reached to push the defibrillator a second time.

CHAPTER TWENTY-FOUR

Billy nudged Roman. "Time to go."

Roman half sat and rested on his elbows. "Who's going back?" He looked to Eliza for answers. "Can you see them?"

Eliza searched the room. Men, women, and children crowded the small area. They were late, so the accident must have happened already. Or was the room always this packed with people? Had Nate already pulled their rides back? Would Roman know if he had?

She left the guys where they lay and pushed her way through the crowd. So many people, none of whom met Nate's descriptions. She glanced back at her brother, catching a quick glimpse of him before the crowds swallowed him up again. He looked beat, ready to give up. She had no idea what the two of them had been through, but she had come too far to throw in the towel at the eleventh hour.

Her heart skipped a beat when she saw the black woman standing in the far corner, looking lost and frightened like everyone else waiting here. Nate had relayed that she was the first to be collected. And he hadn't yet, which meant the other people were also in here somewhere. Eliza shoved her way through the crowd and grabbed the woman by the wrist. She flicked her hand over, elated to find a small, red heart tattooed just above her palm.

The woman started to protest, but Eliza quietened her. "Come with me."

"No."

"I'm taking you back to your family."

The woman's confusion turned to relief. She eagerly grabbed Eliza's waiting hand and followed her back to Billy.

"This lady is returning first." Eliza stood the lady beside Roman.

Roman shook his head. "Billy needs to go first."

Billy stood. "I'm not going first. Eliza can go first."

"I need to stay and find the others." Eliza looked at Roman. "You're in a bad way, Roman. Whatever has happened to you, you're not healing properly in here. It needs to be you."

Roman dismissed her. He struggled to his feet and addressed Billy. "She needs to find the others and you need to be shown how to leave."

"You're in no state—"

A bright light manifested across the ceiling. The waiting people shielded their eyes, and Eliza and Billy did the same.

"You need to hook on," Roman shouted to Billy.

"How?"

"Just jump at her. When I tell you."

"I'm not leaving without my sister."

"She'll be right behind you. I won't let any harm come to her. You have my word. Now concentrate."

Roman shifted his weight. He could hardly hold himself upright. "If this light is coming for her, you need to be hooked on. Just jump and hold on."

The light brightened. Billy began to protest. A flash exploded above them and Roman pushed him against the woman.

When the room returned to normal, Billy and the woman had vanished.

Eliza looked at Roman. "It's that easy?"

"When you know who's going back, yeah, it's that easy. So, who's next?"

Eliza directed her attention back towards the remaining people in the room. "The guy's six feet tall. Blue jumper. Beard."

Roman scanned the crowd. He grabbed her shoulder, spun her a little to her right, and pointed. "There."

Eliza spotted the man immediately. He stood out like a sore thumb and she was amazed she hadn't noticed him during her previous walkabout. She left Roman and approached him.

He was tall. Like, really, really tall. Way over six feet in her opinion. She waved for him to bow to her level.

"Do you want to go home?" she whispered.

The man straightened up. He stared at her and nodded, looking a little sceptical.

Eliza beckoned him to follow her and was amazed when he did.

Roman waited for her. He looked worse than ever. Why weren't his injuries self-healing here?

"Good, you go back with this one," he said.

"No. I need to find the third ride."

"Describe them to me. I'll find them."

"You can hardly stand. How are you going to work the room?"

"Eliza, don't argue with me," he said. But his face had paled beyond recognition. Dark circles rounded his eyes. His lips trembled with every shallow breath he inhaled.

The ceiling brightened, only this time the light was pale green.

"This one is not for us," Roman said.

The light whirled like a tornado and lowered. It swirled through the crowd and latched onto an older man sitting a little way from them. His panama hat blew from his head and a green bolt of lightning descended from the light and struck the top of his skull. Green light flashed out of his nostrils. His eyes glowed emerald then switched to a dull khaki. White steam sizzled from his body like a fine mist. The scent of burning flesh filled the air. His skin browned and his arm hairs scorched and blackened. A large crack erupted overhead and a searing flash killed all visibility. When Eliza's sight returned, the man was gone.

Eliza tried to blink the remaining brightness from her eyes. "What was that?"

"He's going down one of the other pathways."

"What one?"

"Hell." Roman limped towards her. "You need to leave with this guy."

The tall man remained beside them. "When do I get to go home?"

Eliza reached for his arm. "Trust me. You're going home soon."

"How do you know that?"

The white light blossomed above them.

Eliza looked at Roman. "You need to leave."

"No. Tell me who's next. I'll find them and meet you back in Cornwall in less than ten minutes."

The light brightened and the room's occupants shielded their eyes. Eliza grabbed Roman's hand and pulled him into an embrace.

She lightly kissed his cheek. "I'm sorry."

Roman pulled back. Confusion darkened his blue eyes, but it was too late. Eliza had found the motel again. The movie reel inside her head played. Roman's eyes widened. He knew what she was about to do.

"Eliza. Don't."

Roman reached for her, but an invisible force stopped him from touching her. The light brightened and he was catapulted back against the taller man.

Eliza shut her eyes. She couldn't watch him go. Light crackled and popped behind her lids. When she reopened her eyes, Roman and the tall man were no longer in front of her.

CHAPTER TWENTY-FIVE

Roman slipped out of the unconscious body.

The driver didn't move. He remained slumped across the steering wheel of his articulated lorry. Roman dragged himself across to the passenger seat. Agony pierced his abdomen and the goddamn robe he still wore caught on the handbrake. It took him a good minute of cursing to unhook it. He reached the chair and let out a sigh, waiting for the pain to subside.

Through the cracked windscreen, he saw a pile-up of vehicles. A motorbike was wrapped around the central reservation; a second bike lay on the other side of the road. A mangled pile of some eight to ten cars blocked a good part of the road, and a coach, which looked to be full of junior school kids, lay on its side, water dripping from its radiator.

Roman reached for the door handle and groaned. He wanted to get out but, truth was, he could barely move. The injuries he'd sustained in the torture room needed time to heal. And it wasn't just his injuries that stopped him from leaving the cab. It was exhaustion. The journey from Purgatory had taken its toll on him. He couldn't lift his arms and it took all his remaining strength just to hold his head up.

"We have one over here."

A couple of police officers ran his way. They split up in front of the cab. Within seconds, one had the driver's door open and the other was leaning through the passenger door.

"You okay, fella? I can't believe we missed you." The copper looked into Roman's eyes. "Are you hurting anywhere?"

"I'm fine." Roman nudged him away. "Just a little winded."

The officer felt for his pulse anyway. "Okay, pal, just stay here. I'll get a paramedic to look you over."

He disappeared back through the door and Roman watched him run across the road to where a paramedic stood beside a little Fiat 500 that had rear-ended a Merc. The windscreen was smashed in and the female inside looked to have a head injury. Roman sensed she was already dead. That wasn't his concern, though. Eliza was. He swept his gaze over the carnage. Bodies everywhere. The majority of them were tucked away in the wreckage that had once been their cars. Most were dead. No wonder the waiting room had been so full.

Roman kept looking. Past the paramedics. Past the police and their roadblocks. Past the fire crews cutting crushed vehicles apart. Across the backed-up traffic and its occupants. But no matter how carefully Roman combed the area, he couldn't locate Eliza.

The police officer had left the passenger door wide open. Just as well. Roman wasn't sure he had the strength to push it. He swung his legs out and fell onto the road. Shit, he felt so fucking useless right now.

"Roman." Billy limped over to him. "Just give it a minute, man. Your legs will come back; it just takes a while."

"I know. I've done this before, remember?" Roman held out his hand for Billy to pull him up. Once standing, he took a breath. He felt steady enough to walk. "Where's Eliza?"

"Over there." Billy pointed at a man.

Roman recognised him immediately. It was his brother – leaning over the body of a small boy.

"Your brother is with her. The teacher survived. Paramedics have just taken her away. She collapsed with shock, seeing most of the children dead and all."

Roman hadn't seen or spoken to his brother in centuries. His muscles tensed and he walked towards him, pushing any lingering exhaustion from his body.

He locked onto the back of Nate's head. "Where is she?"

Nate didn't look up.

It was no surprise to Roman. His brother hated him. Despised him. It was a mystery how Eliza had gotten him to agree to this Purgatory breakout. Roman glanced down at the child. A white blanket was pulled up over his head.

"Hey. You hear me? Where the fuck is she?"

Nate scoffed but declined to give any other acknowledgement that Roman was there.

Really? This was how his brother was going to play it? Roman reached out to grab him. Pain ripped through his backside and he stopped short.

He paused to take a breath and lowered his hands. "Get her the hell out, Nate."

"It's not time yet."

Roman closed his eyes and unclenched his fists. His body ached to the point of collapsing. "How long?"

"Less than a minute."

CHAPTER TWENTY-SIX

For the briefest of moments, Eliza rejoiced in pulling off the impossible.

She'd saved her brother and Roman. Something Nate had not thought her capable of doing. Something even she'd started to believe was impossible. But reality quickly reared its ugly head and fear rocked her. Because now she was here all alone.

She frantically started to search the room again, desperate to find the child Nate had described to her. The waiting room's occupants didn't seem to thin out, no matter how many were taken by the lights. Eliza pressed through the crowd. People of all shapes and sizes surrounded her. Some moved out of the way; others seemed to block her route on purpose. Several children crossed her path, all causing a flutter of hope that this child was the one to take her home. But not one of them resembled the little boy she was looking for.

Above, the light began to form and Eliza quickened her pace through the horde of people. Her hands began to shake and tears threatened to spill. She pushed up her sleeves, hoping the air would cool her warming body. She'd done her bit. Now she just wanted to go home.

The light overhead brightened. Time had just run out.

Tears streamed down her face. She shoved people out of her way, rushing through the crowd. She couldn't see properly anymore, her vision a tunnel.

There. In the corner of the room. Two identical-looking children. She ran over to them. They clung to each other, scared to death. Eliza's tears turned to sobs. One of these children would be left here alone, like she was now, and her heart broke. The crackle and pop of the light above sounded like a sparkler on fireworks night. Only seconds remained before Nate pulled one of these kids back.

Eliza knelt in front of them and smiled. They couldn't be any older than six or seven. For a moment, she wondered if there was a way they could all go back. Maybe if she grabbed hold of both? Would that work? Could she save them both as well as herself? No. She couldn't. If there had been a way for more than one person to hitch a ride back at once, Nate would have said. She, Billy and Roman could have gone together.

Truth was, though, she couldn't bear to leave one of them behind.

She ran a hand through her hair and lowered her head. The child on her right had blue laces threaded through his white trainers. She looked at the other twin – red laces.

A chuckle left her lips. She wiped her eyes, her decision already made.

The little boy with blue laces stared at her and the white light brightened. Eliza embraced the twin with the red laces and covered his face. The light crackled overhead. She'd given up her chance to return to her life, and she could live with that, but the little boy with red laces didn't have to.

Eliza pushed him towards his brother. Nate would see what she'd done. He would protect them somehow.

"Hold onto each other as tight as you can."

The brightness filled the whole room. Eliza's life was over, but the two little boys' lives were just beginning. She could find comfort in that knowledge when the Sheriff inevitably caught up with her and dragged her off to the torture room.

Someone ran up beside her and a man's arms pulled the red-laced boy from his brother's embrace. Eliza reached out and tried to pull the man back, but he spun and punched her in the side of the face. Eliza hit the ground. The red-laced boy ran to her. The man leapt for the blue-laced brother.

The light disappeared, taking the blue-laced boy with it. The man who'd hit her vanished with him. What the hell had just happened? She glanced down at the small boy curled in her arms and her heart broke for him. She didn't know what to do. She didn't understand how this waiting room malarkey worked. She tightened her hold around the boy. All she could do was stay seated on the floor and pray for something good to happen.

A person approached her, their shadow hovering over her like a dark cloud on a stormy night.

Excitement pumped through her veins. Roman had returned for her. She looked up – and her blood turned cold.

"Hello, Eliza," the Sheriff said. "I've been looking for you."

Eliza moved the little boy from her lap and stood. The Sheriff wore his true form –hunched and pale, his coat stretched tight across his shoulders. He towered over her.

"You're too late. Everyone's gone," Eliza said, moving the child behind her.

"I'm not here for everyone. I'm here for you."

The little boy clung tight to Eliza's thigh. He peered around her, his tear-stained face white with terror. Any escape plans she had bubbling away inside her head immediately fizzled out.

The Sheriff knelt before her. Even on his knees, his head still reached her shoulder. He pointed his bony finger towards the boy and motioned for him to come forward.

"Leave him alone." Eliza pulled the child back. She stepped in front of him again. "He is not yours."

The Sheriff laughed. He stood and held out his hands, inviting her to look at all the people in the room. "All of them are mine."

"I don't believe you. I know how it works down here. I know you only get the ones that have nowhere else to go. I'd bet my life that this little boy is destined for Heaven."

The Sheriff's smile soured. "Maybe he is, but you are fair game."

"I thought it was Roman you wanted."

"It is. But I am tired of chasing him. He will come for you – and you will be with me."

"I'm not going to make it easy for you to take me."

Eliza searched her memories and found the motel room.

The Sheriff grabbed the top of her head, curling his fingers around her skull and pushing her down onto her knees. "Unfortunately for you, witch, I don't have time to play. So, I *am* going to make it easy."

Eliza tried to break free, but the Sheriff held her tight. She tried to concentrate. Tried to hold onto the motel room. Tried to find Roman's embrace. But her eyes began to burn. She cried out and the little boy sobbed along with her. He wrapped his tiny arms around her shoulders, his tears staining the back of her neck.

The motel room started to fade from her thoughts and other memories followed it: Billy looking out of the hospital widow days before floated from her mind. And Roman –standing on her doorstep in the pouring rain, a scar curving his mouth, his blue eyes lighting up when he saw her – vanished along with it. Now he was just a faceless person among a score of others.

Eliza's arms fell limp by her sides. She stared ahead.

Who was she?

CHAPTER TWENTY-SEVEN

"Where the fuck is she?" Roman paced the road.

Nate stood. His height and build almost matched Roman's. He glared, defiance hardening his eyes. "You know how this works. Give her time. She'll leave his body when she's ready."

"Yes, but you brought that kid back five minutes ago. She should be out by now."

"Let's not forget that you're the reason she's in there in the first place."

Roman pushed him aside. He lowered himself beside the child, the white blanket now pulled up to his chin. The kid's eyes remained closed, but small, shallow breaths passed his lips. Beside him lay another blanketed form, identical in size. The sheet covered the child completely; only the red laces tying his trainers were on show. A bad feeling swept over Roman.

He looked up at Nate. "Sibling?"

"Twin."

"Shit. Tell me they're both coming back."

"Just him." Nate crouched beside Roman. "You don't think she'll come back?"

"And leave a child behind, alone?" Roman ran his hands through his hair. "No. She ain't fucking coming back."

Roman stood, winced, and paced the tarmac again. His legs were feeling stronger, but his backside was still tender. He rubbed the back of his neck and his shoulders tensed. He couldn't think straight. Fuck. How could he leave her there? He should have been prepared for her to use her powers and made her come back before him in that fucking lorry driver.

He stopped pacing. "I'm going back for her."

Nate stood. "Don't be stupid."

"Don't fucking call me that." Roman tried to side-step him, but Nate grabbed him by the shoulders and held him still. Roman moved to break free, but his strength hadn't fully returned. He looked his brother in the eye. "I cannot leave her there."

"She made her choice."

"Like you did with me?"

Nate's lips hardened. "I've done my bit. I'm out of here."

Billy stopped him. "Please. You have to save my sister."

"Like I said to Roman, I warned her of the dangers and she made her choice anyway. If you want to blame anyone for the mess she's in, blame my brother."

"No. You made the choice." Roman spun Nate around to face him. "You sent her in there. Alone. On a fucking suicide mission."

"Which I couldn't have done if you hadn't sent her to me in the first place."

"A moment of weakness, believe me." He jabbed Nate in the chest and pushed him back. "What the fuck were you thinking?"

"Hey," Billy interjected. "Now is not the time for a family spat, okay? Let's just put our heads together and work out how to get my sister back."

Roman didn't want to work shit out. He knew what he wanted to do. He wanted to punch the living crap out of something. He wanted to dive straight back into Purgatory and get Eliza out of there. He ground his teeth and swallowed. Tried to relax but couldn't.

He glanced down at the child and saw his chest arch from the ground, ready for a soul to emerge.

"Holy shit, she did come back." Roman lowered himself to the child's side again.

A shadow floated from the child. Roman watched it hover for a moment and then move to the side of the road a couple of metres away. Eliza was seconds from being back. The shadow's transparency clouded and a shape slowly formed. Roman stood. Something wasn't right. The manifestation seemed to be taller than Eliza. More masculine.

He waited, watching the shadow morph into a person, and his fists clenched tight. "No fucking way."

James Hamilton swayed before them, unsteady on his feet.

Pure hatred consumed Roman. "I'm going to fucking kill you." He charged at James, his fists eager to connect.

Roman threw a punch. He hit James and knocked him to the ground. Roman drew back for another swipe but Nate threaded his arms under Roman's armpits. He interlocked his fingers around the back of Roman's neck and pulled him off balance, preventing him from further assault.

"You fucking shit. Where the hell is Eliza?" Roman's frenzy didn't die. He kicked out at James and tried to break his brother's grip.

Nate dragged Roman back. "Jesus Christ, people are watching. You need to calm the hell down." He released his hold and threw Roman against a white van that lay on its side.

Roman slammed against the roof and Nate held him there, his arm pressed against Roman's chest.

He eyeballed Roman, a light sweat glistening across his creased brow. "He can't tell us anything if you beat him to a pulp first."

Two police officers ran over. "What's going on here?"

Still holding Roman, Nate turned to them. "We're all fine here." He held out his free hand.

The officer nodded and shook it, followed by his partner. They apologised for the interruption and returned to helping their colleagues – no more questions asked.

Hell, Roman missed being able to Jedi-mind-fuck people. He stole a glimpse over Nate's shoulder. James stirred but remained on the ground. Roman couldn't wait for Nate and his softly-softly approach to find out what the bastard had done to Eliza. But he was incapable of doing anything while Nate held him. He took a deep breath. Forced his breathing to slow. Made his shoulders relax.

"We good?" Nate said, his attention back on him.

Roman nodded.

Slowly, Nate released his grip and stepped back.

As soon as Roman saw daylight between them, he raced at James again. He clasped Eliza's father by his collar and swung a punch at him so hard, he expected to feel the back of the bastard's skull. "What the fuck did you do to her?"

Blood dribbled from James mouth. "I couldn't stay there. She's stronger than me. She'll handle it better."

Roman swung again.

This time, Billy was on him. "If anyone's gonna kill him, it's gonna be me."

He pushed Roman aside and swung his own punch at his father. He took hold of James's collar, pretty much the same as Roman had, and swung again.

Nate looked on. "Are we all going to beat him up?"

"You can always leave." Roman said.

"Actually, I was going to make the observation that none of this is being handled correctly."

Roman snorted. "What? You'd rather he confess all in a sin box?"

He started to pace again. He itched to kill James. Adrenaline shook his hands, his arms, his entire being.

"Actually, I was going to suggest you drag him over to the verge." Nate walked up behind Billy. "Too many people can see you here."

Roman watched his brother – a man of God – help Billy drag James across the grass verge and into the woodland. Wow. His brother actually had a pair of balls hanging between his legs after all. Who'd have thought? For a small moment, Roman's admiration for his brother's balls of steel softened his interior. But it was fleeting moment and the feeling vanished before it really had time to make its mark.

Roman glanced at the emergency services – all busy getting on with their jobs and not the slightest bit interested in the man Roman was about to kill.

"Hey," he shouted out to them. "We got a live one here." He motioned to the child with the blue shoelaces then followed his brother and Billy into the trees.

James tried to yell for help.

Roman marched straight up to him and struck him across the side of the head. "You'd better start talking because I'm ready to pummel every last shit out of you." He glanced at his brother. "He's the one who started all this mess."

"He sacrificed his own daughter?" Nate tutted and wagged his finger at James. "Now that wasn't a very nice thing to do, was it?"

James whimpered. "Please. There's nothing any of us can do about it now."

"I wouldn't say that." Billy turned to Roman. "What d'you reckon? Killing his sorry arse may make us feel a little better."

Roman grabbed James and lifted him off the ground. He slammed him against a tree and moved real close, almost nose to nose. "Tell me what happened to her or I'll kill you where you stand."

"Eliza. She showed me the child. Made me get in him."

"You're fucking lying." Roman slammed him up against the tree again.

James cried out. He tried to reach behind him, but Roman smacked his hands back down and seized him by the chin.

James struggled, but Roman didn't loosen his hold. He pressed his fingers against James's jaw and tilted his head upwards. "You stole the ride from her, didn't you?"

"N…no. I swear."

Roman leaned closer. Fear wafted off the Cornish mayor in droves; Roman could smell it. But when he stared into the man's eyes, he couldn't find an ounce of remorse. Just regret at being caught.

"Did you hurt her?"

"No! She wasn't coming back. She was sending the other kid back instead."

Roman punched James in the gut and let him drop to the ground.

He turned to his brother. "You owe me nothing, but I'm begging you. Please. Send me back for her."

"Don't be stupid, Roman." Nate crossed his arms.

Roman sprang towards his brother, pushing him across the small clearing until he wedged him against the opposite tree. "Fucking send me back."

Nate shoved him away. "What then?"

Roman took a swing, but Nate easily blocked it. He hooked Roman's arm and twisted him round to face the other direction. Then he locked an arm around

Roman's neck. Roman struggled, but it was all in vain. Nate had him trapped.

His brother leaned in close and Roman felt his breath against his ear when he spoke. "Stop thinking with your emotions. Start thinking with your head. I won't be able to get you out."

"Then it's a win-win for you."

Nate removed his arm. "The past doesn't rule me."

Roman stared at his brother. He wanted to argue. He needed his brother to feed his anger with cheap shots and snide comments. What Roman didn't need was understanding and calmness.

"There must be others around here due to be resurrected."

"There were only four. Eliza needed all the time she could get, so I gave her the final three. The kid was the last one to be resurrected."

"Back to plan A then. I'll kill him." Roman grabbed James. "It's unsanctioned, so you'll have to bring him back. Eliza can hitch a ride with him."

"And how is Eliza going to know that James is her ride out of there? Come on, Roman. Think. You know how all this works."

"Do it anyway." Roman turned on James, headbutted him, and kneed him in the stomach.

James doubled over and Roman elbowed him between the shoulder blades. James dropped to his knees.

Roman hauled him back to his feet. "Jesus Christ. There's no way this piece of shit is staying alive if Eliza dies."

"Eliza is not a soul to bring back. She needs a vessel."

"Then I'll kill one of them out there." Roman pointed towards the accident scene. "Send me back and I'll make sure she's hooked on for when you bring them back."

Roman's voice cracked. He let go of James and stared at his brother. His vision blurred. "Please. I don't care what happens to me. I do care what happens to her."

Nate shook his head. "I'm not going to let you kill random people for your own gain."

Roman's throat tightened. "You think I want her because she's a mind mover?" Bitterness consumed him. His brother thought the worst of him and rightly so, even if he was offering up his own life to save hers. "Nathaniel, don't let our history be Eliza's downfall."

"You're a wanted man, Roman. You'll be caught the moment I send you back and then we'll be back at square one again." Nate turned his back. "I'll go."

"You?" Roman narrowed his eyes.

"Yes, me."

"You'd be breaking the rules."

Nate shrugged.

"And you'd do that? For me?"

"Who said I'd be doing it for you?"

"Then why?"

"Because she's an innocent caught up in your mess. My conscience can't leave her there."

Roman wanted to pull his brother close and thank him. To apologise for every wrong he'd ever inflicted upon him in the past. Instead, he just stared at him. Aiding Eliza's escape would be his brother's undoing. Roman knew he should stop him. Tell him not to throw his life away. "Do it."

Nate nodded and threw him a set of car keys. "White Ford's mine."

And he faded away.

CHAPTER TWENTY-EIGHT

The waiting room was full to the rafters.

But, then, it always was. Scores of people arrived and departed by the minute.

Nate walked through the crowd. Eliza wasn't anywhere that he could see, or sense, and a bad feeling gnawed at his gut. To his right, over by the far wall, he saw the door that led through to the Purgatory tunnels. He sensed the hellhounds. Not in the immediate vicinity, but nearby. Outside. Waiting. The Sheriff had not turned up at the accident site and that was worrying. Now, with the mutts outside, he was certain the Sheriff had returned here after the accident. With Eliza MIA, he could only imagine the Sheriff had taken her. He sighed. Bringing her back wasn't going to be the get in, get her, and get out scenario he'd first anticipated.

On the other side of the room was the door that led through to the Elders. It had not been Nate's intention to have a conversation with them, but with Eliza not being here, he'd have to chase down the Sheriff – and no way was that meeting going to end without some kind of retaliation. He pushed through the crowd of people, opened the door, and headed down the narrow corridor to where the centurion waited for him.

Nate bowed, knowing a show of respect was expected. "I have a request."

The centurion stepped aside. Nate bowed again and entered through the black gate. He stepped inside the room, waited half a minute for the stone entrance to materialise, and entered the white room. He stood on the pentagon mark in the middle of the floor and prepared himself for the panel of Elders to come forth.

One by one, they appeared before him, until all five curved around the table.

"You have a request?" the Elder in the centre said.

"Sire, I am here to ask for the return of an innocent soul."

"Innocent how?"

"She is being held here, against her will and before her time. I have come here to seek your consent to collect her and immediately return her to her life."

The Elder glanced at his peers. No words were exchanged.

He turned back to Nate. "We are aware that several illegal entities have entered Purgatory over the last few days."

"Not illegals. They too were innocents."

"But now they are gone?"

"I believe so."

"And, yet, this girl remains?"

"Yes."

The Elder waved him on. "You have permission to elaborate."

Nate straightened and clasped his hands behind his back. "Sire, I am sure the Sheriff has her and, as such, is acting illegally not only in having taken her, but also by withholding his actions from you."

"What evidence do you have to support your claim?"

"I believe the Sheriff wants my brother."

"We know of the Sheriff's vendetta against your brother. He has been ordered to stand down."

"My brother is no longer sort after?"

"Your brother's bounty is centuries old and still active. But we declared it not to be actionable at this time."

"Sire, I do not wish to speak out of turn, but the Sheriff has ignored your orders. Just yesterday he came to me, seeking the girl. I am now certain he has taken her hostage so as to entice my brother to return."

"Then your brother will return and be back where he belongs."

"True, but my brother is not my concern. The girl is. She ought not be used as a pawn."

Again, the Elder glanced at his peers. Each nodded their agreement.

The middle Elder turned back to Nate. "Your comments have been noted. The Sheriff's current duties within Purgatory will be discussed in private."

"Then I have your permission to collect the girl?"

"No."

"But you agreed—"

"Your brother is not a priority of this court. However, if he deems it necessary to return here, for whatever reason, then he will be imprisoned to finish out his sentence. You are ordered to leave both the girl and the Sheriff alone."

"And what happens to the girl after my brother is apprehended?"

But the Elders vanished and Nate was left standing alone in the white room. He clenched his fists and turned to the stone arch. He crossed the room to where the centurion stood beside the open gate. He didn't bow as he left.

Back in the waiting room, Nate squeezed through the people and headed towards the Purgatory tunnels. For the entirety of his reaping afterlife, he'd played by the rules – respected them, even. But for the Elders to condone an innocent person's imprisonment...it sickened him, regardless of any punishment they might hand down to the Sheriff. Everybody seemed to be making up their own rules; now it was time for Nate to make up his.

He opened the door and entered the tunnels. As expected, hellhounds waited on the other side. They leapt up the moment the door opened, barking and snarling. Saliva dripped over their yellow fangs. Nate clicked his fingers. He pointed to the ground beside him and, immediately, the barking ceased. The hounds lowered their heads and cowered into the space beside him, whimpering their obedience.

Ahead, a multitude of tunnels branched out into the darkness. Each one led deeper into Purgatory – and towards the torture room. Nate closed his eyes and concentrated. Eliza had been here; he detected her essence in the air. He also picked up Roman and Billy and various others – probably the Sheriff's guards. He tried to push the trace of everybody else away and focus solely on Eliza, but it had been way too busy down here recently.

Nate knelt before the hound to his right. He scratched behind the mutt's ear and clutched his head in his hands. "Where's the girl?"

The beast tilted his head. His ears pointed and he stared at Nate. Then, as if on cue, he took off down the middle tunnel. The second hound quickly followed, leaving Nate to bring up the rear.

He didn't have to run far, a small blessing considering time was an issue. The Sheriff walked a little way ahead. He wasn't rushing, as Nate had thought he would be, and there were no guards around that Nate could detect. Clearly, the Sheriff hadn't contemplated a rescue attempt this early on.

The hounds barked and the Sheriff turned. He scratched his head and frowned when he saw the dogs.

Nate jogged out of the darkness.

"Not the Holbrook I was expecting to see." The Sheriff threw back his shoulders and sauntered towards Nate. Just not close enough for Nate to grab him. "So, what brings you down here?"

Beyond the Sheriff, Nate saw Eliza. "I see you found the girl,"

Eliza stood frozen to the spot, her arms hanging lank by her sides and not an ounce of recognition lightening her face when she looked at Nate.

Nate looked back at the Sheriff. "You know, my car has a whacking big dent in it because of you."

"Is that why you're here? Because of what happened at the church?" The Sheriff shifted forward a little more. "You took your revenge on the road. Clever manoeuvre, taking the bend at speed like that. Caught me unawares."

Nate stood his ground and smiled. The Sheriff hadn't positioned himself to fight but, rather, to obstruct his view of Eliza. He was smart not to trust Nate and clever to block Nate from getting his hands on her.

The Sheriff narrowed his eyes. "So, what are you doing here, then? You certainly didn't come all this way to discuss our driving habits."

"More to the point, what are you doing here?"

The Sheriff's face took on a quizzical expression. He straightened, looking like he was trying to assert a little authority with his stance. "I'm collecting an intruder."

"Who? The girl?"

"Yes."

"Under whose orders?"

"The Elders."

"Really?" Nate stepped closer. "Because I've just been speaking to them."

The Sheriff stiffened. "You've spoken to them?" He stepped back, keeping his distance.

"Hmm..." Nate took another step forward, this one slower, not as obvious. "They want a word with you."

The Sheriff moved Eliza further behind him. He looked Nate up and down and narrowed his eyes.

"Twice you've had my brother and twice you've lost him," Nate continued.

The Sheriff pursed his lips. "I have not lost him."

"So, he was released, then?"

The Sheriff marched towards Nate, his index finger outstretched. "You listen to me, reaper. You have no business questioning the way I run things down here."

"Maybe not. But the Elders do. You had no authority to take the girl."

The Sheriff remained silent, his expression strained.

"In fact, you had no authority to go after my brother either." Nate could see that the Sheriff's lack of dominance over this conversation annoyed him. "So, I'll ask you again. What are you doing down here with the girl?"

The Sheriff flashed him an uneasy smile. His irritation was clearly on the verge of spilling over. He nodded back in Eliza's direction. "Your brother will return for her."

Nate laughed. "You're an idiot. My brother's long gone."

"A couple of days ago, I would have agreed with you. But I have seen a difference in him. He has deep affection for this girl."

"My brother cares for no one other than himself. He's used the girl to make a fool of you." Nate tilted his head and looked at Eliza. She stood motionless, zombie-like. No emotion on her face. No life in her eyes. "I see you stunned her?"

The Sheriff stiffened. "She has powers—"

"Hell, we all have powers." Nate edged further forward. "But you're wasting your time with her. My brother would never sacrifice himself for another."

"I disagree. She is the key to catching him and elevating my standing with the Elders."

"He's trackable now. Why not just go get him?"

"This way is easier."

"Or maybe it's because you've been told to step down?"

Nate sighed. Too much time was being wasted. He'd tried to retrieve Eliza the easy way, causing the least amount of fuss possible. The Sheriff wasn't biting. Hell. Nate had to take Eliza back the messy way. He grinned. "You are disillusioned, my friend. Whatever the Elders have in store for you, it certainly isn't a promotion." Plan B it was. He reached for Eliza.

The Sheriff knocked Nate's hand away. "We could join forces. You hate your brother as much as I do."

"Maybe. But I hate you more."

The Sheriff sneered. "Then I guess we must do battle."

"You're making the wrong decision taking me on," Nate said.

"See, I have this nagging doubt, right back here." The Sheriff patted the back of his head. "And it's screaming deceit and dishonesty – on your part." He wrapped his arm around Eliza's shoulders and pulled her close. "I don't think the Elders have granted you permission to take this girl either, and that means you'll lose your reaper status if you do. You'll be just like your brother – fair game."

The Sheriff turned from Nate, spinning Eliza with him, and started off along the passageway towards the chamber.

Nate curled his fingers until his hands formed fists. He let out a short, sharp whistle and the hounds attacked.

The Sheriff heard the order. He spun back around in time to see the first mutt strike. He pushed Eliza aside and raised his arms, blocking the razor-sharp teeth from sinking into his shoulder. The second dog attacked low. It bit into the Sheriff's calf and dragged the Sheriff onto one knee.

Nate dashed for Eliza and pulled her from harm's way. The dogs needed space to do what they did best: maul, maim, and mutilate.

The first beast clawed at the Sheriff, snapping left to right, trying to find any unprotected flesh to rip apart. The Sheriff moved quicker, serving up his forearm to take the brunt of the lacerations. The two grappled for domination. Saliva spat from the animal's mouth. The Sheriff bellowed, caught hold of the dog's neck, and snapped it. The hellhound's head flopped to one side, his black tongue swinging from the side of its mouth. Its wilted legs ceased kicking and the Sheriff flung its lifeless body against the wall.

The second hound attacked harder. It ripped into the Sheriff's leg, tearing flesh and muscle from the bone.

The Sheriff screamed, but it sounded more from frustration than pain. "I will see you burn in Hell for this betrayal, Nathaniel."

"Right after my brother, eh?"

Along the hall, Nate heard the trample of guards racing to the Sheriff's aid. It didn't matter. Nate had what he'd come for. He clasped Eliza's hand and linked his fingers with hers. His life would be different now. But he was doing the right thing. Now he just had to get her back safely. One thing was for sure – he'd be damned if he'd let Roman get his hands on her again.

He stared down at the Sheriff. The hellhound had torn his lower leg apart. But that wouldn't kill the Sheriff. He couldn't die from something that simple. The hound might have the upper hand for now, but he would soon lose his life. The Sheriff would quickly heal. And then it would be game-on once more.

But Nate was ready. He was a Holbrook, after all.

CHAPTER TWENTY-NINE

The Sheriff looked down at the dead hellhound.

Its lifeless body lay slumped in a heap beside the Sheriff's feet. Blood – the Sheriff's – reddened its fur, but otherwise it looked to be asleep. It had taken all the Sheriff's strength to snap the mutt's neck. Shame. The dog had been his favourite.

The Sheriff brushed the dirt from his coat and limped back along the corridor. His mauled arms had healed, but his pride hadn't. As soon as the Sheriff dragged Roman back to Purgatory, he was returning for the younger brother. And this time he would walk away the victor.

He was metres from the waiting room when one of his aides caught up with him. "Sir, the Elders have sent for you."

The Sheriff had expected as much. He'd never doubted Nate's admission that he had spoken to them. "Inform them that I have already left."

"Sir?"

The Sheriff opened the waiting room door. "The instruction is simple. It will not be repeated."

The aide bowed but made no attempt to leave.

"Is there something else?"

"Sir, the Elders were insistent that you attend the white room immediately."

The Sheriff exhaled. "I cannot attend if I did not receive the message."

The aide bowed again and stepped back. He didn't speak again.

Satisfied, the Sheriff turned and entered the waiting room. He hated this place. The stench of innocence usually far outweighed that of the condemned, and today was no different. He pushed through the crowd but went unnoticed. His presence could not be detected in this room unless he deemed it necessary. When he reached the gateway, he paused and sniffed the cool air that floated through from beyond. He closed his eyes and concentrated. He knew Roman's scent better than his own and, as Roman had recently escaped, his aroma was strong.

The Sheriff locked onto his essence and smiled. Roman had returned to Cornwall, England. He stretched his neck and felt his shoulder blades crack into a different form. His arms shortened and his torso contracted. He felt his long hair lift from his shoulders. When he opened his eyes, his coat had been replaced with the familiar police uniform.

He straightened the hat and stepped through the gateway – following the odour that would lead him to Roman.

CHAPTER THIRTY

The Ford's engine turned over but didn't start.

Roman whacked the steering wheel. Lately, his luck with cars was total shit. He took a deep breath and turned the key again. The engine groaned…and did very little else. He sat back, chewed his lip, and felt the mounting frustration ready to spill over. Eliza was at the forefront of his mind. He couldn't shake her away. What the hell had she been thinking choosing to stay in the waiting room so some kid could come back instead?

Roman folded his arms across his chest and rested his head against the back of the seat. He'd been ready to return and save her from Purgatory. He would have stayed there just to get her home safe. Instead, he'd entrusted the responsibility to his brother. His brother who hated him. His brother who'd lost a wife and child because of him. His brother whose goddamn car wouldn't start.

Roman tensed. Surely Nate wouldn't use this chance to take his revenge?

Billy appeared at the window. "It's been hours. Where are they?"

"What?" Roman snapped out of his dark thoughts.

"I said, shouldn't they be back by now?" Billy opened the door to get in, but Roman got out.

He walked to the front of the car and hopped onto the bonnet. Lifting his feet onto the bumper, he prayed the thing wouldn't fall off, and rested his elbows on his knees.

Billy left the door open. He approached Roman but didn't join him on the bonnet, opting instead to lean against it. "What do you think's happened to them?"

Roman shrugged. "Five minutes down there is like an hour up here. They're fine; I'm sure they are." Of course, he wasn't sure.

"So, this time thing is normal, then?"

Roman turned away. Ambulances had become thin on the ground; most of the victims had been driven to nearby hospitals and the majority of bodies taken to the morgue. Hordes of police still swarmed the area, some collecting the last of the statements, others trying to piece together what had happened here today.

Roman put his head in his hands. He'd never been good at the waiting game and not knowing what was happening was killing him. He should have gone back himself.

"Nate will bring her back," Billy said.

"Will he?" Roman looked up but didn't make eye contact with Billy. Instead, he fixed his gaze on the police activity. "You don't know the history between us."

"You're right; I don't. But I know you. You wouldn't trust her life to just anybody. And neither would I. You trust your brother, which means I have no choice but to trust him as well."

Roman snorted. He wanted to trust his brother but, truth was, the longer he waited, the more he thought he'd been wrong to let Nate go instead of him. He located the little kid with the red laces – one of the last bodies to remain on the ground. A white sheet still covered his tiny body and a forensic officer photographed the area around him. Roman remembered the son he'd lost. Many centuries had passed, but it was still no easier to accept. Shit. Nate had lost that son too. Roman hung his head. There was no way on earth his brother was bringing Eliza back to him.

Billy tapped Roman's arm.

Roman glanced up. Nate stood beside a fire engine. Eliza stood by his side.

Billy raced towards them. He wrapped his sister in his arms, held her at arm's length to look her over, and then pulled her close again. Roman yearned to do the same but held back. Eliza looked bewildered, a little lost. It couldn't be the exhaustion. That only happened when a soul left a host. So, what was it? Roman slid off the bonnet. Billy was too busy cooing over her to notice her expressionless face. The distant look in her eyes. The lack of response when he hugged her. Fuck. Only the Sheriff could have done this to her.

Roman raced through the commotion of crashed vehicles. "He stunned her, didn't he?"

"Are you surprised?" Nate held out his arm, preventing Roman from reaching her. "This is your fault."

"I didn't do this! She's a fucking zombie. Look at her."

"You're the reason she was there!"

Billy stepped back and examined Eliza more carefully. He looked at Nate. "What's wrong with her?"

"The Sheriff wiped her mind."

"Wiped her mind? How? Will she be all right?"

"She'll be fine." Nate turned back to Roman. "No thanks to you."

"Don't keep spurting that crap at me."

Roman dodged past Nate and pushed Billy aside. He stood in front of Eliza. He didn't know what to say. He wanted to scream at her for staying in Purgatory. He wanted to yell at her for even entering it in the first place. He wanted to shout about how fucking stupid and pig-headed she'd been for not doing what he'd asked. Most of all, he wanted to hear her argue back.

Eliza glanced at him as though seeing him for the first time. Roman tried to speak, to reassure her, to apologise to her, but the words stuck in his throat. He stepped forward and wrapped her in his arms. It was all he was currently capable of. He rested his chin on top of her head, inhaled the odour that Purgatory had left behind, and still found the faint scent of strawberries in her hair. He remained like that for a moment, just breathing her in – happy to stay that way forever.

"Roman, she needs to come with me." Nate's voice was steady, but there was an undercurrent of urgency.

"You're not taking her anywhere."

"She's not safe with you."

Roman glared at his brother over Eliza's head. "I said she's not going with you."

"The Sheriff is coming for you."

"Then let him come. I'm ready."

"But is she? He hates you. He defied the Elders coming after her – to get to you. He'll do anything to see you back in the chamber. He's used Eliza against you once already. He'll do it again."

"So? You think she's better off playing house with you?"

Nate stepped forward. "I can keep her safe. What can you do?"

Roman eyed Nate, but his brother wasn't scared of him, and for good reason. Nate still had strength – powers that not even the Sheriff could overcome. Roman held his stance. His rigid body ached. He continued to glare but, inside, he knew Nate was right.

Nate grabbed Roman's arm. "Prove to me you're no longer the selfish bastard I once knew."

Roman shrugged himself free. He glanced at Eliza, only to meet her vacant stare. His brother was right. He'd done this to her.

His hands slipped from Eliza's arms and he turned to Billy. "We need to get moving."

"Together, right?"

Roman glanced back at Nate. "No. We're on our own now."

Nate took Eliza by the arm and gently pulled her to him. "You're doing the right thing."

Roman couldn't look at him. He nodded towards the car. "Keys are in your ignition. James is in your boot."

"Where are you going to go?"

"Better you don't know."

Nate turned Eliza towards his car.

"Hey," Roman called out.

Nate glanced back at him.

"Keep her safe for me."

Nate nodded. "I put the Sheriff down. Should buy you some time."

The smallest of smiles tugged the corners of Nate's lips. Then he turned and Roman watched him walk Eliza towards his car and out of his life forever.

Nate settled her into the passenger seat and walked around to the driver's side. He didn't look at Roman again. Miraculously, the car started and Nate reversed back along the hard shoulder. Roman watched until he could no longer see it.

"Are you sure you know what you're doing?" Billy said.

Roman had no idea what he was doing. He kept watching the hard shoulder, almost hoping Nate would return.

"What are we going to do now?" Billy said.

Roman blinked. He turned and looked around. "We need a car."

"And then what? Where are we going to go?"

Again, Roman had no idea. He hadn't planned this far ahead. He glanced back at the hard shoulder. Still no Nate. Or Eliza. She was gone and he had to forget her if he was going to stay alive.

"We can't stay here," he said finally. "This will be the first place the Sheriff comes looking."

"Then I suggest three rows back. See the Fiat?" Billy pointed past the police cordon. "The slow lane," he added, when Roman didn't react. "I found it earlier when I thought we needed a ride."

Roman stared at the cars, finally spotting the Fiat. "Couldn't you find anything smaller?"

"Hey, what d'you want? A bus? There's only two of us, remember." Billy pulled some keys from his pocket. "And it had these in the ignition."

Roman ducked under the police line and approached the car. It wouldn't have been his first choice. Rust spots nibbled the bonnet and a small crack marked the windscreen. But it was occupant-less, hadn't been totalled in the crash, and it was running.

Billy rushed to the driver's side and Roman couldn't be bothered to argue with him. He climbed into the passenger seat. His foot caught on the underneath of the dash and the plastic moulding snapped away from its bracket. It hung mid-air just above his feet. Jesus, of all the cars Billy could have chosen. He sighed, knowing it would annoy the crap out of him during their journey.

Billy revved the engine. He reached for the manual crank and wound down the window.

Roman welcomed the cool air. He watched Billy force the car into reverse and waited while he pulled back a couple of inches, swung the car around onto the hard shoulder, and put it back into first gear.

Billy held the car still and turned to Roman. "So, where to?"

"As far away from here as possible."

A hand rapped on the driver's door and the Sheriff peered at them through the open window.

Billy turned to Roman, his face drained of colour. "What do I do?"

Roman ignored him. He turned his attention to the Sheriff. "You must really hate me."

The Sheriff smiled. "I'm beyond hatred." He reached for the handle and opened the door.

Billy tensed.

"Stay calm," Roman said.

Billy's hands tightened around the steering wheel. His knuckles whitened and perspiration drenched his forehead.

The Sheriff squatted. He looked past Billy and stared at Roman. "How did you escape the chamber?"

"You still wanna know that?" Roman chuckled – he needed to buy some time while he thought of a way out. "I'm afraid that's a secret that will die with me."

"Then die with you it will." The Sheriff scratched his chin. "And then I'm going after your brother and the girl."

Quick as a flash, the Sheriff grasped Billy around the throat.

Billy tried to prise the Sheriff's fingers free. Roman leaned across and pulled at the Sheriff's hand.

The Sheriff's grip couldn't be broken. Billy's face reddened. He struggled for air. The Sheriff could have easily snapped his neck, but he was playing with him – dragging out Billy's death for as painfully long as he could.

"Clutch," Roman yelled.

Billy's bulging eyes looked at him and realisation of what Roman was asking flooded through the fear. Billy's leg straightened and his foot pressed down on the clutch. Roman pushed the car into gear and, without any prompting, Billy hit the accelerator.

The car shot forward along the hard shoulder, dragging the Sheriff with it. But still his hand retained a grip around Billy's neck. The tiny engine screamed for second gear and, again, Billy's leg straightened so Roman could make the shift.

The gears grated and the car jolted. The door slammed against the Sheriff and he released Billy's throat. He grabbed for the door, curling his arm through the open window and wrapping it around the frame. His feet scrambled to find purchase, but the car was moving too quickly; he had no choice but to let the car drag him along.

Billy bypassed third gear and punched the car into fourth. The little Fiat accelerated along the hard shoulder, the wrong way. Drivers still waiting in the queuing traffic watched with slack jaws.

"Get him off," Roman shouted.

"I'm trying." Billy accelerated.

The Sheriff continued to hold on.

"Brake."

"What?"

"Brake!"

Billy braked. The wheels locked and the car skidded forward. The stench of burning rubber infiltrated the vehicle. The Sheriff catapulted forward and slammed into the open door, forcing it clean off its hinges. Both he and the door careened forward. He rolled across the ground, tarmac shredding his police shirt and grating several layers of skin from his body.

Several people left their vehicles and ran to help him.

Billy pulled the little Fiat around the carnage and sped off down the road.

"Change of plan," Roman said. "We're going to Morwenstow."

CHAPTER THIRTY- ONE

Nate pushed James down into a chair.

Immediately, James stood again. "I'm a wealthy man. I can give you anything you want."

Nate rested against the kitchen table. He rubbed his chin and folded his arms. The Sheriff aside, it wasn't in his nature to harm others. He was a man of God. He saw the good in the worst of people and tried to help them overcome their sins.

However, with James Hamilton, he didn't feel any of his usual empathy. "I have one question for you."

James eyed him. "If I answer, am I free to leave?"

Nate watched him. James was good at hiding his fear. "Maybe."

"I need to know what the offer on the table is before I can agree to it."

"Did you sacrifice your daughter?"

Surprise dissolved James's tight control. He side-stepped the chair, clocked the back door and, very casually, backed towards it.

"You can run if you want. But you should ask yourself how far you think you'll get before I catch you."

James faked a laugh and held up his hands. "I was just checking out the scenery."

He walked back to the table, swung a different chair out, and sat. He glanced up at Nate but avoided eye contact.

"I'm waiting for an answer."

James looked worried. His skin paled and he looked away.

For the first time, the man's nerves were evident.

"Who are you?" he said.

"You don't see the resemblance? Most people spot it straight away."

"You're a Holbrook?" James cleared his throat and narrowed his eyes. "Does that also mean you're a reaper?"

The kettle started to whistle. Nate got up and walked to the stove. He caught James stealing another glance at the back door, but this time he didn't make an obvious play for it.

"I'm still waiting for you to answer my question."

James sat up straight and placed his hands on the table in front of him. "You don't appear to be as hot-headed as Roman."

"You may think differently soon, if you keep avoiding my question."

Nate lifted the kettle from the stove and the whistle died. He didn't switch off the gas.

"Remind me what the question was again."

Nate's shoulders tensed. "Did you sacrifice your daughter?" He gripped the kettle's handle and turned to face James. Steam floated from the spout, evaporating seconds after hitting the atmosphere.

"Is that what your brother told you?

"Is it true?"

James eyed the kettle and that flicker of fear returned to his gaze. "Are you going to kill me?"

"You'd be dead by now if I was. I just want you to answer my question."

James chuckled. It was a nervous laugh. "I think sacrifice is a strong word."

"Then explain it with a simpler one."

James pushed the chair back from the table but didn't stand. "You know what Eliza is, don't you?"

Nate's grip tightened around the kettle's handle.

"It's what she was created for, her destiny."

Nate slammed the kettle back down on the stove.

"I was dying."

"You still are."

"Then you understand why I had to do what I did. Tumours and cancer run in my family. No Hamilton man has ever lived beyond fifty-five. I didn't want to become one of those statistics."

"And you think that rationalises murdering your own daughter?"

"I was taught about mind movers like other kids are taught about Father Christmas. It was normal for me to do what I did."

Nate stared at him, at a loss for words. The guy truly believed his actions were justified. He walked to the cupboard and retrieved two mugs. It was all he could do to stop himself from sending the man straight to Hell.

"So, what happens now? Am I free to leave?"

Nate scoffed. "That decision lies with someone else."

He set the mugs down on the work surface and took two tea bags from the ceramic pot that sat just left of the fridge. He needed to be busy. If he stopped fiddling with things, he worried he might not be able to control the rage that bubbled away in the pit of his stomach.

The kitchen door creaked open and he looked up. Eliza stood in the doorway. Her cheeks were a little flushed. She smiled briefly – more of a twitch, really – but it was something he needed to see.

"Hey," he said gently. "You should be resting."

Eliza looked at him. The faint after-effects of her ordeal still clouded her eyes, but she recognised him now. A small smile pulled at the corners of her lips – a real smile this time. Then she turned and saw her father.

Her smile faded. "What's he doing here? Where's my brother and Roman?"

"Roman and Billy are somewhere else."

"Are they safe?"

"Yes," Nate lied. He'd lied to Eliza a lot since he brought her back. "This man here was just telling me why he sacrificed you."

Eliza remained quiet.

"The decision as to what happens to him now is yours, Eliza."

Eliza sat on the chair opposite her father. "I want to know about my mother."

James eyed her. "You know all there is to know about your mother."

"Not that mother. My real mother."

The kettle began to whistle again and Nate reluctantly left Eliza and removed it from the stove. This time he switched off the gas.

"Is she still alive?" Eliza asked.

"Look," James said. "Why not leave the past where it is? Let sleeping dogs lie and all that."

"Sleeping dogs?"

The kitchen light began to flicker and the two mugs on the work surface rattled.

"I'd tell her what she wants to know," Nate said. "Somehow, I get the feeling you already know what she's capable of doing."

James looked up at him. "Okay, okay. She's in South America."

One of the mugs rattled towards the edge of the counter. It toppled and smashed across the floor.

"In a hospital," James quickly added.

"What hospital?"

"St Agnus. It's a nunnery."

"Why?" Nate asked. "What happened to her?"

"She went mad."

"Mad?" Eliza whacked her fists on the table.

A chair overturned and skidded across the kitchen.

"When I took you, I swapped you for my own daughter. She knew, but nobody believed her. It ended up being her downfall."

"So you sent her away? Hid her?" Eliza abruptly stood. Her chair toppled backwards and the cutlery draw shot open and fell to the floor. "*You* were her downfall."

A knife rose from the drawer and catapulted towards James. Nate reached out. The blade sliced his palm and he grabbed the handle. He quickly strode up to Eliza and cupped her face. Tears glazed her eyes and her chest rose and fell with every breath.

She focused on him. Slowly, the lights brightened and the kitchen calmed.

"You okay?" Nate said.

Eliza nodded. She looked down at the knife he still held. Blood reddened his hand.

Her eyes widened in horror. "I'm so sorry. I didn't mean to hurt you."

"You didn't." Nate opened his hand. The wound had already healed. "Why don't you make the tea?"

Eliza glanced back at her father. She wavered for a moment. "What are we going to do with him?"

"What do you want to do with him?"

Eliza turned back to him. "He can't go free. He belongs in prison."

Nate nodded. He waited, giving her the time to process her thoughts. Finally, she walked to the cupboard, retrieved another mug, and went to the stove. She glanced down at the cutlery scattered across the floor, forgot about the tea, and knelt to pick the silverware up.

Nate placed the knife on the table and settled into a chair.

He waited until Eliza had put all the cutlery back in the drawer before he addressed James again. "I think you need to start at the beginning."

James turned to Eliza.

"Don't worry about her," Nate said. "Just concentrate on me."

"What do you want me to say?" James shifted in his seat. "Eliza's mother was the mind mover I always intended to use. But in case I couldn't obtain all the pieces of the True Cross before she died, I needed a back-up." James glanced at Eliza again.

"Jesus Christ." Nate leaned back in his chair and clasped his hands behind his head. "I should let her kill you, you know."

Eliza placed a cup of tea in front of Nate. "Why don't we let the Sheriff take him?"

"Because the Sheriff isn't looking for him."

Eliza frowned. "I don't understand. He escaped the waiting room by hitching a ride back – just like Jacob did. Like my brother and Roman."

Nate shook his head. "Your brother and Roman escaped the torture chamber. Their existence in Purgatory was logged. As far as I am aware, your father wasn't caught—" Nate turned to James. "You weren't caught, were you?"

James shook his head.

"Then his existence was sensed, but his identity would have remained unknown, hence, he cannot be hunted."

"So he just gets away with everything he's done?"

"He has a tumour that's terminal. Isn't that comfort enough?"

Eliza laughed. "Nowhere near."

Nate nodded. He'd thought as much. "Eliza, I don't know what else I can offer you."

James piped up. "Why don't you hand me over to the police?"

Eliza drummed her fingers on the counter. "Because you'll spin it that you were the victim."

"Well, you can't keep me here." James stood.

Nate also stood. He glared at James until he sat back on the chair.

"I have one last question," Eliza said. "My mother's name. What is it?"

James looked away from Nate and stared at Eliza for a second before dropping his gaze. "Amanda Taylor. Her name is Amanda Jane Taylor."

CHAPTER THIRTY-TWO

Eliza was relieved when Nate walked back into the kitchen.

"What did you do with him?" she asked.

"Put him back in the car boot." Nate closed the door and walked to the sink. He washed his hands and dried them on a tea towel. "Do you want a tea?"

Eliza shook her head.

Nate looked at the kettle. "Me neither."

He looked lost, as though he were searching the kitchen for something to occupy him.

"I'm going after them," Eliza said.

"Not this again. Eliza, I said I'm not discussing it anymore." Nate hooked the towel over the stove.

Eliza twisted in her chair. "Good, because neither am I." She stood. "I'm telling you, they need our help."

"It's not safe."

"Nothing about this past week has been safe."

She glanced at the floor and inhaled. She didn't want to argue with Nate. When her agitation calmed a little, she looked up. Nate stood with his back towards her, staring out of the window. Outside, rain had started to fall, clouds casting darkness over the previously serene landscape.

Eliza sat back down. She lifted her feet up onto the chair and wrapped her arms around her knees. "I am not asking for your permission."

Nate's shoulders sagged. He leaned on the work surface but kept his gaze fixed on the fields outside. "You wanted them out of Purgatory and, against my better judgement, I agreed to help you. Can't you leave it at that?"

"Roman may be able to put up a convincing fight, but my brother has nothing. He will die if the Sheriff catches up with them."

"The Sheriff is not after your brother."

Purgatory logged him and he escaped. Regardless, he will pay the price just for being with Roman."

Nate turned to face her. "The Elders ordered that the Sheriff stand down. Roman is not on the most wanted list anymore."

"If you believe that, then why am I sitting here?" Eliza lowered her legs. She stood and walked over to Nate. "You know I have to go, don't you?"

Nate looked up. His eyes were the perfect shade of blue, just like Roman's. They held her gaze and he gently clasped her arms.

The back door flung open.

Roman rushed into the kitchen. He saw the two of them standing by the sink together and stopped dead. He stared at them both and the urgency he'd entered with dissipated.

Nate dropped his hands from Eliza's arms. "Roman? What are you doing here?"

Roman's glare hardened.

Eliza went to him and reached for his hand. "Where's Billy?"

Roman stiffened under her touch and pulled his hand away.

"What's the matter? Where's Billy?"

Panic took hold. Eliza left Roman and ran to the back door. She heard her brother's grumbling before she saw him.

"Is he here?" Billy bounded around the corner of the church.

He looked fine, if a little exhausted. "He? You mean Roman?"

Billy rushed past her into the kitchen. "Have you told them yet?" he said to Roman.

Eliza followed him back in. "He hasn't told us anything yet."

"The Sheriff is coming for you. Both of you," Billy said.

"What?" Nate walked to the back door. He glanced outside and then closed it. "How do you know this?"

"He just told us." Billy moved over to the sink. He grabbed a glass from the drainer and filled it with water. He gulped it down and refilled it. "We need to get out of here."

"No." Nate stepped away from the door. "We are better equipped here."

Billy turned to him. "How?"

"Because I am stronger than the Sheriff."

"So, you can kill him?" A touch of relief lightened Billy's voice.

"He can't be killed," Roman said, speaking for the first time since he'd entered the room.

Eliza looked at Roman, but he avoided her gaze. Tension still hardened his features and his glare remained on his brother.

"We've tried killing him," Eliza said. "He just doesn't die – a bit like someone else I know."

If she'd hoped to lighten the mood, she'd failed. Roman remained standing there like he was made out of stone.

"So, what? We all stay locked in this church for the rest of our days?" Billy said. "We need to either run from him or find a way to kill him."

"Even if we could kill him, then what?" Eliza said. "Wouldn't another Sheriff be appointed the job of coming after us?"

"His hunting us is a vendetta, not a job. It's unsanctioned by the Elders." Nate checked outside again. "Nobody else will come looking."

Billy clenched his fists. "So, we're back to either running or killing."

"And I said, he cannot be killed," Roman bit out, tension curled around every word.

"That's not entirely true." Nate turned from the door and leaned against it. "Everything can be killed."

Roman clenched his jaw. His whole face tightened. "Tell me."

Nate scoffed. "You'd never pull it off."

"Try me."

"Forget it." Nate pushed away from the door. He looked at Eliza. "The safest thing is to stay here where I can protect you...all of you."

"And what if the Elders remove your powers?" Roman demanded. "You still think yourself capable of protecting her?"

Nate eyed him for a second. "What is your problem?"

Roman snorted.

"You want to watch her die?"

Roman pushed past Eliza. He stormed towards his brother. "Is this your idea of revenge? I took your girl so now you're taking mine?"

Nate straightened. He squared up to Roman. "If this girl dies, her blood will be on your hands."

"Ah, finally. I see where this is going." Roman stepped back. "You still blame me for Jane's death."

"Okay." Billy leapt between them. "Let's take this down a notch."

The two brothers stared at one another, neither one wanting to back down.

"Roman." Eliza gently took his arm. "This is not the time."

Roman glared at her venomously. "Of course, you would agree with him."

"I'm not agreeing with anyone. I just think this conversation would best be left for another time — maybe when we're not waiting for the Sheriff to turn up and kill us?"

Roman shrugged his arm from her grip. He looked at his brother then at Billy. Finally, his gaze landed back on Eliza. His chest expanded and deflated, over and over. Anger still ruled him, but Eliza registered sadness in his eyes. He blinked it away and reached for the back door.

"Where are you going?" Eliza called out after him.

He slammed the door in her face.

Deafening silence hung in the air.

"Shouldn't someone go after him?" Billy finally said.

Eliza shook her head. However angry he was, he wouldn't leave them. Leave her. "He's probably gone to the pub."

She sat back down at the table and put her head in her hands. As if things weren't bad enough, now she had two warring brothers to deal with.

"I didn't mean what he implied." Nate sat opposite her. "I'm not out for revenge and I don't blame him for my wife's death."

"I know." Eliza looked up. "The only person who blames Roman is Roman."

"So, what do we do now?" Billy said. "I mean, the clock is ticking. The Sheriff is going to follow us here."

"You're right." Nate stood. "We need to decide what we are doing."

Eliza got up from the table. She walked to the back door, paused beside Nate, and rested her hand on his shoulder. "It's his guilt that spoke to you. Deep down, he still loves you."

CHAPTER THIRTY-THREE

Roman saw Eliza enter the pub.

He lowered his head, pretending he hadn't clocked her, and continued to carve a star into the wooden table. But it didn't take long for her to spot him.

She pulled out the chair opposite him and sat down. "You need to come back."

Roman ignored her. He'd nearly finished etching the star and didn't plan on stopping until it was completed.

"For Christ's sake. Will you get over yourself and come back to the church?"

"You don't need me. Nate can look after you."

Eliza stood. "Fine. You wallow. I'm going to find a way to get us out of this mess." She turned and left.

Roman continued to scratch at the star. What a first-class dick he was being. But walking in and seeing her and Nate together in the kitchen – with him holding her so close. That shit had thrown him. He didn't want to believe Eliza liked his brother more than she liked him. He looked out of the window and watched her trample across the grass to the leafy path that led down to the church.

Shit, she was right. He needed to go back and help them. He got up from the table, left the pub, and jogged back to the church.

The kitchen door was closed and he worried about what he might see when he walked in this time. To his relief, when he pushed the door open, he found everyone sitting around the table.

Billy stood. He'd changed his clothes, the robe replaced with what Roman assumed to be one of Nate's jumpers and a pair of his slacks.

"These are for you." Eliza patted a pile of clothes beside her – a folded pair of jeans and another jumper.

Shit. She'd known damn-full-well he'd follow her back.

Roman declined to sit at the table. Instead, he honed in on the work surface and leaned against it. "I want to know how to kill the Sheriff."

To his surprise, it was Eliza who answered him. "We have to burn his bones."

"That's it?"

Nate looked at him. "I'm surprised you didn't know it already."

"Why would I know that? And how is it that Eliza knows it?"

"Because we talked rather than storming off to the pub," Eliza said. "Apparently, it's the same for everyone, even the Elders."

"Okay, so where are these bones?"

"In Hell," Nate said.

"And, like with Heaven, only Christ can open the gateway." Eliza got up from the table. She chucked

Nate's spare clothes to Roman. "Or someone with his blood."

He caught the jumper. The jeans landed at his feet. "I always thought the gateways to Hell were a myth."

"Yeah, well, they're not. It's just nobody knows where any of them are," Nate said.

"I know where one is."

"Oh? How's that?"

"*Semita ad immortalitatem*," Roman said slowly, picturing the chalk figure deep in the Catacombs where he'd retrieved a piece of the True Cross. He paused and watched recognition dawn in his brother's eyes. "I've seen it."

The Sheriff entered the church.

He could smell Roman and the cop had been here and that pleased him. The fact that they were no longer here didn't. The Sheriff cracked the agitation from his neck and closed his eyes. Taking the cop's human form constricted his body and the constant cramping made him want to kill someone. He straightened the police uniform and tilted his head towards the rafters. Roman's scent was everywhere. To his left, to his right. Even in the trees outside. But, although the smell was strong, it tasted twenty minutes old.

The Sheriff yelled and his frustrated vibrations echoed around God's house. He clenched his fists. He risked his whole existence in Purgatory by ignoring the Elders' orders to stand down. But he wanted revenge on Holbrook more than anything else. And he'd be damned if he'd allow Roman to get the better of him again. He allowed the building anger to consume him and marched to the front of the church, where a door led through to an office. Off that room, another door led to a corridor. He followed it, finally reaching the kitchen.

He was surprised by what he found – a man tied to a chair.

Relief flooded the man's eyes when he saw the Sheriff. "I knew you wouldn't leave me, son."

The Sheriff smiled. "You're the cop's father?"

James frowned and the relief quickly changed to fear. "Billy? Untie me, son."

The Sheriff approached him. He stroked James hair and ran his fingers down his face.

He cupped his chin and yanked James's head up until they were eye to eye. "I sense..." The Sheriff leaned closer and sniffed long and hard. "You've been to Purgatory?"

"No."

The Sheriff leaned back. "Where'd they go?"

"I don't know. They tied me up and left."

The Sheriff dug his fingers into James's face. Slowly, his talons pushed through the tips of his fingers.

They cut into James's cheeks and he cried out. "Honestly. I don't know where they went. They had me locked in the car boot."

"Then you are of no use to me."

The Sheriff slapped his hands against James's ears, wrapped his fingers around the back of James's head, and yanked upwards.

James started to scream. His head tore free from his shoulders and the screaming stopped. The Sheriff lifted James's head, the spine swinging from his severed neck, and studied the shocked expression frozen on his face.

The Sheriff lifted the end of the spine to his mouth and tasted it. He closed his eyes, savouring the evil that had been the cop's father. Then he leaned his head back, widened his mouth, and swallowed the spine whole.

He bit the spine free at the neck and licked his lips, the flavour energising him and feeding his need to hunt down the Holbrook brothers more than ever.

He inhaled the air again and found Roman's scent. Along with it came images – rows of cars, followed by a flash of men in uniform identical to the one he wore. The Sheriff searched the hallucination, looking for further evidence of where Roman had gone. Blurred wording on a sign sharpened and came into focus. Roman was at Liskeard Police Station.

The Sheriff opened his eyes. Protocol called for him to return to the waiting room and travel to his next destination via the gateway. However, he was not following protocol. The Elders would soon have people combing Purgatory for him. To return now would be a grave mistake. And one he might not survive.

CHAPTER THIRTY-FOUR

"Wait here," Billy said.

"Are you sure you know where to look?"

Billy glared at Roman. "How many passenger footwells does your Aston have?"

Roman bit back a retort. He wasn't used to being on the receiving end of such sarcasm – well, other than the constant acidity thrown at him by Eliza.

"Hey." Billy slapped him across the shoulder. "You with me?"

Roman nodded. "Just be careful in there."

"I'm a police officer. This is a busman's holiday for me."

Billy got out of the Fiat and Roman watched him jog across the road to the police station. He entered the main doors at the front and disappeared inside.

The digital clock displayed 16:04. Roman drummed his fingers against his knee and waited. He checked the rear-view mirror and saw Nate and Eliza sitting in the Ford behind. He exhaled and, for a moment, allowed himself to mourn not having her beside him. They had battled the odds time and again over the last week and survived, convincing him that this thing between them

– whatever it was – had a glimmer of hope of blossoming into something more.

Taking the two cars had been his idea. If the Sheriff caught up with them again, he'd told Nate to take off with Eliza and keep her safe. He looked in the rear-view mirror again. Was he tempting fate allowing his brother to get close to her?

He whacked the mirror away so he couldn't see them anymore. Outside, shoppers and workers alike went about their day. None of them glanced at the Fiat or at Roman inside. To them he was just another individual living a mundane existence.

Boredom quickly set in. Maybe he should head over to the station and check on Billy. Or maybe he could get around back unnoticed and locate his car for himself.

He glanced back at the clock. 16:19. Roman shifted in the uncomfortable seat. His foot knocked the dash and the plastic dropped onto his leg again. He kicked it back up. It fell back down.

Shitty fucking car. He sighed, refusing to get angry with it, and switched on the radio. A song was playing – an upbeat pop thing by a band whose name escaped him. He switched it off. Silence had to be better than the manufactured drivel today's youth called music. Dire Straits – now that was music. He glanced out of the window again. Still no sign of Billy. What if he couldn't find the car? What if he'd been caught? Fuck, he was asking a lot of *what ifs*.

Back to the clock. 16.34. He'd waited long enough. He opened the door. Billy should have returned by now. Roman crossed the road to the station but stopped short of the main doors.

Billy exited, his gait a hurried jog.

He bounded across the forecourt towards Roman, grabbed his arm, and hurried him back towards the Fiat. "Did you know I was wanted for murder?"

"Did you get the shirt?" Roman asked.

Billy flashed him a glimpse of some material hidden beneath his jumper and got in the car.

When Roman had settled beside him in the passenger seat, Billy threw him the shirt. "Who the hell am I supposed to have killed?"

"Some kid you used to work with."

"What kid? Not Eddie?" Billy's face paled.

"Maybe, I don't know. You finished off his female friend too."

Roman rummaged inside the front pocket of the shirt. There it was. He extracted a business card – the details of the French woman who'd accosted him outside the Catacombs and offered him a fortune to go back in.

"And you didn't think to tell me?"

"Honestly? I totally forgot." Roman threw the shirt on the back seat. He glanced at Billy. The man looked on the verge of falling apart. "Hey."

Billy glanced at him.

"Mourn later. We have bigger fish to fry."

Billy wiped his forehead and blinked away the sadness. He leaned closer. "You sure we need this person's help?"

"Like I said back at my brother's, I know a guy who could get us into France under the radar. But it will take time to arrange and we need to get away now. Plus, we're gonna need supplies if we're heading into the Catacombs. Again, I can't get that sort of equipment together in the time we have."

There was a phone number on the card and Roman punched it into Nate's mobile. The call was answered on the second ring.

"Natalie Laurent?" he said.

"*Oui?*"

"This is Roman Holbrook. We met outside the Catacombs. I believe you have a job for me."

CHAPTER THIRTY-FIVE

Natalie Laurent put down the phone.

She stared at it for a moment, giving herself time for the excitement to settle. This phone call had been a long time coming. And, although not in as straightforward a fashion as she'd first anticipated, her plan was finally going to get the ending it deserved.

"Our plans have changed." She looked at the man sitting opposite her – André, her longest serving and most trusted aid. He looked totally relaxed – his legs crossed and his fingers spinning a silver letter opener. "Mr Holbrook is coming to us."

"Oh?" The letter opener stopped spinning.

"Not quite as we planned, but the outcome will be just as acceptable."

"What do you want me to do?"

"Holbrook has given me a list of instructions – some equipment he needs. Sort it out as quickly as you can." Natalie got up from her desk. "With regard to our other plan, send Dax and François to set it up."

André nodded. He uncrossed his legs, put the letter opener on the desk, and stood. "Are you sure this is fool-proof?"

"Admittedly, this Mr Holbrook has others coming with him, but they shouldn't be a problem."

"How many others?"

"Three – two men and a woman. We'll make sure they don't hinder us."

André nodded. "I will prepare everything and report back shortly."

Natalie smiled. She could always count on her friend. "Thank you, André."

She waited for him to leave the room then sat back down at her desk. She reached for the phone and pressed in a number. After listening to the ringer for a minute, she hung up.

She stood and went to the window. She gazed outside, across the rooftops, and studied the top of the Eiffel Tower – something she always did when she was thinking.

The circumstances were not ideal, but she would use their time in the Catacombs to her advantage. She just hoped her accomplice didn't let her down at the last hurdle.

CHAPTER THIRTY-SIX

Eaglescott Airport consisted of three or four buildings in a really big field.

It was perfect for getting over to France without going through all the rigmarole of a fully functioning commercial airport.

Roman got out of the Fiat. Eliza and Nate had already exited the Ford and were walking towards him – side by side, their hands almost touching. Roman's fingers curled into a fist and he looked away. He had to overcome this jealously. He couldn't think straight for worrying about what may or may not be happening between them.

"Wait here," he called over his shoulder.

Several cars lined one side of the field. Real nice ones too. More than one caught his eye and he thought of his Aston the way it had been before he'd ditched it. He looked back at the cars – and focused on the dark green Range Rover farthest from him. Two men sat inside. The passenger exited as Roman approached.

"You Roman?" the passenger asked.

Roman nodded.

"Your helicopter will be here at seven o'clock."

"What helicopter? I thought we agreed a plane."

"You wanted a plane. You're getting a helicopter. White. Eagle on the door."

Roman pulled back the sleeve of his jumper and remembered he wasn't wearing a watch. "Well, what time is it now?"

"Nearly six."

"That's too long. We need to move now."

"That's the time. Take it or leave it."

Roman sighed.

"That's what I thought." The man handed him an envelope. "Your passports are inside. You will wait here for your flight." He turned and got back into the car.

"And the rest of the equipment?"

"It will be waiting for you."

Roman opened the envelope. Inside were four passports. Roman checked them: different names, but the four pictures were theirs all right. "How'd you get these photos?"

"DVLA."

The Range Rover reversed back onto the worn path. Roman watched it head off towards the buildings, a cloud of dirt spitting from its back tyres. When the dust finally settled, the car was gone.

Behind him, a small charter plane descended towards the runway. It landed, tyres squealing as they touched tarmac. The plane's speed decreased and Roman watched it travel along the runway, turning off into a field near hanger three.

A long, unbroken blast of the horn came from the Ford and Roman spun around. Eliza was running towards him.

He went to her, meeting her at the edge of the airfield. "What's wrong?"

"It's your brother. Something's wrong." Eliza swallowed. Catching her breath, she grabbed Roman's arm and pulled him back towards the car. "He just started convulsing."

The driver's door was open. Nate lay stretched out on the ground, his shirt unbuttoned.

"I checked him over. I can't see what's wrong," Eliza said.

"He's out cold." Billy was crouched beside him. "At least he's stopped shaking."

Roman knelt and felt for a pulse. He found one beating strong and fast. He lifted Nate's eyelids; his pupils had dilated.

Roman leaned back. "He's okay."

"What? Are you sure? What happened to him?" Eliza said. "It was like he was having a seizure."

Roman stood. "He's been stripped of his reaper status."

"Why?"

Roman shrugged. "The Elders must know he helped you."

"So, now he's like you?"

Roman nodded. "Exactly like me."

"So, he can still save lives?"

"As well as take them away. He can alter and close the gateways, just like me. But he won't be as strong as he was and his jetting off to Purgatory days are over."

"Meaning?"

"Meaning things just got a whole lot easier for the Sheriff."

"How much time do we have?"

"Before the Sheriff arrives? Don't worry, we'll be long gone by the time he gets here."

Eliza raised a brow. "I mean, how long until our plane arrives?"

"Not long." Roman paused. He really didn't want to tell her they still had an hour to wait. "And it's a helicopter."

He left her to digest that piece of information and walked back to the Fiat. He opened the boot and busied himself with absolutely nothing inside.

Time ticked on and Roman went to check his watch again for the umpteenth time. Fuck. No watch. He really had to get a replacement from somewhere. It had to be close to seven, though. He grabbed his brother's phone but didn't bother looking at the time. He recalled the number on the screen – Natalie Laurent's number. It rang. And rang. And rang.

Roman hung up and slipped the phone into his back pocket. The aircraft should be here any minute. He glanced at the Ford. Eliza sat on the car bonnet, Nate alongside her. Again, jealousy tightened his chest. They both rested against the windscreen. Hell, they were almost lying on top of one another. They spoke a little and then watched a charter plane land and another take off. They'd been doing the same thing for three quarters of an hour now, ever since Nate had felt strong enough to stand – with her assistance, of course. Roman knew because he'd watched them from behind the Fiat.

He shook his head, annoyed at himself for vilifying Eliza's attempts to help his brother – even if his thoughts were in the privacy of his own head. This last week had been hell. If he'd only turned down the offer to find the True Cross, then none of this shit would have happened. Eliza would still be a nurse. Her brother would still be a copper. Jacob would never have escaped Purgatory. Nathaniel would still have his reaper status. And the Sheriff wouldn't be hot on their tail right now.

Truth was, though, with or without his help, James would have eventually located the pieces. Eliza's destiny was to die on that cross. If not her, then her children. At least, this way, Roman had been able to put a stop to it all. Now he just had to destroy the Sheriff and save her again.

Nate slid off the bonnet, thumbs hooked in his trouser pockets, looking cool and collected. He showed no signs of the earlier trauma he'd suffered. He'd aged well – Roman would give him that. But he no longer held reaper status – a small fact Roman felt responsible for. Maybe he should apologise to him.

Nate sauntered over. "You think this woman's going to come through for you?"

"I do," Roman replied, despite the fact he was beginning to doubt this pilot of theirs was ever going to turn up.

"How do you even know her?" Eliza said. She'd followed Nate over.

Roman paused and a guilty sweat broke out across his forehead. His body warmed. "I met her in Paris."

"Oh." Eliza turned back to the runway, her curiosity seemingly satisfied.

Roman exhaled slowly. He really didn't want to admit he'd met Natalie Laurent the day he'd gone into the Catacombs to retrieve a piece of the cross.

Nate narrowed his eyes and cocked his head to one side, the same way he had when they were young men and Roman had lied about why he'd returned home late; the same way he had when they were reapers and Roman had lied about hunting down a mind mover.

"What were you doing when you met her?" he asked.

Roman felt his body temperature rise again. Sweat dripped down his back. Eliza turned back to face him, interested again. Even Billy seemed to stare him down.

Roman looked away, turning his attention to the airfield. A helicopter arrived, its landing skids kissing the tarmac. His heart skipped a beat. Was this their ride out of here? No. There was no eagle on the door.

"Roman?" Eliza said.

Roman inhaled. He held the breath and turned back to them. "I was getting a piece of the cross."

Eliza reached for her neck, as though to grab a necklace that wasn't there. "When?"

"You were in the cabin." The words choked him.

Nate scoffed. "What is wrong with you?"

Roman ignored his brother. "Eliza, it was before I knew you."

"Just how friendly are you and this Natalie?"

"We're not. That's the only time I met her. She's just trying to find her brother."

"And she just happened to be hanging around outside the Catacombs when you were there?"

Now it was Billy's turn to chime him. He ran a hand through his hair. "I have to admit, mate. It does sound a bit convenient."

"Or it's a lie," Nate said.

Roman spun to face him. He clenched his fists around Nate's jumper and yanked him close. "I am not lying."

Whoa." Billy ran around the car to intervene.

"Course you are," Nate said. "It's what you do: cheat, deceive, scam, sweet-talk...the list is endless."

Roman didn't let go. His jaw tightened. "You don't know me anymore, little brother."

Nate remained calm, unaffected by Roman's outburst. He raised a brow and almost smirked. "Then tell me. What's so different about you now?"

Roman glared at Nate, but he had no words to fight back with. How could he argue with what he knew to be true? He looked at Billy, still standing there, his arm wedged between their chests. Admitting defeat wasn't something he was used to, but he loosened his grip and released Nate's jumper. He didn't want to look at Eliza but turned anyway. She, like Billy and Nate, stared at him. Only, in her eyes, he sensed a tinge of embarrassment for him – and for herself.

It nearly killed him to see her look at him in that way. He scratched the back of his neck. The right thing to do would be to apologise for his actions. To offer Nate his hand and put their differences to one side.

"Fuck you all," he said instead.

He left them and stormed around the closest building. It was quieter this side of the airport. At least he could think a little clearer.

The hairs on the back of his neck spiked and an uneasy feeling swept over him. Had their luck just run out? Had the Sheriff found them? Roman turned and looked towards the airport entrance. It was little more than a small turning off a country lane. Nobody was there. All he heard was the faint chatter of the birds and the muffled noise of aircraft engines.

His hand tightened around the passports. Still no Sheriff materialised.

He shook his head and forced himself to relax. "Holbrook, you're a fucking idiot."

He turned his back, his goal now to get back to the others – whatever they thought of him – and watch out for the helicopter.

An engine purred behind him. Roman glanced over his shoulder. A red Peugeot entered the airport. He narrowed his eyes but couldn't see inside. He pushed his paranoia to one side and continued walking. At some point, he'd have to apologise to his brother. And Eliza. Heck, weren't the passports he'd gotten them a big enough apology?

The Peugeot's engine revved. Tyres squealed and the smell of burning rubber polluted the air. The horn screamed for his attention and Roman spun around. All he saw was a flash of red.

The car smashed into him head on.

Roman felt his legs snap. He catapulted backwards and smash-landed on the ground. The car accelerated again and the flash of red raced towards him. Roman rolled onto his side and kept rolling. Tyres breezed past his face then skidded to a stop a little way past him. Roman rolled onto his front, biting back the pain. He heard the Peugeot's gears grind before two white lights blinked to life.

The car reversed, aiming straight for him, and Roman rolled again, ending up on his back. He cried out and tried to sit up. But he couldn't get up – his broken legs completely immobilising him. He glanced down at them. His splintered left tibia pushed against the inside of his trouser leg. He held his breath and snapped it back into place.

The Peugeot's door opened and a police officer strolled towards him. A normal looking dude, were it not for the fact that he looked exactly like Billy. But it wasn't Billy. Evil hid behind these dark eyes.

"Really?" Roman forced a chuckle. It was all he could do to mask the agonising pain his lower body was in. "You need a car to take me down?"

"Where are the others?" the Sheriff asked.

"Ditched 'em."

Roman searched for some kind of weapon: a large stick, a rock, anything. He saw the passports strewn across the ground. Shit. He must have dropped them when the car hit him.

The Sheriff knelt beside him and placed his hand on Roman's shin. "Where are they?"

"They were slowing me down."

The Sheriff squeezed.

Again, he forced a laugh to cover the scream. "You stupid fuck. Is that the best you've got without that chamber of yours?"

The Sheriff sighed. He ran his hand down Roman's leg and clasped his ankle. Standing, he dragged Roman towards the car. Stones scratched Roman's head. Gravel slipped through his fingers. Darkness whirled behind his eyes. Nausea filled in his throat. The scene around him faded. The Sheriff released his ankle and Roman's foot dropped to the ground. Pain exploded up his leg and the darkness behind his eyes lifted. The red paintwork of the Peugeot popped into view again. Roman was lying in front of its front tyres.

"I'll crush you inch by inch until you beg to tell me what I want to know."

Roman tried to sit up. He couldn't quite manage it. He heard the Peugeot's door open. Bollocks. This was going to hurt like fucking hell. Suddenly, the torturous rack didn't seem so bad. He waited to hear the engine growl to life, for the car to edge forward and the tyres to crush his bones. None of it came.

Roman lifted his head.

The Sheriff lay on the ground some way back. He looked dazed, but managed to scramble to his feet. Again, Roman waited for his attack to commence, but the Sheriff's focus was on something else. Something behind Roman.

Roman rolled away from the tyres and onto his front. Eliza stood by the corner of the building. She stared at the Sheriff, her face set in stone.

Billy and Nate ran past her. Within seconds, they were by Roman's side. Each grabbed an arm and lifted him off the ground.

The Sheriff marched towards Eliza, roaring at her like an angry tiger.

Roman reached out to her, but she didn't even glance his way. She closed her eyes and inhaled. The Sheriff flew back some twenty metres towards the airport entrance. Eliza opened her eyes, but still she did not look Roman's way. She'd learned to use her powers. When had that happened?

"The passports," Roman said. "On the ground behind me."

"You got him?" Billy said to Nate.

Nate nodded. He bent at the knees and lifted Roman into a fireman's carry. He wrapped his arm around Roman's legs and Roman couldn't stop the muffled cry that erupted from his throat.

Billy returned, four passports in hand. "What now?"

"Find a pilot. Any pilot." Roman said.

Nate started for the airfield. He paused when he reached Eliza. "You need to put this guy down."

Eliza nodded, closed her eyes, and took another deep breath. The Sheriff got to his feet. The Peugeot's front wheels lifted off the ground and the car flipped over. It landed upside down – on top of the Sheriff.

Her eyes lit up when she opened them and surveyed her handiwork.

"Good girl," Nate said. "Wherever this emotional place of yours is…keep going there."

The four of them rounded the building, Roman hanging helpless across his brother's shoulders. He scanned the field and spotted the black logo – an eagle – on the waiting helicopter. A pilot sat inside, the copter's blades rotating so fast above him that they were a blur.

"There. The copter," he said. It was all he could manage.

Nate ran towards it and Roman lost sight of Eliza and Billy. He heard their voices, though, and then Eliza ran into view and opened the helicopter's door. Nate half threw half placed Roman on the seat and jumped in beside him.

Roman grabbed his hand. Eliza was out of earshot; this might be the only time he'd have alone with his brother. "Eliza opens the gateway, but I go into Hell alone. If I don't return, then you have to keep her safe."

"Roman—"

Roman winced. "Just leave the bones to me."

Billy jumped in and they pulled both doors shut.

"Okay, go," Nate shouted at the pilot. He glanced back at Roman and frowned.

Roman turned to the window. He was no fool. The chances of him finding the Sheriff's bones, killing him, and getting out of Hell – unscathed – were remote at best. But there was a chance to put this shit right. And that had to be enough.

The Sheriff staggered around the building. He locked eyes with Roman and paused. The two men stared at each other, neither looking away. The Sheriff straightened his index finger and ran it across his throat.

"We need to get out of here," Roman shouted.

The Sheriff started sprinting towards the helicopter.

Nate slapped the pilot's shoulders. "Now." He whirled his finger and pointed towards the sky.

The Sheriff closed in and Roman gripped the door.

The helicopter left the ground.

The Sheriff was metres from them. He reached for the landing skid.

The helicopter tilted forward, sweeping across the field, rising higher and higher above the trees and surrounding countryside.

Billy stared out of the window. "Did we do it? Are we free and clear?"

The helicopter bore right and Roman glanced below.

The Sheriff stood in the middle of the airfield.

"Yeah. We're clear."

CHAPTER THIRTY-SEVEN

Roman looked at peace and Eliza felt guilty waking him. He'd been through so much and he needed the rest more than any of them.

"Roman?" She lightly shook his shoulder.

Roman opened his eyes.

The flicker of blue focused on her and she met his gaze with a smile. "We're here."

"Here?" Roman straightened and looked past her. "Another small airfield, eh?"

"Another small airfield that's in Paris." She unclipped his belt. "Can you walk?"

Roman rubbed his legs. Nodding, he jumped out of the helicopter.

He winced upon impact and tried to cover his discomfort with an exaggerated yawn. "Where's Nate?"

Eliza motioned around the helicopter "He's with some men."

It was dark. Only the headlights of two vehicles lit up the small group of men.

"Who are they?" Roman said.

Eliza shrugged. "I assume they're with Natalie."

"Then I need to get in on the conversation." Roman rounded the helicopter. A slight limp marred his step; he clearly still hurt.

Eliza followed him. A black limousine was parked alongside the aircraft. One man spoke to Nate. Another two men waited by the limo. Billy watched them.

Nate saw Eliza and Roman and waved them over.

The man he conversed with turned to look. He seemed unimpressed with what he saw.

He turned back to Nate. "*Qui est-ce?*"

"*Mon frère.*"

The man took a second glance at Roman, looked him up and down, and addressed Nate once again. "*Il n'est pas grand chose à regarder, est-il?*"

Roman's shoulder's stiffened. "What's he saying? Is he fucking with me?" He barged towards the man, but Nate got between them.

The two men beside the limo, suited like their counterpart, stepped away from the car.

Nate waved for them to calm down. He gently pushed Roman back. "He wondered who you were. He's concerned you don't look up to the job at hand."

Roman glared at the man. "You wanna test me, frog?"

"*Fucking porcs anglais avec vos attitudes vanites.*"

"Whoa." Nate turned to the man and chuckled. "You got a death wish or something, pal?"

Roman's shoulders tightened even more. Eliza had witnessed him do it a hundred times this past week. It was his thing when he'd had enough and was about to blow. Sure enough, Roman spun the man around to face him. He grabbed his tie and jabbed the knot tight into the man's throat. The two men beside the car leapt forward to help their colleague. Billy brought one of them to a halt, twisting the suit's arm up behind his back. Nate stopped the other.

Eliza rushed forward. Bloody men. All they knew was how to argue and fight.

She removed Roman's hands from the man and gently pushed him behind her.

She turned back to the man. "We are not pigs, nor are we conceited, Sir. Now I suggest you speak English so we can all understand you. Then I suggest you take us to the Catacombs, as I'm sure your employer has ordered you to do."

The man narrowed his eyes. He glared at Roman.

Roman smiled, ear-to-ear and totally exaggerated. "Well? You heard the lady."

The man tried to loosen the knot in his tie. He gave up and crossed his arms. The two men behind him settled down. One made a phone call then stared into the darkness behind them.

Eliza looked too. Two headlights brightened in the distance, their beams lighting the group up, and a second limo pulled forward. Jeez, what was it with rich people and black limos?

Everybody waited in silence while the car crossed the airfield. It pulled up behind the first limo and the driver's door opened. A man got out – also suited, and similar in looks to the other three. He promptly moved to the back door and opened it. Two slender legs swung out. It was dark, but Eliza recognised Christian Louboutin's when she saw them.

A woman emerged from the car. The elusive Natalie, no doubt. She walked towards them and, for a moment, the headlights silhouetted her frame. It was only when she was within a couple of metres that Eliza could see her properly. She looked similar in age, maybe a year or two older. And she was beautiful. Her size-eight figure was clad in a stylish, navy skirt and camisole. Glossy, blonde hair bounced around her shoulders. And red lipstick painted her perfectly shaped lips.

Eliza felt her own hair and glanced down at Nate's oversized joggers and jumper.

Natalie saw Roman and her eyes sparkled. She approached him, her strut mimicking that of a catwalk model. She had yet to acknowledge anybody else around her.

"Hello." She smiled and spoke in heavily-accented English. "I see you survived whatever it was that so urgently called you back to England."

She stepped forward and took Roman's hand, pulling him close and double-kissing his cheeks.

Eliza's heart sank a little. This was the woman who was supposed to help them? Eliza was the one who'd flipped over a car and squashed the Purgatory Sheriff. And, yet, Roman had called her?

Roman threw Eliza a sideways glance, almost as though he'd heard her thoughts.

Eliza bit her lip and watched their hands. Why were they still holding hands?

"I hope your journey was a comfortable one?" Natalie cooed.

"It was very well timed."

"Good." Finally, she released his hand. "I have booked a hotel. I assume you would like to rest up?"

"No. Actually, we'd like to go straight to the Catacombs."

Natalie hesitated for a moment.

"Is that a problem?"

"Not at all. Everything is ready for you." Natalie smiled. She turned to Eliza, finally choosing to acknowledge the rest of them. She smiled and offered her hand. "I am Natalie Laurent."

She even had the perfect name. Eliza shook her hand. It felt smooth and manicured. "Eliza Hamilton."

"I'm Roman's brother, Nate. And this is Billy," Nate interjected.

Natalie double-kissed Nate then moved onto Billy. Her gaze remained on him much longer than Eliza deemed necessary.

Finally, she looked away and pointed at the first limousine. "This car will take you to the Catacombs."

One of the men opened the back door and Roman motioned for the others to get into the car. Nate and Billy obliged.

Eliza held back. "Are you sure about this?"

"We'll be fine."

Natalie smiled. "You need not worry. You will follow behind my vehicle."

Roman looked up. "You're coming?"

"*Oui*. My men will also accompany us." She pointed at the man Roman had argued with. "André you're already acquainted with." Then she turned to the two men waiting beside the car. "Beau and Dax will ride with you."

"What? Everyone's coming?"

She smiled at Roman. "I need to make sure my money is being well spent and that you're making suitable efforts to find my brother."

"What money?" Eliza said.

"The money I am paying you to find my brother, *oui?*"

"I am not happy with this arrangement," Roman said.

Natalie smiled. Confidence oozed off her in waves. Only smart, prepared women were this confident.

"Of course," she said smoothly, "you are well within your rights to terminate this arrangement. Just as I would be well within mine to notify French customs of your unauthorised visit to my beautiful city. And all that equipment you asked for? It will be gone."

Roman ran his fingers through his hair. His shoulders stiffened, and Eliza saw the argument inside him brewing once again.

She stepped in front of him. "No, those terms are fine."

She pushed Roman inside the car and climbed in behind him. The door closed and Beau and Dax – if Eliza remembered their names correctly – climbed into the front.

Roman leaned forward. "Hey, how about some privacy back here?"

Dax nodded at Beau, who pressed a button above his head. A blacked-out partition lifted behind their seats and divided the car in two.

Now they could talk.

"How are we going to find Hell if this lady thinks we're looking for her brother?" Billy said in a hushed voice.

"We can still head towards the gateway," Roman said. "Natalie will just think we're searching for her brother."

Billy frowned. "How do you even know where to go? Because this Natalie doesn't look like the kind of woman who'll fall for your bullshit, Roman."

"Look, forget Natalie." Roman inhaled and lowered his voice. "She's not going to know where we're going once we're among the bones. I dropped glow sticks. Their fluorescence will have died, but the plastic tubes will still be on the ground. We just follow them back to the gateway."

Eliza sat quietly, listening. Roman made it sound easy, like Hansel and Gretel and a trail of breadcrumbs. But there was one thing that nobody had questioned.

"Say we achieve all this," she said. "Do you even know where to find these bones? I mean, do you even know what Hell is like?"

Roman and Nate shared a look.

"We've been there before," they said in unison.

CHAPTER THIRTY-EIGHT

The car hit gravel and Eliza wound down the window. They were driving through some kind of pit or ditch. Eliza peered out further. It was hard to see in the dark, but they looked to be following railway tracks.

Roman leaned over. "Don't worry. Trains haven't used this line for decades."

His revelation didn't bring her much comfort. Headlights caught sections of the bank where grass and weeds sprouted between the rocks and boulders. Above it, a wall had crumbled away from years of disrepair.

"Where are we?" she asked.

"The outskirts of Paris."

"And this is the way into the Catacombs?"

"One of them. The only one I know of."

The car slowed and came to a stop.

Roman leaned over her and opened the door. "We're here."

He jumped out before Eliza had chance to respond.

Nate didn't wait either. He, too, climbed over her and got out. Billy followed, leaving Eliza in the back of the car alone. She couldn't see the two suits up front but heard their car doors close. Everyone was outside – except her.

She heard Natalie's French tones summon Roman and took that as her cue to get out. When she did, she saw the area had been floodlit

"Is this a good idea?" Eliza said. "Shouldn't we be doing this a little more low-key?"

Natalie looked at her. She'd changed her outfit and now wore a navy T-shirt – the front of which was tucked into tight, black, three-quarter-length jeans. Her Christian Louboutin's had become white Converse and a navy baseball cap sat on tied back hair. Even her red lips had changed to light pink. The casual attire made her look more beautiful than ever.

"My family are very influential," she said. "Nobody will bother us here tonight."

Eliza stood beside Nate. Roman had moved to the front of Natalie's car, where yet two more suited men – both of whom Eliza hadn't seen before – stood guard over a bunch of stuff covered by a blue tarpaulin. Roman ignored them and pulled back the plastic sheeting. Underneath was a stack of wooden boxes, rucksacks, and other equipment.

"Exactly what you asked for." Natalie leant against one of the boxes.

Roman pulled off a couple of the lids. He took out a torch, turned it on and off, and tossed it to Eliza, followed by a rucksack and a dozen batteries.

He threw the same items towards Billy. "Nate, you wanna help me?"

Nate grabbed a rucksack and began to fill it. "I'm having second thoughts about all this."

"Too late for second thoughts," Roman replied. "You remember what I said?"

Nate didn't glance at him. "I need to go with you."

Roman continued to search through the equipment, uncovering several hard hats with lights set on them and torches bigger than the one Eliza had put inside her rucksack. Then there were flares, ropes, pickaxes. The list was endless.

"She's gonna need you more than I do," Roman said quietly, oblivious to the fact Eliza could hear them.

"Haven't you noticed? We're the ones who need her."

Roman paused. "Just promise me. I need to know that you'll get her out if I can't."

Nate looked at his brother. He nodded, a strained expression on his face.

Their muttered conversation over, Roman flicked the wheel of a Zippo. Getting the flame he wanted, he snapped the lid closed and tossed it Eliza's way. Again, he did the same for Billy.

Back to the boxes, and he ripped open another lid. Inside this one were first aid kits and bottles of water and lighter fluid. Another box was filled with walkie-talkies, chalk, and glow sticks.

"Get at least one of each," he said.

Eliza and Billy didn't waste any time. Eliza filled her bag with as much as she could squeeze inside.

"Here." Roman passed her a hard hat. "It's the smallest size. Grab yourself some waterproofs, boots as well."

Eliza looked at the waterproofs. The most oversized and unflattering clothes she'd ever seen. She wondered if Natalie would also wear them. If she did, she'd probably still make them look designer. Eliza flapped open the overalls and stepped in.

Natalie laid a sheet of paper a little smaller than A3 across one of the open boxes. "This is as accurate a map as I could find."

"How accurate?" Roman said.

"It is meant to be very accurate, although I cannot guarantee it."

Roman leaned over and made a good show of examining it, tracing numerous outlines with his finger. "Here."

He grabbed a marker from one of the other boxes and circled an area near the top left-hand corner. Eliza had to assume he'd marked an area somewhere near the gateway.

Roman looked up at Natalie and smiled. "Good a place as any to start looking. You have any more copies?"

Natalie waved her hand over her shoulder and her man, Dax or Beau – Eliza couldn't tell them apart – went back to the car. He returned with some more pages and handed them to Roman.

Roman circled the same corner on each of the maps then handed them out, giving the last one to Natalie.

"I have to ask. What makes you think your brother is in there?" Eliza said.

Natalie folded the map. "He told me he and a friend were coming here."

Eliza zipped up the overalls. Natalie still hadn't made any attempt to pick up hers. "So, we're looking for two people?"

Natalie nodded.

Billy looked up from packing his bag. "What were they doing in there?"

Natalie turned to him and her whole demeanour changed to one of warmth. Her voice lowered a pitch when she spoke. "Excitement probably. Why do kids do anything they shouldn't?"

Billy threw the rucksack over his shoulder. He also ignored the overalls.

Eliza pulled on a woolly sock and reached for a wellington boot. Suddenly, something about heading down into the Catacombs didn't sit right with her.

Roman slung his own backpack over his shoulders, clearly not opting to wear the overalls either.

He caught Eliza's gaze. "You okay?"

Eliza nodded.

Natalie glanced her way. "Do you want to stay out here?"

Roman grabbed an anorak. "She stays with me."

Natalie said no more.

Roman threw Billy an anorak. "Okay then, let's finish up and get going. Sooner we go in, the sooner we get out."

"We still need to discuss your money," Natalie said. She still hadn't picked up any overalls or boots, and one of her men held her packed rucksack for her.

"We can sort that out afterwards," Roman said dismissively.

Eliza pulled Roman to one side. "You are planning on coming out again, aren't you?"

Roman flashed her one of his confident smiles that lit up his eyes. He kissed her forehead, the first affection he'd shown her since Nate had brought her back from Purgatory, and turned to Natalie. "If you're coming, you carry your own supplies."

He took the rucksack from the suit and lobbed it at her. Then he headed for the disused tunnel entrance.

Natalie failed to catch it. The bag landed by her feet and her inadequacy brought Eliza a moment of contentment.

One of Natalie's guys bent down to collect it, but Natalie waved him away.

She picked it up herself and turned to Billy. "Could you help me with this?"

Billy took the bag, holding it while Natalie threaded her arms through the straps.

She turned and smiled. "You are a gentleman."

Billy stared at her. He coughed away a nervous chuckle and shifted his balance. Eliza could hardly believe what she was seeing – the speed in which Natalie had charmed her brother was impressive, if not a little creepy.

Eliza shook her head. She caught Billy's attention and rolled her eyes. Men were so predictable. She looked at Roman. He stood by the entrance, staring into the dark abyss that was the tunnel.

Nate stepped up next to her. He pulled down on his backpack's straps and tightened them. "You ready for this?"

Eliza replied with a nod. A bad feeling gnawed at her insides, and it wasn't from having to locate the gateway and open the door to Hell. She looked towards the tunnel. She didn't want to enter the Catacombs, but she had no choice. The Sheriff was coming after them, which meant they had find and destroy his bones.

Nate left her and walked to Roman, grabbing some waterproofs on the way. Eliza watched them trade words, but she couldn't make out what they were saying. Whatever it was, Nate did not look happy. She approached them and they immediately stopped talking.

The three of them stared into the tunnel.

"You thinking someone else may be in there?" Eliza muttered.

"I never saw anyone when I was down there," Roman said. "Natalie's brother and his friend just got lost. That's all."

"All these years and you still haven't mastered the art of lying," Nate said.

"If I didn't know you better, I'd swear you were making a dig at the past." Roman turned to him. "Whatever shit there is between us, we need to bury it until this is all over. I need to know we have each other's backs in there."

"I wasn't making any reference of the sort." Nate repositioned his backpack. "And I agree with the latter."

Roman turned to the rest of the group. "Okay, people. Let's get going."

Billy walked towards them, a newfound strut in his gait. Natalie stuck close beside him, her four goons following close behind her. Only one person remained – the suit guarding the cars and leftover equipment.

Roman took Eliza's hand. His touch sent shivers up her arm. "Here goes nothing."

CHAPTER THIRTY-NINE

Roman wished he were anywhere but here.

It was no secret the French authorities were quickly sealing off any and all entrances into the Catacombs. Roman just wished this had been one of them.

He led his newly appointed team through the tunnel, sticking close to the railway tracks – the light fading the further in they ventured. Eliza still held his hand and he liked it. It calmed him. And, by God, he needed to stay calm if he was going to wriggle through that tiny hole in the wall again.

"I wonder what happened to my father," Eliza said.

Roman scoffed. "You know, you never cease to amaze me."

"Why?

"The guy murdered you and you're still worried about him."

"Not worried. I just wondered if he was still tied to the chair."

Roman paused. He didn't want to start an argument and he didn't want to admit he'd left James in the kitchen knowing the Sheriff would find him. "He's probably free by now. I didn't tie his binds too tight."

He was relieved when she changed the subject.

"So, how far in do we have to go?" she asked.

"About a mile."

Roman reached over and switched on her helmet light. It brightened the tunnel in front of them. A mass of objects littered the edges: old sleeping bags, discarded rubbish – all stuff he hadn't seen when he was here previously without the aid of a strong light.

"What are we looking for?"

Eliza didn't seem nervous at all. Surprisingly calm, in fact, given her earlier question about the possibility of them not being alone in here.

"There's a hole in the wall. A small hole." He flashed a smile. "Hope you've been counting those calories lately."

Eliza rolled those big, brown eyes of hers. She looked beautiful, walking alongside him in her oversized overalls, clunky wellies, and yellow hard hat.

He cleared his throat. "I've been meaning to say, that was some handiwork back at the airfield. How did you learn to control your powers?"

"Your brother. He told me to tap into my emotions."

"I see." Roman's body tightened. Yet another thing Eliza had shared with his brother. "He's obviously a better teacher than I am."

She shot him a look and he cringed. What the hell was wrong with him?

Behind them, Natalie's French tones caressed the air as she questioned Billy about his job, his lifestyle, his private life. Roman shook his head – their conversation was so...normal. Why couldn't he have that with Eliza? All they'd discussed in the last week was sacrifice, betrayal, and death.

He focused forward again. The last time he'd been here, he'd thought of it as just another theft – a simple grab-and-go. He knew different now. He remembered how claustrophobic it had been down among the graves.

Darkness completely swallowed the daylight. One by one, the entourage behind flicked on their hard hats, the beams zipping past him to help light the way. Roman followed suit and switched on his lamp. He tilted his head and lit the GPS strapped to his wrist. Almost a mile in. He'd nearly reached that bloody hole. He fumbled and took a torch from the side pocket of his backpack.

He aimed its light towards the edge of the passage, finding a worn trainer, a couple of carrier bags, some badly drawn graffiti, and...was that a used condom? He definitely hadn't seen any of this during his first visit. He kept walking. Kept searching for the elusive hole.

And, then, there it was. The perfectly formed circle.

Roman stopped and brought the group behind him to a halt. He dropped his bag beside the hole, opened it, and pulled out a bunch of glow sticks. "Eliza, I suggest you get yours out too. We're gonna need them. Stick them in your pocket."

He cracked one. Its amber glow brightened the tunnel and he promptly dropped it through the hole. Like on his first visit, it splash-landed in a puddle a level below them. And, like the last time, the puddle swallowed most of its light, making it almost impossible to see any threat that could be waiting for them.

Roman took a deep breath and glanced up at Eliza. "You come through after me." He turned to Nate. "Make sure everyone gets down okay, backpacks first."

Roman slipped the other glow sticks into his back pocket and pushed the backpack through the hole. It landed in the puddle on top of the glow stick, cutting off the light completely. *Shit*. He couldn't see jack down there now. He contemplated dropping another stick, but he wanted to conserve what supply they had. He inhaled and lowered himself through feet first.

He landed, feet spread either side of the backpack. He picked it up, grateful Natalie had had the foresight to supply waterproof ones, and threw it back over his shoulders. "Okay, Eliza."

Her backpack dropped through the hole, missing his head by an inch or two. He picked it up and threw it to the side. Eliza's feet came through the hole, followed by the rest of her. Roman embraced her calves and guided her down as her body slithered through his arms. Her hands found his shoulders and her arms wrapped around his neck. The baggy overalls couldn't disguise the slim body beneath and, for a brief moment, he was back holding her in the motel room.

Her feet touched the ground and she glanced at him. He held her close, giving himself that one moment to be with her. He'd treated her so badly since they'd all escaped Purgatory and he wanted to apologise, to say how sorry he was. But the words stuck in his throat.

"Your bag's behind me," he said.

Eliza released his neck and he tried not to think about the possibility he might never hold her again.

"Okay, next one," he shouted up towards the hole.

A bag came through and, this time, one of the suits lowered themselves down. Roman didn't give him the same attention he had Eliza.

The man landed in the puddle. *"C'est génial. Ruiné mes chaussures."*

"Oh, geez." Roman felt his shoulders tighten. "Enough with the French crap, already."

Eliza held the man's bag out for him. "He's just peeved he ruined his shoes."

"Well, he shouldn't have come down here looking like a bloody office boy, then."

Roman called for the next person. He caught the bag and passed it to the suit to hold. Billy lowered Natalie through. Like he had with Eliza, Roman wrapped his arms around her legs and guided her down. But as soon as Natalie's feet touched the ground, he released her.

Bag after bag dropped through the hole. Billy and two of the other suits followed – including André. Roman scowled at that prick.

There was only Nate and one last suit to go. The bag came through and so did the man's feet...but not much else.

Roman waited for him to lower himself through. "What's going on up there?"

"He's too big," Nate shouted down. "He's stuck."

"For fuck's sake." Roman looked at Natalie. "Who is it?"

"François. He's my driver."

Roman glanced back up at the hole. Actually, this could be a blessing in disguise. "He'll have to wait up there. He can keep guard and radio us if there's any sign of trouble." *The Sheriff, for example*. He called up to Nate. "You hear that, bro?"

"I heard."

The man's feet slowly slithered back out of the hole.

Nate stuck his head through. "Shall I leave my bag up here for him?"

"Just the radio, a bottle of water, and a torch. He has no use for the rest of the stuff."

A few moments later, Nate's bag landed at Roman's feet. Roman picked it up and moved over, allowing his brother to jump down beside him. Roman handed over his backpack.

Now they had an extra bag, which Roman chose to carry for a while. He moved to the front of the group, keeping Eliza at his side. He wanted her close-by while they were down here. At least until they opened the gateway and Roman ventured into Hell. Then she was Nate's to protect. He shone his torch over his map. This first part was pretty straightforward. He only had one way to go. But, further on, other tunnels came into play and he didn't want to get lost. Anyone unlucky enough to take a wrong turn down here stayed down here.

"Everyone stay close." He shone his torch towards the back of the group – on the suit in front of Nate. "What's your name?"

"Beau."

"Right, Beau. My brother has your back, so you'd better have his while he's behind you. Got it?"

Beau nodded. He gripped the straps of his backpack.

André stood in front of him. Roman didn't have anything to say to him.

He shone his torch forward one person, to Billy. "You good?"

Billy nodded.

Roman moved the torchlight forward again. Natalie stood in front of Billy and, in front of her – guarding his employer – was the last of the suits. "And you are?"

"Dax."

Roman's torch found Nate again. "Grab the glow stick off the ground and bring it with us."

Roman caught Eliza's gaze and winked then faced forward and started to walk. If the Sheriff arrived before Roman had the chance to find and burn his bones, Roman didn't need any unnecessary light indicating where they'd entered the cavern.

Fifty paces in, Roman chalked a white cross onto the brick wall, still omitting to use the glow sticks. He should feel confident being down here with seven other people, but he wasn't. This first level was just the beginning. He knew what to expect the lower they ventured. The others didn't have a clue what horrific conditions awaited them.

He continued onwards, following the passage into a pit of darkness. Only the immediate ten metres or so lit up under the torchlight. Artwork, scribbled names, and spray-painted graffiti adorned the walls – maybe from previous explorers or maybe from party revellers feeling the urge to mark their territory.

Roman glanced at the walls, but his attention quickly turned to the darkness ahead.

"Do you know where you're going?" Eliza muttered in his ear.

Roman paused. He reached a small ledge and jumped down. Then he turned around and held out his hand for Eliza. She took it and jumped down.

She checked the digital display on the watch she'd taken from one of the crates outside the tunnel entrance. "We've been in here a while now. How much longer do you reckon?"

"We haven't even scratched the surface."

"That long, eh?"

Roman grimaced. "It's going to be a good few hours. You up for that?"

"I seem to be up for all sorts since I met you." She grinned.

Just like her to keep him calm when he needed it the most. He pulled his map from his pocket and unfolded it.

Dax jumped down and turned to help Natalie.

"Are we going the right way?" Natalie said, sounding a little weary.

Roman lifted his boot and stared down at the used glow stick he'd dropped during his first visit. "That's what the map says."

"That map hardly made any sense on ground level under the spotlights. How can it possibly make sense to you down here in the dark?"

"It makes sense."

Roman turned away from her. He glanced at the map one more time, refolded it, and slipped it back into his pocket. Swapping it for a glow stick, he cracked the light and dropped it to the ground beside the old one. From here, they would let the light lead them back.

"You still with us, Nate?" he said.

"I'm still here."

Roman started off again along the passage. He led the group in silence until the ceiling scraped the top of his head.

He hunched his shoulders. "Watch your heads."

He cracked another glow stick and stopped. He was by another hole in the wall.

Roman removed his backpack. "If you grabbed wellies, now's the time to put them on."

He got onto all fours and crawled through the tiny opening. The corridor on the other side was lower by two feet. Roman's toes found a narrow ledge and he shone the torch around. Water flooded the tunnel – not too deep, but Roman knew it would get worse. He wedged his torch in between two crumbling rocks and stuck his head back through the hole.

Eliza and the others still waited on the other side. Eliza was the only one wearing wellingtons, though.

Roman grabbed his rucksack and pulled it through the entrance. "Careful as you come through. Try and stick to the ledge."

He left his torch wedged in the wall and, with his back pressed against the side of the corridor, made his way along the ledge. The further he went, the slimmer the ledge became, until the toes of his boots hung over the edge.

Natalie screamed. Roman spun around and Eliza's torch blinded him. He blocked the light with his hand.

"She's just seen a rat," Eliza said, matter-of-factly.

Natalie whimpered. "Heaven knows what diseases we will catch down here."

"Jesus fucking…" Roman turned and rubbed his chin. He'd almost forgotten what high-maintenance women sounded like. He looked back at Natalie, now being comforted in Billy's arms. "She okay now?"

Billy looked up. "She's fine. Keep walking."

Billy released his hold and muttered something to her. She nodded and, still holding Billy's hand, continued to edge forward.

Roman smiled. Billy was in there with the French princess; that was for damn sure. He continued onwards, the ceiling getting lower and lower, and the ledge more and more narrow. Finally, he had no choice but to step off it. The water clouded white and covered his boots, washing around his ankles. He waded through, loose bones snapping under foot.

He heard Eliza jump in and, splash after splash, the others followed. Roman pushed on. The ceiling continued to lower and mumblings of unrest started to echo around the passage. The water rose past his shins and up to his knees. The air was stuffy and breathing was becoming a struggle. His chest tightened, his lungs unable to expand as much as he wanted. Several times, his foot caught on a bone and he tripped.

When Eliza tripped behind him, he stopped. "Give me your leg."

Eliza grabbed his shoulders and lifted her foot. Roman removed the wellie and emptied the water from it.

He slipped the boot back on her. "The other one." Eliza lifted her other foot and he repeated the action. "Just a little further and there'll be another ledge."

He turned away from her and continued walking. The quicker he found that ledge, the quicker they would get out of this water. The stench of it was enough to make him gag.

The ceiling was lower again – or the ground was rising. A small ridge jutted out of the wall. A little further, it widened into a ledge. Roman lifted Eliza onto it then climbed up himself. Sure enough, he was almost doubled-over, his back still scraping the top of the passage. He edged forward until, eventually, there was no room to stand. He got down onto all fours and started to crawl. Eliza was able to go on a little further before her height became a problem, then she too had to resort to crawling.

Crumbling walls blocked their path. Roman cleared the way, sweeping broken stone and brick into the water. He shone his torch into the hidden rooms beyond. Rats scurried away from the light, scampering across the bones that littered the ground. Every so often, he heard Nate crack a glow stick and leave it on the ledge behind him.

Finally, the water dispersed. Now the sea of bones across the ground was visible to the eye. Roman climbed off the ledge. The bones snapped beneath his boots. It was a sickening sound, but one they were going to hear a lot over the next few hours.

"Roman, hold up," Billy called out.

Roman stopped and turned to find a multitude of spotlights all aimed his way. He shielded his eyes. "What's up?"

"We need to take five."

Roman watched Billy perch on the ledge beside Natalie. There wasn't time for this. Roman needed to get to Hell's gate before the Sheriff found them – Billy knew this. Why was he pandering to the French queen's inadequacies?

Eliza took Roman's hand. "We've been walking for hours. We could all do with a quick break." She sat on the ledge and pulled him down beside her. She reached into her pocket and pulled out a chocolate bar – a Snickers. She unwrapped it and broke it in half. "Found this in my bag." She passed half to him.

Roman took it. He loved Snickers. He took a big bite and started chewing. He looked along the group. Everyone had sat. Some, like them, ate chocolate. Nate sat at the end, swigging from a water bottle.

"You think the Sheriff's here yet?" Eliza said.

Roman shrugged. "Maybe. Who knows?" He looked past her, towards Billy and Natalie. "He's getting too close to her."

Eliza turned and glanced at her brother. "Like you did with me?"

Roman waited for her to turn back to him. He met her gaze. Now was the time to apologise to her. To tell her that meeting her was one of the best things that had happened to him.

"And look how that's turned out," he said. "We're sitting with thousands of dead corpses hundreds of feet beneath ground level."

Eliza cupped his face, her cold fingers sending electric jolts through him. She leaned towards him and pressed her lips against his.

"It ain't over yet," she murmured and kissed him again.

Roman melted into her. He wrapped his arms around her shoulders. His hands cupped her neck. His fingers dove into her hair. Her kisses warmed his mouth. His pulse raced and his quickened blood-flow heated his whole body.

Some way back, one of the guys cleared their throat. Eliza pulled back and Roman glanced along the line. He caught Nate watching them. Roman glanced back at Eliza. He stared at her, taking a moment to drink her in.

Then he stood, still having to hunch a little because of the low ceiling. "Okay, people. Break time's over."

He trudged onwards, still chalking crosses on the walls and dropping glow sticks every hundred metres or so. He descended through another hole, down another level. Bones were piled several feet high beneath their feet. Skulls stared up at him. The graffiti had disappeared some hours ago and now symbols etched the walls, telling him that he was nearly there.

He clambered over the endless broken skeletons and, finally, at the end of the passageway, his torchlight found the familiar chalk figure of a man — his arms and legs outstretched, leading the way down to Hell.

CHAPTER FORTY

Even in the lack of light, Nate saw his brother's shoulders tense.

He looked down towards the hole lit by Roman's hard hat and a shiver ran down his spine. A sick feeling churned inside his stomach and he swayed, assaulted by sudden light-headedness. Every essence of his being wanted to turn and run. There was no doubt Roman had been right; the gateway to Hell was in the next room. They were so close he could taste it.

Roman glanced at him. "Here goes nothing."

Nate turned to Billy. "Eliza and Roman are going to check the room out on the other side of this wall and report back."

"Why? Do you think my brother's in there?" Natalie said.

Billy turned her to face him. "He may be. But, in case he isn't, we can cover more ground if we split up and search for him."

"Billy's right," Nate added. "Let them check inside. The opening's small. It would take time for us all to go through and it might turn out to be a dead end."

"No. We should not split up," Natalie argued. "Not down here. We should all enter."

Billy turned Natalie back to face him. "Let them go check. We'll wait out here."

Natalie glanced at Nate. "I think I should go with them."

Nate said nothing. Whatever happened down here, Roman had to find the Sheriff's bones and destroy them first.

"Roman's like a bad penny," Billy continued. "He always shows up. Besides, we have radios, remember?"

Annoyance flared in Natalie's eyes, but she said no more.

Roman got onto all fours. He glanced up at Eliza. "You come through straight after me."

Nate watched him pull himself through the hole. Eliza crawled through after him.

"I still think I should go with them," Natalie said.

"We wait here," Nate said.

"But my brother could be with them." Natalie rushed towards the hole.

Nate stopped her. "We all wait here."

Natalie scowled at him. "Are you forgetting what we came down here for?"

Again, she made a play for the small opening. She glanced back at Dex, who followed her.

This time, Nate blocked the entrance. "Stop. I'll go though. You wait here."

He lay on his back and started to pull himself through the hole, feet first. He stopped when he was halfway through and looked up – first at Natalie, then at Billy. "Wait here."

CHAPTER FORTY-ONE

Twenty minutes had passed since the Sheriff's arrival at the French airport.

Roman's scent had been easy to follow. But, standing outside the disused railway tunnel, the Sheriff was a little confused. Of all the places Roman could have fled, why on earth had he come here? Was he trying to hide hundreds of feet below ground? Even with his minimal intelligence, Roman would know the Sheriff would still find him.

The Sheriff had to assume it was some kind of trap.

"*Hé toi.*"

The Sheriff turned.

A man, dressed in a black suit and tie, emerged from one of two limousines parked by the tracks. He hurried forward, a menacing look hardening his face. He was unfamiliar to the Sheriff – definitely not someone from the Cornish airfield.

He held out his hand as a warning for the Sheriff to stop where he was. "*Ce tunnel est fermé.*"

The Sheriff narrowed his eyes. "Closed tunnel or not, I am entering."

The man reached into his jacket, but the Sheriff didn't wait to see what he was going to pull out. He slapped his palms against the man's head and pressed. Blood flooded the whites of the gentleman's eyes. The man screamed and hit out, trying to loosen the Sheriff's grip. It was a feeble – and pointless – attempt.

"How many are in there?" the Sheriff asked.

The man still struggled. His eyes bulged from their sockets.

"How many?"

"*N...neuf.*"

"Thank you." The Sheriff squeezed his palms together and one of the man's eyes popped from its socket.

The man screamed louder. The Sheriff pressed harder and the man's skull cracked like an egg. A line of blood streamed from the man's nose. The Sheriff dug his talons into the back of the man's head until he felt the softness of the man's brain upon his fingertips. He savoured the texture for a moment then he ripped the man's head in two.

The headless body dropped to the ground.

The Sheriff raised his arms. Each hand held half a skull. Like a jigsaw, he pressed the head back together and studied the face. He definitely hadn't seen this man before, so whom had Roman joined forces with? And why?

The Sheriff cast the pieces across the railway tracks and onto the bank. The left side of the man's face hit shrubs and stayed put. The right side hit a rock, wavered for a second, then rolled down over the dirt, finding its final resting place against an old shopping trolley.

The Sheriff inhaled the air around him. Roman's stench was everywhere: near the vehicle farthest from him; around the turned out crates that were piled everywhere; and, most importantly, at the tunnel entrance.

There was no doubt Roman was inside. As was the cop. His smell lingered just as much as Roman's, and if they were still together, the Sheriff had to believe that Nathaniel and Eliza were with them. The Sheriff looked back at the decapitated body lying on the ground. Smart, suited, and French. Who the devil was he to Roman? And, as he assumed four of the people inside were the cop, the Holbrooks, and the girl, who were the other four?

The Sheriff entered the tunnel. In hindsight, he should have interrogated the man a little more before he killed him. Maybe found out exactly what his connection to Roman was, and what he and his new crew were up to.

He ventured further into the tunnel. The floodlighting had long since faded, eaten up by the looming darkness. Roman's scent was as strong as ever inside the tunnel, the lack of air making it hard for the odour to easily dissipate. The Sheriff followed it, marching forward, not wanting to waste any more time hunting the Holbrook brothers down.

Nearly a mile in, he paused. Up ahead, the sound of light breathing caught his ear. He listened harder, straining to hear what his eyes couldn't see. It was human breathing – not animal.

He moved forward, keeping his steps soft and silent. A soft, yellow light illuminated the tunnel like a dull beacon a little way ahead. It looked low to the ground and the glow didn't stretch very far at all.

A radio crackled and a French voice called for François to give him an update. The Sheriff paused, listening for any other people.

"*Tout est clair ici*," François replied.

It seemed only François blocked the Sheriff's current path and that was music to his ears. He stepped forward and the man froze.

"*Qui est là?*"

Unlike the man at the entrance, this guy didn't try to put on a pretence of bravery. The darkness down here had done a damn good job of scaring him half to death already.

The Sheriff stepped into the light. "What is Roman doing in here?"

François frowned. "*Je ne connais aucun Roman.*"

The Sheriff sighed. "You know exactly who Roman is. He came in here. English guy. Dark hair. So tall." The Sheriff hovered his hand about six feet from the ground. "I strongly suggest you reply in English. I'd hate for any information to get lost in translation."

François stepped back. A wise move, not that it would save him.

"They went down that hole," he said shakily.

"They?"

"Seven of them." François paused and studied him. "You...one of them was like you."

The Sheriff glanced down at his apparel and remembered he still looked like Billy. "Ah, yes. Let me just clear that up." He stretched his body.

François's screams reverberated through the tunnel, drowning out the sound of the Sheriff's body cracking back into his own, more comfortable form.

"Now," the Sheriff continued. "Was an English lady also with them?"

François nodded. Tremors visibly rocked his body.

"And these others. Who are they?"

Inaudible words whimpered from the Frenchman's mouth.

"You need to calm down. I cannot hear you." The Sheriff hunched lower and looked him in the eye. "Tell me what I want to know and, this time, make sure I can hear you."

"M...m...my employer and h...her security."

"Why are they down there?"

François swallowed. "Search and r...rescue mission."

"For who?"

"My employer's b...brother."

The Sheriff rubbed his chin. None of this made sense. Roman should be on the run. Instead, he was down here doing this? He picked up the glow stick and shone it towards the hole. He leaned closer and breathed in the staleness from the other side. Couldn't Roman have found a bigger one to crawl through?

The radio button clicked and François yelled in to it. "*Dax, nous avons compagnie. Un homme—*"

The Sheriff twisted. He grabbed the Frenchman's leg and snapped his knee. François screamed in pain, ending his radio call for help.

The walkie-talkie fell from his hand and he stared down at his leg. The Sheriff kicked the second kneecap backwards. François dropped to the ground and the Sheriff leaned over him. Before François had chance to scream, the Sheriff grabbed his throat. He squeezed his fingers around his larynx, smiled, and then ripped it out.

He dropped it, swapping it for the radio. Nobody had replied to François's outburst. Maybe the Frenchman's warning hadn't reached its recipient. The Sheriff wiped his hand down his shirt and turned back to the hole.

Now for Roman Holbrook.

CHAPTER FORTY-TWO

Natalie felt the rage building inside of her.

She glanced at the hole. Her plan was falling apart. She was losing control and she hated not being in control. She looked at Dax. He also looked worried, as did Beau.

André stepped closer to her. "Maybe we should go through."

Billy looked up. "Nate told us to wait here."

Natalie walked towards the hole regardless. She lay down, getting in position to pull herself through the gap, but Billy dragged her back up.

"I'm serious," Billy said. "We wait here, okay?"

Natalie sighed. "Billy, you seem like a nice man and I don't want to see you hurt. Please, move aside and let me enter."

Billy tilted his head, clearly not understanding that the dynamics between them had changed.

Natalie waited. She gave Billy a minute to comply with her request.

When he still stood fast, she sighed again. "So be it."

She flicked her wrist and Billy catapulted to the other side of the tunnel. He hit the wall and fell to his knees. He remained on all fours and shook his head clear. Then he stood, unsteady, but with a determined look on his face that she almost had to admire.

Natalie raised her hand and lifted Billy from the ground. The low ceiling wouldn't allow her to lift him as high as she would have liked.

Billy's head hit the ceiling and he kicked his legs, his feet finding nothing but air.

He glared at Natalie. "You're a mind mover?"

Natalie smiled. "Your knowledge surprises me. I am impressed."

"Yeah, well, you're not the first mind mover I've come across."

"So, you know what I can do?"

"I know."

"And you will now comply with my request instead of fighting against it?"

Billy glanced below him. "Do I have a choice?"

"Not really."

"Then I guess I comply."

Natalie lowered him back to the ground.

Billy rubbed his head. He glanced at Dax and Beau and took a step closer to Natalie. "How is all this going to help find your brother?"

Natalie laughed. "I don't have a brother."

Billy gaped at her. "So, what are you doing down here?"

"Originally, I was guarding a piece of the True Cross. That wood is bad news for us mind movers, you know. But when Roman was the one who turned up looking for it, I let him have it. I wanted him more than the wood."

"I don't understand."

"I've been searching for Roman for a long, long time. I'm sure you are aware that a man like Roman cannot be stopped – not even by a mind mover. Even if you kill him, he does not stay dead. I had no choice but to let him leave. My lost brother story was the tale I used so he would contact me again. Well, that and a million pounds."

"That still doesn't explain why?"

"He killed my family. That hole he and his brother have just crawled through leads to the perfect prison. But I get the feeling you already know that."

Billy shook his head dazedly. "So, this whole charade is about revenge? Why not just go to the police?"

"The family I speak of were killed in 1657, in Salem, and they deserve justice."

"Maybe, but not at the expense of others." Billy shifted his feet. "There are innocent people down here with us."

Natalie crouched beside the hole. "Not everyone is as innocent as you think."

"What is that supposed to mean?"

"It means I have explained enough. I cannot kill Roman, so I am going to send him where he belongs."

Billy took another step forward, but André grabbed him. Billy turned and punched him away.

André fell back and Billy rushed at Natalie again. "You have to let Roman finish what he's doing first."

"I know all about Purgatory hunting him. Unfortunately, Roman's downfall will be by my hand, not theirs."

"No, you don't understand." Billy grabbed her arm.

Natalie looked at him and again Billy flew back against the wall. He hit it with more force than before and fell to the ground in the same spot as before. This time, when Billy tried to get to his feet, André planted his elbow into the back of his neck. Billy collapsed.

"Take him to the pit," Natalie said.

André motioned to Dax and Beau. They hoisted Billy up off the ground by the arms and dragged him down a corridor to the left of the chalk man.

André turned to her. "What now?"

"Now we finish this."

CHAPTER FORTY-THREE

Nate couldn't stand upright.

He was in a small room. Bones filled the entire floor and the ceiling was lower than in the previous room. Eliza and Roman were crouched on the far side, blood already dripping from Eliza's hand. When he looked above them, the words *Semita ad immortalitatem* lit up under his hardhat's lamp.

Roman glanced up. "What are you doing here?"

"The Pathway to Immortality." Nate crawled closer to the sign. He touched the paintwork and sniffed his fingers. It was written in Lucifer's blood. "Are you sure about this?"

"There's no other way."

"We've only been in there once. It was by invitation and we arrived through the main entrance. You remember what it was like in there? How hard it was to survive?"

"Of course I remember."

"This back door here could have anything behind it."

"Hey, if you know another way in, I'm all ears."

Nate didn't. He squatted beside them. "So, how're you going to do this?"

"Exactly as we discussed. I go in, find the bones, and burn them." Roman turned to Eliza. "Remember, the gateway into Hell works exactly the same as the Cross did with Heaven. Your blood will open it. I'll contaminate and close it with my blood after I get out."

"You sure this will work?"

Roman shrugged. "It's a gateway."

He gestured for Eliza to press her bloodied palm against the Latin words.

"Wait," Nate said, halting Eliza from touching the sign. He turned to Roman. "I'm coming with you."

"No, you're staying here with Eliza, remember?"

"I have to come with you. If I'm with you, I can't be used to close the gateway early."

"What are you talking about?" Roman frowned. "Why would you want to close it early?"

"He doesn't," Natalie said. "I do."

Nate turned to see Natalie crouched by the opening. "You need to be outside, Natalie."

"But it sounds like you are trying to back out of our deal."

"I'm not, but Roman needs to do this first."

"What deal?" Roman said.

Nate couldn't look at Roman. It was even harder when he turned to face Eliza. "I'm so sorry."

Eliza stared at him. A light frown creased the top of her nose. "You know her?"

Nate nodded. "For years now. She came to me last week. Wanted help stopping Roman, but I didn't want any part of it. Then you turned up at the church. You were decent and kind. I couldn't let Roman drag you into his crap."

Horror filled Eliza's eyes. "But I explained that he'd changed."

"I didn't believe you." Nate glanced at Roman. "He has a history of easily manipulating women."

For once, Roman didn't argue with him.

Nate looked back at Eliza. "You were so brainwashed that I agreed to lure Roman here. Natalie was to open the gateway and I was to close it."

"You agreed to imprison him?"

"He has his reasons," Roman butted in. "Don't blame him."

"I can't believe you're defending him."

Eliza turned back to Nate. "Why didn't you just leave him in Purgatory?"

"Because you were hell-bent on saving your brother. If I didn't help, you would have undoubtedly found another way in."

"So, all this was to save me?" Eliza shook her head. "And you were okay sending Roman off to kill the Sheriff knowing he wouldn't be able to come back?"

"It doesn't matter," Roman said. "I'm okay with it."

Eliza turned to him. "Well, I'm not."

Roman reached for her hand. "It needs to be done. The Sheriff will be dead and you will be free to go have a normal life again."

"I'm past being normal." Eliza glanced at Natalie. "And what's your story?"

Natalie smiled. "I am like you."

She flicked her wrist towards Roman, sending him sprawling against the skeletal wall. Loose bones fell around him.

Eliza made ready to attack, but Nate held her back. The last thing he needed was for the two mind movers to commence battle against one another. He felt Eliza's rigid body push against his arm. She wasn't about to back down.

"Hey," Nate said softly.

He waited for Eliza to look at him. When she did, he discreetly eyed the sign above their heads.

Eliza glared at him. "I don't trust you."

"You don't have a choice."

Roman crawled towards them. "Listen to him."

Eliza glanced from one brother to the other. Then she slammed her hand against the wood. The bones beneath their feet started to tremble and more loose bones fell from their place in the wall. Light circled above their heads. Fire bolts descended and exploded across the ground around them. One landed beside Natalie and she pressed back against the wall.

The bones beneath the sign burst outwards in a blaze of heat. Eliza covered her face and dived to the side of the doorway for cover. The heat scorched Nate's body, but this was his chance. He grabbed hold of Roman's shoulder and hauled him though the gateway.

Nate landed on the other side. Roman landed beside him. The intense heat seared his skin. When he turned back to the portal, he saw Natalie glaring at him.

Roman grabbed his arm and twisted him around. "What the fuck are you doing? You were supposed to stay and look after Eliza."

Nate looked at his brother – the man prepared to give his life to save a woman he'd vowed to kill. "Maybe Eliza's right. Maybe you have changed."

He got up and glanced above him. If there was a ceiling in here, he couldn't see it. "We need to get moving. The Sheriff could be here soon."

Roman got to his feet and halted him. "I'm not going anywhere until you explain who I'm leaving Eliza to deal with."

Nate glanced back at the gateway. Eliza had joined Natalie at the opening, the two of them standing side by side, watching their progress but not entering.

"Natalie only wants you to suffer. She has no argument with Eliza. They're practically family, after all" He repositioned the rucksack, pulled down on the straps, then started off along the pathway.

Roman grabbed his arm. "If you're wrong..."

"I'm not."

Nate started off along the path again. It was a different passage, but this place looked just how he remembered it from his first and only visit – back when he became a reaper.

Roman caught up to him. "So, what did I do to fuck off this Natalie chick?"

"You did Salem."

Roman stopped walking and Nate turned.

The colour drained from Roman's face. "That girl is Natalie's ancestor?"

Nate nodded.

"Does she know you sent me to Purgatory for that?"

"For killing her?"

"It was an accident."

Nate bit back a cutting retort. "She knows."

"Then what the hell...?"

"It's not enough. She wants you imprisoned in Hell."

Nate started off along the path again.

Roman caught up and quietness fell upon them. Nate glanced back. Only Eliza remained at the gateway.

"I should never have agreed to any of this," he said.

"But you did. And I get it." Roman looked back. "I feel uneasy leaving Eliza with that psycho."

"I told you, she'll be fine. Natalie may be a problem later – after we get out of here – but for now she isn't a threat."

"Later I can deal with." Roman halted. He flung his arm across Nate's chest, stopping him dead in his tracks. "I remember this bit. Or, at least, something like this." He knelt and pointed towards a small hole bored into the wall. He waved his hand in front of the hole and a dart fired out and hit the wall opposite. "Still using this Indiana Jones shit, it would seem."

Nate started to search the walls for more holes and, together, they walked on, cautious and vigilant. He halted beside another gap. Like Roman, he waved his hand in front of it and allowed the dart to shoot out. It hit the wall and bounced to the ground.

Nate picked it up. "These have poison on them."

"So?"

"So, they may come in handy later on."

Roman nodded his approval and when he waved his hand over the next hole, he too collected the dart from the ground.

They must have collected fifteen darts each by the time they reached the end of the path. They stopped and glanced down at the black tar that oozed along the track.

"I'm beginning to remember why I hated this place so much," Roman said, stepping into the substance.

His boot slipped and he fell back, landing on his arse. Nate helped him up.

Roman flicked the goo from his hand. "Just when I thought things couldn't get any worse."

Nate smiled. Centuries had passed since he and his brother had shared a joke. It was definitely an odd thing to do at a time like this.

It didn't last. The passageway came to an abrupt end and the smile dropped from Nate's lips. He stood on the edge of the chasm. Thousands upon thousands of bodies were set into the walls. Nate peered down into the circular abyss. The walls moved with living bodies. A few hundred feet below, at the bottom, a fire roared. The cliché Hell's pit.

He looked up. More arms reached out – way too many to count. Bodies writhed together. Groans and murmurs echoed around them with no end in view. Just an incessant sea of souls.

Roman stuck his head out and glanced up. "You remember the etchings?"

Nate nodded.

"We need to go up."

"Why don't we look for the easy way, like we were shown before?"

"Something tells me we won't find it."

Roman reached for the wall of bodies and grabbed an ankle. He swung outwards and started to climb.

Nate followed him. He grabbed the same ankle, pushed the toe of his boot into an armpit, and hoisted himself up. Roman waited until he caught up and the two brothers climbed side by side. The bodies cried out and clawed at their clothing. Some begged for freedom, others groaned in anger. The rest, those with their tongues torn out or throats ripped apart, didn't say anything.

Face after face, Nate saw missing eyes, missing ears. Skin with third-degree burns. Limbs stripped completely to the bone. Each carcass tried to hold him back, tried to drag him down, but he fought on.

Every few metres, spy-holes appeared between the bodies. Through them, more human walls surrounded flames higher than Nate remembered when he, Roman, and a bunch of other young reapers had visited during their tour of Hell. The heat was unbearable. The scorching atmosphere swept through the spy-hole and scorched Nate's face. Sweat dripped into eyes. Blisters bubbled on his skin.

He whipped his head away.

"How high do we have to climb?" he yelled across at Roman.

One of the bodies grabbed Roman's wrist. Roman bent the bearer's fingers back until they snapped and released him. "Not sure. I just remember there wasn't any fire where we were."

Nate continued to climb. So many bodies. So many tormented souls. He saw Roman grab a carcass's shoulder and pull himself higher. Blunt teeth chomped down on his hand, and Roman whipped his arm away, toppling off balance. His foot slipped and he fell backwards.

Another body in the wall seized him around the waist and pulled him close. Bodies either side clutched his arms and pinned him, their fingernails clawing into his skin. Roman kicked out. He glared at the face in front of him. Teeth gnashed for his ear, his throat, his face.

Nate climbed past him and kicked the prisoner in the head. The guy's face crumbled apart, but still those teeth tried to bite.

"Don't worry about me. Just find the bones," Roman said, headbutting the prisoner as hard as he could.

Nate lowered himself again. He pried one of the hands from Roman's arm, allowing Roman to quickly free the other. The prisoner still clung tight around his waist. He stared at Roman, his yellow eyes bloodshot from an eternity of being imprisoned down here. Roman pressed his thumbs against them and pushed inwards.

The prisoner groaned. Pus oozed from the tear ducts and his hold around Roman loosened. Roman's foot slipped but his thumbs still hooked into the prisoner's eye sockets. He curled his fingers around the back of the prisoner's head and held on, dangling in the air, only his hold on the prisoner stopping him from plummeting into Hell's fiery pit.

Nate grabbed the cuff of Roman's jumper. Roman tried to get a better footing, but the prisoner's head lolled forward under Roman's weight and the back of its neck started to sever from its shoulders.

Nate lowered himself further and tried to get a better grip on his brother.

The prisoner's head tore free and Roman plummeted towards the flames.

"No!" Nate quickly descended.

Roman reached out for the wall, limbs slipping through his grasp as he fell. Random arms flapped and flailed around him. He seized hold of an arm and tightened his grip. He hung there, suspended.

"You okay?" Nate yelled down, praying the limb would hold his brother's weight and not tear free like the head had.

"Just dandy."

Nate quickly descended until he was beside him. Roman pushed his foot back in between the bodies and found a secure footing again.

He glanced at his brother. "If I go down, you make sure you burn those bones. Don't let all this be for nothing."

Nate swallowed and wiped the sweat from his brow. "How about you make sure it doesn't happen again."

Roman threw him a nervous smile. "That's a deal I'm happy to make."

The two began to climb again. This time, Nate stayed even closer beside Roman. Together, they scaled the bodies, pulling themselves higher and higher. The heat, although still uncomfortable, no longer scorched their skin. The higher they climbed, the cooler it got and the closer they were to finding the Sheriff's bones.

"Hold up." Nate paused. He wiped the cuff of his shirt across his face.

Roman waited for him, looking glad of the rest. The heat had dehydrated them both.

Light-headedness muddled Nate's thoughts and he struggled to focus.

Roman frowned. "You good?"

Nate nodded and Roman started to climb again. Nate followed. Up and up. Higher and higher. Fighting their way past every tortured body they encountered. The top was still nowhere in sight and when Nate glanced down, the pit had become a tiny pool of orange.

Finally, the flames behind the bodies disappeared. Heat no longer burned its way through the portals and Nate's skin began to cool.

"I think I see something," Roman yelled across at him.

Nate clambered closer and looked through the small portal. No flames burned on the other side. Instead, he peered at what looked to be water glistening against a cavernous rock face.

"See the etchings?"

Nate searched harder. Sure enough, three small triangles were etched into pillars just as he remembered. "The hole's too small. How're we supposed to get in?"

A child's body curled around the edge of the portal like a mint polo. Roman grabbed the boy's leg and started to pull it away from the wall.

It was in bad taste, being a child and all. But the kid must have done something bloody horrendous to be in here in the first place. Nate took the kid's arm and, along with his brother, prised the tiny torso away from hole.

"What do we do with him now?" Nate said when the child was finally free.

Roman glanced down.

"Oh no. I can't do that to a kid."

"Well, what do you suggest?"

"Can't we just fling him across to the other side and let the other bodies hold him?"

Roman shrugged. "I couldn't care less what you do with him, as long as he's away from the portal."

"Okay. On the count of three," Nate said.

Together, they swung the child towards the other side of the pit.

The kid plummeted through the air like he was on a trapeze and crashed into the waiting bodies opposite. They pulled the child in close and proceeded to rip his tiny body limb from limb.

"Maybe they don't like squatters," Roman surmised. He looked unbothered by the massacre and turned back to the portal.

He pulled himself through the tiny gap and into the room on the other side. Nate quickly followed. He fell into a pool of water beside his brother. His blistered his skin cooled in its icy temperature. He quickly stood. Water lapped around his ankles and he looked for somewhere dry to stand. There wasn't anywhere.

"I don't remember it being this cold." Roman wrapped his arms around his body. "I can feel frostbite on my feet."

"They'll heal soon enough." Nate grimaced. He waded through the water to the pillars and studied the etchings, remembering exactly how cold it had been the last time he was here.

Roman joined him. "This is definitely the chamber."

Nate glanced around the cavern. "So, where do we start looking?"

He searched the rock face. Tiny crevasses jutted here, there, and, oh hell, every bloody where. He didn't have a clue where to begin looking. And he sure as hell didn't have the time to search them all. He glanced down at his feet freezing their nuts off in the water. Roman was right. Frostbite had already started to set in. Their toes would snap off before the hour was out, something they couldn't heal from. They had to find the Sheriff's bones and quick.

The crystal-clear water rippled around Nate's ankles.

"Stand still," he said to Roman. Roman halted and Nate waited for the water to settle. "Look."

Roman glanced down and clocked the iron cages sporadically buried in the bed below the water. Each one was padlocked and each contained a sack.

"How many do you reckon there are?" Nate said

"Does it matter? We only need to find one." Roman reached down for the padlock, waited for the water to settle again, and examined the small impression carved into the iron. "Here. This must identify the occupant."

"What is it?"

"Looks like a bird of prey. An eagle, maybe."

"A hieroglyphic?"

"Maybe." Roman moved onto the next one. "What's three dots mean?"

Nate shrugged.

"This is stupid. How are we supposed to find the Sheriff's bones if we can't read the bloody symbols?"

"Maybe we should burn them all. Be on the safe side."

"Nice thought." Roman tugged on a box. It was fixed solid into the bed. He scratched his head. "My feet are fucking freezing."

"Look, we know we have the right chamber. We've been here before and we were told it's the only one that houses Purgatory workers' bones."

Roman nodded. He glanced back at the cages. "Okay, we do it your way. We'll burn all the bones."

"How're we going to open the cages?"

Roman smiled. "You never picked a lock before?"

CHAPTER FORTY-FOUR

Eliza climbed through the hole. "What the hell do you think you're doing?"

Natalie waited on the other side, flanked by André. "That man, Roman, is a murderer."

Eliza got to her feet. She wanted to defend him, but what Natalie said was nothing less that the truth. "Who did he kill?"

"A family member from long ago. Roman wanted to sacrifice their child."

"Wanted to?"

"She died when he tried to kill her parents and she intervened."

"She was the reason Nate sent him to Purgatory?"

"Yes, and my ancestors – your ancestors – have been seeking their revenge ever since his escape."

Eliza paused. She looked at the mind mover before her. It hadn't dawned on her that she'd ever meet another like herself.

An uneasy feeling swept over her. "So, what happens now?"

"I will wait for Nathaniel to come out and trap Roman inside like we planned."

"Then we have a problem because I won't allow that." Eliza straightened. She clenched her fists, ready to fight.

Natalie smiled. "We are family, you and I. Bonded by the same blood. Our powers do not work on each other, as you know."

Eliza swallowed. Natalie seemed to presume she had extensive knowledge of her heritage and she sure as hell wasn't going to tell her otherwise. She glanced at André then searched for Natalie's other two suits. They were nowhere to be found. Neither was Billy. "Where's my brother?"

"I had Dax and Beau take him for a walk."

Eliza stepped towards Natalie. "Why?"

"Because he was trying to stop me."

"Tell me where my brother is before I lose my temper." Eliza hardened her stare. "And trust me when I say I don't need the use of my powers to make you bleed."

A flicker of uncertainty widened Natalie's eyes and she glanced towards to the chalk figure on the wall. Eliza followed her gaze and saw the passageway to the left of it.

"Good. Get moving," Eliza said.

"I am not going anywhere. I am waiting for the reaper to return."

Eliza grabbed Natalie by the arm.

André made to intervene, but Eliza shot him a look. "I'd rethink whatever it is you're about to do."

André glanced at Natalie then reluctantly stood back.

"Good decision." Eliza turned back to Natalie. "I may not be able to make you go with me telekinetically, but I am more than capable of forcing you physically."

Natalie rolled her eyes. "You English – always using violence to get what you want."

Eliza didn't dignify her remark with a response. "André, you go first."

André headed for the passage.

Eliza shoved Natalie behind him. "Take me directly to Billy and don't try anything."

The three of them walked in silence. Eliza guessed a good twenty minutes had passed before the light on her hard hat illuminated what looked to be some kind of a well – waist height and maybe three feet in diameter. Dax and Beau stood beside it. They both turned when they heard André approach.

Eliza's heart beat hard. "Where's my brother?"

The two men looked to Natalie for an explanation, but Natalie shrugged. "It's okay. You can tell her."

The men didn't move. Confusion creased their brows.

"We have the same blood running through our veins," Natalie said by way of clarification. "So, for the moment, we do as she says."

The men turned and glanced at the well.

Eliza ran to the wall and peered over the top. Rocks and boulders whitened under her torch beam. The bottom loomed somewhere beneath the darkness, but the light couldn't quite reach it.

"Billy?"

Billy never answered.

Eliza turned and faced the group. "What have you done?"

Natalie glared at Beau and Dax. "I told you to bring him here so you could detain him – not throw him in the pit."

Eliza turned back to the well. "Billy," she shouted out again.

"Maybe the fall knocked him out," Dax offered.

Eliza's lips tightened. She turned to Beau. "You. Grab the rope. You're going for a little climb."

Beau peered over the edge of the well. "I cannot go down there."

Eliza leaned next to him. "You can either climb down or I can force you down. But you are going to the bottom."

"It's all right, Beau," Natalie said. She looked at André. "*Prends la corde. Nous allons vers le bas.*"

André nodded. He stepped towards the well and unravelled the rope from his backpack. He secured one end around his waist, cracked a glow stick and held it over the well. The extra light did nothing to reveal how long a drop it was – or if Billy was down there. André dropped the stick and both he and Eliza watched it plummet to the bottom of the chute. It hit the ground with a dull thud. The light barely illuminated the bottom, but it was enough to show that Billy wasn't there.

"There must be a passage at the bottom," André said.

Eliza frowned. "If he's hurt, I swear to God…"

"*Beau, vous allez en premier*," Natalie said.

Beau looked uncertain. He peered over the side of the well again, his stance rigid. He glanced at André then turned to Natalie. Neither spoke to him and he looked over the edge of the well for a second time. He wiped his mouth.

André planted his feet against the base of the wall and tugged the knot around his waist. It was Beau's cue. He sat on the wall and spun his legs over the top. His hands shook as they took the rope. Another uneasy sigh and he rolled onto his stomach. He glanced at Natalie one last time and then slowly began to climb down. When he reached the bottom, he shouted up – in French – but the echo distorted his words.

"Use your walkie-talkie," Eliza said into her radio.

"He's not here," Beau reported back.

"What do you mean, he's not there? Where is he?"

"There are tunnels…"

Eliza cursed. She needed to get down there herself but didn't trust that André would pull her back up. She waved her torch at Natalie. "Okay, you next."

Natalie glanced back the way they had come. Eliza's demeanour didn't seem to frighten her at all and Eliza fully expected her to make a dash back to the chalk man. Instead, she spun towards the well, her blonde ponytail swinging about her face, and climbed onto the ledge.

Dax stepped forward. "*C'est dangereux là-bas.*"

Natalie paused. "*C'est une superstition stupide.*"

As Beau had done before her, she rolled onto her stomach and started her climb down.

Eliza glanced at Dax. "What do you mean *it's dangerous down there?*"

Dax stared down the chute. "The lost people live down there."

"Lost people? Nobody could possibly survive down there."

"The ancient do."

"That makes no sense." Eliza watched Natalie lower herself down and disappear into the darkness below.

A second glow ignited at the bottom of the shaft and Natalie's French tones spoke over the radio. "I'm here."

André untied the rope from around his waist and passed it to Dax. "Natalie's right. It is nothing but local superstition." He stretched his arms, cracked his neck.

Dax held the rope but ignored him. He turned back to Eliza. "Hundreds of years ago, Paris cemeteries overflowed with too many bodies, bringing with them the stench of decomposing flesh and disease, especially to people of Les Halles. They complained – for years – and the dead were eventually excavated and moved to what we now know as the Catacombs."

Eliza glanced at him. "You can find that information in any tourist pamphlet."

"Do your pamphlets also mention the other undead people that were put here? Beggars, street vermin, criminals. Anyone classed as undesirable was dumped down here. It was a way the government could clean up Paris."

André laughed. "None of it is true."

"No? Then how do you explain the anomalies?"

"What anomalies?" Eliza butted in.

"Stories circulated—"

"False stories." André sighed. "Even if it is true, these people would have died a long, long time ago."

Dax continued. "Stories circulated that some people did not die. That they survived on vermin and dirty water. That they ate each other. And, over the centuries, they reproduced. Each new generation adapted to the conditions down there. It is their home now."

Eliza glanced at André. He rolled his eyes and shook his head, clearly not convinced.

She stared at Dax. "It sounds like folklore gone mad to me."

"It is not folklore," Dax protested.

"Then, where are they – these people? Why hasn't Paris ever seen any of them? Why haven't *we* seen any of them?"

"Their lungs cannot process the cleaner air, so they live lower down."

"I'd hardly call this air clean."

"People come here, you know. Like your English mobsters dispose of bodies in the foundations of bridges, here the criminals use these pits."

"People use these pits because they know the bodies will never be found. That's all," André said.

Eliza glanced down the well. She couldn't see any sign of anyone down there. Just two glowing sticks. She pushed the button on the radio. "Can you see my brother down there?"

No answer. Just static.

"Beau? Natalie? Are you there?"

Dax waved his hands. "I am not going down there. That drawing back there on the wall – that was a sign. A warning."

"You talk rubbish." André said.

"More people believe the story than not. How many people come down here and never come back?"

"That is because they are stupid people who get lost." He tied the rope around Dax's middle.

There was still only static from the radio. Eliza hesitated and glanced at the other two men. Dax looked scared. André looked bored. Dax's story was so far-fetched it was stupid. But, then, so was the notion of being sacrificed on the True Cross. And never in her wildest dreams would she have believed Purgatory existed. She bit the inside of her cheek and glanced back down the well. Her stomach tensed. This could be a trap of Natalie's, but she needed to find Billy.

She tucked the radio into her jacket pocket, climbed onto the edge of the well, and spun her legs over the edge.

CHAPTER FORTY-FIVE

"Is that all of them?" Roman said, pulling the last bag from the cage.

Nate held up his hands and Roman counted nine. With the thirty-one he had piled around his feet, that made a round forty.

Nate lowered his arms. "Shall we just toss the lot in the pit?"

Roman shrugged. "Sure as hell can't see any point in keeping hold of them."

He walked over to the portal, pushed the first sack through, and tipped it upside down. A ton of bones fell out, a good hundred or two. They plummeted down towards the fire, each bone exploding like a firework when it touched the flames.

Roman reached behind him for another sack. He shoved it through the hole and emptied the bag out.

More fireworks popped and fizzed.

Nate handed him another bag. "How are we going to know if we've destroyed the Sheriff's bones?"

"Well, if he's waiting for us outside the Catacombs, then I think we can safely deduce we haven't." Roman pushed more bones through the hole.

He thought of Eliza waiting in the Catacombs for him and his need to hurry intensified. He pushed another twenty bags through the hole, no longer bothering to empty them. The sacks hit the flames and an eruption of fireworks cackled below him. He held out his hand for another bag. None came and he turned.

A black mist floated across the walls. A dozen or so red eyes glowered within it.

Roman slowly bent to pick up the remaining bags. "How many you got?"

"If we're talking demons, then I have eight eyes to my left. Four in front. Six to my right."

Inch-long nails protruded from bony fingers and reached out of the mist. They crawled across the walls, dragging the mist behind them like a cloak. They circled Roman and Nate, hissing their displeasure and a lust to kill.

Roman glanced above, just to be sure there were no surprises. "Any suggestions?"

"We ain't getting out of that portal without a fight, that's for sure."

"Yeah, I figured the same." Roman searched the room. "Fuck. You got any ideas?"

"Right now? I got nothing."

"You ever seen these ugly muthas before?"

"Nope. You?"

Roman shook his head. He wet his lips and considered how many more sacks he could throw out the portal before the bastards got him.

"How d'you want to play this?"

Roman grinned. "The way I always play it."

Nate sighed and cursed under his breath.

Roman held out the four bags he held. "Take these and get out through the hole. I'll keep these sons-of-bitches off your tail for as long as I can."

"And miss out on the action?"

Nate backed up against the portal. He turned and ran his hands over the surrounding wall.

"What're you doing?"

"These walls aren't rock."

"So?"

"So..." Nate dropped the bags.

He placed his palms flat against the wall and pushed. The wall stretched and bowed outwards. Nate thrust his whole body against it. It arched outwards. He was trying to make the hole bigger.

The mist continued to curl across the walls. Skeletal hands clawed the rock face, veins bulging underneath a thin layer of skin. A skull appeared, teeth like razors, red eyes glowering like evil tail lights. What the fuck were these things?

Roman turned and rammed himself against the wall. His brother was right; the wall wasn't made of rock. It was rough and leathery...like old skin.

"Is this still the prisoners?"

"Feels like it."

Roman pushed harder. The mist closed in around them. The wall of skin started to split apart. Roman shoved one last time and bodies tore free, falling into the flames below.

A grey, gaunt hand reached out of the mist. Roman ducked. Another hand seized Nate and dragged him from the wall. Roman clenched his sacks. He threw them all towards the enlarged hole, hearing the explosion when the pit below devoured them.

Roman bent for Nate's bags. If he and his brother were going to die, it would be after they destroyed these bloody bones. Two skeletal figures leapt from the mist. They pounced on Roman, shoving him against the human wall. The bags fell from his grip and splashed back in into the water.

Nate made a play for the bags, but three more skeletal figures dived out of the mist and struck him away. Roman was powerless to help his brother or to get to the bags. The demons bit into his neck and Roman felt the oozing blood warm his chest. He fell backwards against the human wall and it tore outwards. Bodies split from each other and the glow of the pit broke through. Carcasses tumbled away from the wall and Roman toppled backwards with them, plummeting towards the fire.

Warm air engulfed him as he fell. He reached for the wall, hit a prisoner, and grabbed hold. His body jerked to a sudden stop and one of the demons lost their grip on him. Roman watched it fall into the flames, causing the biggest firework yet to explode upwards.

The intense heat burned hotter than ever. Sweat dripped from Roman's body and his skin blistered. He clung to the wall of bodies, his perspiring hands making his hard to keep a tight hold. He kicked into the side, trying to find a footing to hold his weight. Prisoners clutched his ankles, but still Roman kicked. Finally, he made a hole.

The second demon still clung around his waist. It clawed at Roman's backpack and pulled itself up Roman's body.

The wall of carcasses clawed at Roman's arms. He glanced up. The passage to the gateway was maybe fifty metres above him. A long way above that, water trickled from the hole he and Nate had made in the side of the chamber. Shit. He'd fallen a couple hundred feet at least.

"Nate?"

He had to get back up there – for his brother and the remaining bags.

He released one of the prisoner's arms, leaving it to his left hand and his right foot to stop him from falling into the scorching pit below. He tried to twist his arm free of the rucksack's shoulder strap, but it caught on his elbow.

A carcass clasped Roman's waist and dragged him in against the wall. Another clawed at his trousers. A third chewed through his clothes. Roman let go of the wall completely, letting the bodies hold him while he shrugged out of the shoulder straps.

The prisoner hugging his waist chewed into his flesh and Roman screamed out his frustration. The straps dropped over his shoulders and the rucksack fell away from his back. The demon fell with it, disappearing into the fiery pit below.

Roman didn't wait for the fireworks. Above him, water had started to pour from the portal, washing away further bodies from the wall. Water hit him in the face and swept over his body, hampering his ability to hold onto the prisoners. He kicked free from his man-made ledge and began to scale the flesh again.

Water gushed forth. The flames in the pit began to diminish and the heat reduced.

"No. no. no."

Roman climbed quicker. If the flames died, he'd have no way to burn the bones.

A bag was tossed over the edge of the chamber above him. It plummeted past Roman and hit the fire. Fireworks sparked from the flames, but they weren't as fierce as the ones before.

Shit. "Nate!"

Another bag hurtled through the hole. A few bones fell free; the others remained inside the sack. Roman watched them hit the flames. The fireworks were a mere sparkle. The fire would soon be washed out and the bones would be unburned – lost to them forever.

"Nate, hold the bags!"

Roman kept climbing.

A waterfall surged from the opening, carrying away several more bodies from the wall. Black mist washed through the hole with it. It dropped past Roman, its bony hands reaching for him. The talons sliced through his shirt but couldn't find a grip. It fell past and grabbed a prisoner some feet below. Red eyes glowered up at him. Then the demon inside the mist began to climb.

Roman moved faster.

Another mist demon washed through the chamber's hole and Roman hugged the wall for cover. The demon crashed into the mist below, knocking his colleague from the wall. Together, they plummeted into the dwindling fire.

Roman glanced up. He was still so far from reaching the portal.

"Roman?" Nate peered out over the edge.

Roman closed his eyes and took a breath. It was good to hear his brother's voice. "I'm down here."

"Can you get to the entrance?"

It was about twenty-five feet from Roman's reach. "Yes."

"I'll meet you there." Nate swung out of the hole, five sacks tied securely to his belt, and grabbed hold of the wall.

Roman started to climb. Past groping carcass's, all eager to devour any part of him they could get their teeth into. He fought each and every one of them off until he reached the passage and hauled his exhausted body over the edge. He stood and rested his hands on his knees. Taking a breath, he looked out to see how Nate was faring.

Nate had descended the wall much quicker than Roman had climbed it. A black mist floated from the portal – three more demons encased inside it.

Nate reached the entrance and Roman pulled him through.

He fumbled to untie a couple of sacks from his brother's belt. "Company's on the way. We need to get the hell out of here."

Nate nodded, untying the other sacks as he ran.

They were going to make it back. Roman just prayed the Sheriff's bones were already in the fire.

CHAPTER FORTY-SIX

The glow sticks had been a nice touch.

No doubt Roman's idea, and one the Sheriff would be sure to thank him for. He paused in front of the chalk man. Roman's aroma led through to the crypt on his right. The other scent, the one belonging to the cop, trailed off in the opposite direction.

The Sheriff sniffed the air. He bent down and tried to look through the hole in the wall. He sensed what was inside. He'd been to Hell several times, but never through a gateway. Those locations were unknown – well, except this one, it would seem. He stretched his neck, but his size stopped him from seeing anything other than a fiery glow that lit up yet more bones.

No Roman, though.

An uneasy feeling churned his stomach. What was Roman up to?

He straightened as much as his height would allow and sniffed the air, inhaling deep and long. Roman had been here recently – within the last couple of hours. There was no way on earth he could have lost him. He looked at the passage to the left of the chalk figure but couldn't pick up Roman's scent at all. Where had he gone?

The Sheriff shook his head and clenched his fingers. His neck tightened and he rolled his shoulders. His hunched body was so cramped inside these tunnels; he'd be glad to get back outside.

He thought for a moment. There were more bodies down here than even he could count and the stench of death surrounded him. He didn't want to believe it for one moment, but maybe being down here around all these people was throwing off his senses.

He turned in the direction of the cop and decided to follow the trail. Even if Roman wasn't with the girl's brother, maybe the girl was. And Roman would definitely come looking for her.

He followed the passage for a while, stopping when he sensed someone ahead. A man was sat on the ground, his knees pulled to his chest. Not Roman or the cop. This person looked similar to the guard at the tunnel's entrance.

The man saw him and shot to his feet. "You're one of them."

The Sheriff charged towards him.

The man turned to run, but the Sheriff knocked him against the wall. The man fell to the ground and cried out. He crawled onto all fours, still trying to get away.

The Sheriff rounded the well, grabbed a handful of the man's hair, and lifted him from the ground. "Where are the others?"

The man glanced towards the well. "How can you breathe up here?"

The Sheriff tilted his head. He turned towards the well and dangled the man over the opening.

He released his grip and the man dropped.

CHAPTER FORTY-SEVEN

"Did you hear that?" Beau said.

It was the tenth time he'd said it in as many minutes. Regardless, the group stopped and listened.

"Must have been a rat," André stated.

"A big bloody rat," Beau said.

Eliza ignored them. She faced forward and lit another glow stick. The air was thin down here and she couldn't get a satisfying lungful, no matter how hard she inhaled. She wiped her clammy hand down her overalls and cast a look around the small passage. She felt like she was being watched.

"Billy?" She kept her voice low – not much louder than a whisper – and it still echoed along the corridor further than she'd have liked.

She called out again in the same hushed tone.

"I'm telling you, he should have been at the bottom of the well," Beau said.

Eliza twisted, her hard hat light finding André.

He shrugged. "I must admit, I cannot see how he got up and walked away."

Eliza hated to admit it, but the Frenchman had a point. "You'd both better pray he did or neither of you are walking out of here. Understand?"

"Billy?" André called out.

Eliza shone her torch along the passage. It wasn't until Beau and André's lights joined hers that she spotted her brother some way off in the distance.

"Billy." She ran towards him. He lay on his front, unmoving and silent. Eliza felt his neck. "He has a pulse. He's alive."

André joined her and together they carefully rolled him over. Eliza caught her breath and André sat back. Claw marks lined one side of Billy's face. His clothing had been shredded and hung from his body.

"Billy," Eliza shook his shoulders, but Billy didn't respond.

She turned to André. "No fall caused this."

"I agree."

"Is there a chance these lost people are real? Could they have done this?"

Natalie leant beside them. "It is just a story."

Eliza lowered the torch back to Billy's torn body. "I'd say this proves otherwise."

Natalie reached for Billy's face. "I just wanted him out of the way. He seems a good man. I wouldn't have done this had I known."

Eliza ignored her. She slipped off her backpack and took out a roll of gauze.

"Hold his head," she instructed Natalie. Natalie complied and Eliza worked quickly in covering Billy's wounds with the bandage. "I suggest we get out the hell out of here, and quick." She slid her arms back through the rucksack.

A high-pitched shriek raced through the air.

Eliza lifted her hands from Billy's body. The group's torches swung this way and that, their beams haphazardly dancing across the walls, trying to find the source of the noise.

"What the hell was that?" André said, his light darting around the passage.

Eliza had no idea and she wasn't waiting to find out. "André, bring my brother."

André quickly lifted Billy over his shoulders.

Another shriek pierced the atmosphere. Nearer this time.

Beau started to freak out. "Dax was right. The stories are true. It's the people."

Natalie slapped him. "Get a hold of yourself. We will be fine."

"No, screw this." Beau took off. He sprinted past Eliza and headed into the darkness.

"You're running the wrong way," André shouted after him.

Another shriek rang out. Right behind them. Shit.

"*Nous devons nous déplacer*," André said. He ran after Beau, pulling Natalie along with him.

Eliza didn't quarrel. André was right. They did have to move. She sprinted alongside them, watching Billy bounce on André shoulders. The shrieking stopped the moment they took off running and she reckoned they'd covered a good half a mile before they finally caught up with Beau. She paused to catch her breath.

"Did we lose it?" Beau said, swallowing.

"I don't know. I think so," Eliza replied.

André shone his light behind them. The passageway looked clear.

"We should head back towards the well," Eliza said.

Beau completely freaked. "You want to go back that way?"

"Not particularly. But I don't want to get lost down here either."

"She has a point," André said.

"You're crazy," Beau cried.

Eliza slipped off her backpack and knelt. She unzipped it and rummaged around inside until she found a flick knife and a couple of flares.

She glanced up. "I suggest you guys do the same."

André lowered Billy to the ground. He reached behind him and slid a pickaxe from the hook of his bag.

He turned to Beau. "She is right. We head back."

Another shriek pierced the air.

"Shit. It's back," André said, quickly hoisting Billy onto his shoulders again.

Eliza unscrewed the cap of a flare and struck the end like a match. A flame fizzed to life, the passageway coming alive in the smoky, orange glow.

"There!" she cried.

A white flash darted across the wall, just above Beau.

André shooed Eliza and Natalie in front of him. "Run!"

Beau charged through them all and took the lead.

The shrieking quietened the more distance they put between them and the white thing on the wall. They ran and ran, cavern walls passing by under the spotlights of their hardhats. Eliza saw the two glowing dots of the glow sticks at the bottom of the shaft. She stopped suddenly, halting Natalie along with her. Dax's broken body was slumped at the bottom of the well. And the hunched figure of the Sheriff stood over him.

André lowered Billy to the ground. He raised the pickaxe, ready to do battle. "What the hell is that thing? Is it one of the people?"

Eliza remained frozen. "No. That is something else."

Beau turned to retreat but the Sheriff pounced on him. Eliza squeezed her eyes shut. Tried to find the motel room. Tried to find Roman's embrace.

Beau's screams assaulted her ears and she covered them.

Then Beau's screaming stopped.

CHAPTER FORTY-EIGHT

Roman reached the gateway to the Catacombs and fell through it.

Nate shot through straight after and both men landed on their backs, loose bones snapping beneath their weight.

Roman quickly rolled onto his back. "Quick, alter the path."

Black mist floated towards them. Demons bounded nearer and nearer to the gateway. Nate bit into his hand and Roman saw blood – reaper's blood – drip from his palm. Nate slapped his hand against the Latin words on the wall. The gateway darkened. A loud roar grumbled through the opening, bringing with it a tornado of wind. Demons shrieked and clawed at the ground as the cyclone started to suck them in. The gust caught hold of Roman's feet and he too started to move towards the whirlwind.

Nate grabbed the wall, keeping on the edge of the tornado. Roman slid forward, every bone he grabbed for support breaking away. He hit the gateway and spread his legs, planting a foot either side of the portal. The tornado roared and Roman cried out. Nate reached out to help him but got caught in the gust. He pulled his arm clear and back against the wall, unable to do anything.

A white light brightened the entire room and the cyclone died. Roman covered his eyes, but the light still penetrated his fingers. Then the brightness disappeared and he lowered his arm. He blinked away the dots hampering his vision. The gateway was closed. The demons were gone.

His and Nate's rapid breathing echoed around the small crypt.

"How the fuck did you get away from them up there?" Roman gasped.

"How did you?"

Roman allowed himself to grin.

"You sure those things can't get in here?" Nate said, sitting up.

"I haven't the fucking foggiest." Roman stood. "Let's just burn these bloody bones."

Nate stood. "How big do you want this fire?"

Roman looked around the small room. "Torch the bloody lot." He piled the sacks against Hell's door. "Let's get this party started."

Nate stared at him. "Got your lighter fluid?"

"I don't have my bag."

"Where is it?"

"Bottom of the pit. Yours?"

"Under a couple feet of water."

"Do you have a match? Anything?"

"I lost the lot."

Roman ran his fingers through his hair. He slapped some life into his cheeks. "Okay, grab the sacks. The others will have a lighter. We'll burn the bones then."

"What about Natalie?"

"We keep her away from the portal."

"So, we just walk out of here?"

Roman shrugged. "Why not? She can't hurt us."

"No, but she could make things difficult – she's a mind mover, remember?"

"So is Eliza." Roman crawled to the entrance. He peered through. "I can't see anybody."

Nate crawled beside him. "You think the Sheriff is here?"

Roman didn't want to think about it. He and Nate had just pulled off the impossible. To fail now, at the last hurdle, was not something he could accept.

He lay on his back and looked at his brother. "Only one way to find out."

He pulled himself back into the tunnel.

CHAPTER FORTY-NINE

Eliza opened her eyes.

Beau stumbled past her. He held his face, blood seeping through his fingers. "I need to get out of here."

Natalie tried to stop him, but he pushed her aside and fled into the darkness.

"Beau," Natalie called out. But Beau was gone.

André raised the axe. "If that isn't one of them, then what is it?"

"That's from Purgatory," Eliza said, her heart sinking. Did the Sheriff's presence here mean Roman and Nate had died?

"It killed Dax," Natalie said blankly.

Behind them, a shriek rocketed down the passageway.

"Screw this. We need to get up that shaft." André raced towards the Sheriff.

The Sheriff blocked his attack and smacked André across the jaw. The axe dropped to the ground and André thudded against the wall.

Eliza raced to his aid. She pulled him to his feet, and half carried half dragged him back to Billy and Natalie.

"We have to move," she said, aware Billy still lay unconscious at her feet. But there was no way they could outrun the Sheriff.

Natalie stood fast. She glanced at the axe lying on the bed of bones and closed her eyes. She flexed her hand and the axe rose from the ground. A flick of her wrist and it spun through the air, aiming for the Sheriff. Eliza released Andre. She could help Natalie. Two mind movers had to be more powerful than one.

Natalie opened her eyes and watched the axe embed itself in the centre of the Sheriff's chest. The Sheriff dropped to his knees.

Eliza held out her hand. The axe tore free from his flesh and flew into her waiting palm. "I'll finish you off once and for all, you bastard."

André yelled and Eliza turned. He no longer stood beside her brother. She glanced up in time to catch a flash of white dragging him up into the darkness above them. Natalie leapt for him and grabbed hold of his kicking ankles, but her weight wasn't enough to bring him down. Her feet left the ground. She lashed out at the air, trying to find a footing, but was lifted up the wall along with her friend.

André gurgled and his struggling legs went rigid. Blood splattered the wall, wetting Natalie's hair and face. André's body jolted and shivers rocked his legs. One of his shoes slipped from his foot and Natalie fell to the ground.

Eliza moved to help her, but the Sheriff had risen to his feet.

He caught hold of Eliza by the scruff of her neck and dragged her backwards. His grip tightened and he lifted her.

Eliza's feet left the ground and she dangled mid-air. She felt his face press against her hair and his breath warmed her ear.

"I haven't finished with you yet," he said.

The axe whipped free from Eliza's hand, but it wasn't the Sheriff's doing. Natalie caught the axe and smiled at her. Then the axe catapulted upward. Another shriek split the air and André dropped from the darkness. Blood covered his face and claw marks scratched open his chest. The white creature fell beside him.

Eliza kicked to be free, but the Sheriff held tight. On the ground, she saw the flares had fallen out of André's backpack. She closed her eyes and one flew into her hand. She struck it alight and reached behind her. Feeling the Sheriff's head, she jammed the lit end of the stick into his ear.

The Sheriff yelled and let go of her.

Eliza landed on her feet. She turned and swiped the Sheriff's legs out from under him. "Hurry, another flare."

Natalie threw one her way.

Eliza struck the end. "Smile, you bastard."

She jammed the stick into the Sheriff's gaping mouth, its glow colouring his otherwise pale cheeks. He fell back and Eliza leapt away from him.

She grabbed the rope that still dangled from the well. "Let's get the hell out of here."

Natalie left Andre's mutilated body. She ran to Eliza. "André's dead."

Eliza had figured as much. "Just get up there."

"What about you and your brother?"

"I'll tie the rope around his waist. You'll have to try and drag him up."

Natalie pressed her foot against the wall. She gripped the rope and pulled herself off the ground but the rope fell and snaked around her feet and Natalie fell onto her backside.

Eliza offered her hand and pulled her back to her feet. Oh, this couldn't be happening.

"You'll have to climb," she told Natalie. "Take the rope with you and tie it to something...yourself."

"I should stay and help you."

"We can't kill him. We can only put him down for a while. I can do that while you sort out the rope."

Natalie glanced up into the shaft. She curled the tips of her fingers around the rock and started to climb.

The Sheriff got to his feet. He spat the flare from his mouth and shook his head. He glanced up at Eliza and anger hardened his eyes.

He pulled the other flare from his ear, stepped towards her, and tutted. "It will take more than a candle to stop me."

Eliza searched for another flare but couldn't see one. Above her, Natalie didn't even look to be halfway up the shaft. Billy stirred, but there was no way he was going to be strong enough to climb. Eliza backed away from the Sheriff, struggling to keep her balance on the loose bones in the darkness. She searched the pockets of her overall and found the flick-knife.

Behind the Sheriff, the end of the rope rose from the ground. Natalie couldn't have climbed the last half the shaft that quick. Eliza watched the rope. It rose, like a snake from a wicker basket, and flicked towards the Sheriff. Its end wrapped itself around the Sheriff's neck – clearly Natalie's doing – and pulled taut.

The Sheriff spun towards the shaft. Eliza extended the knife's blade and swiped it across the Sheriff's legs. It caused little more than a scratch. She closed her eyes and welcomed the sudden warmth as it flooded her body. In her mind, she willed the Sheriff into the air. She heard him yell, and when Eliza opened her eyes, he dangled above the ground in front of her.

The Sheriff struggled helplessly mid-air, the rope pulling tight around his neck. André lay on the ground, his body mutilated almost beyond recognition. Eliza felt for a pulse but could find none. Natalie had been right in her earlier diagnosis. She turned to Billy and tried to hoist him up.

He groaned.

"You need to help me, Billy."

She dragged him to his feet and together they made their way towards the shaft. Her back crippled under his weight. His arm slipped from her shoulder and he fell to the ground.

White figures descended the wall.

Eliza adjusted her hold and lifted Billy's arm around her shoulder a second time. Her legs buckled under the strain, but she staggered forward. She needed to get to the rope, but the rope restrained the Sheriff.

"Natalie!" she shouted up.

The Sheriff struggled free of the rope. The white shapes crawled closer towards them.

Eliza couldn't take them all on. She had no choice but to turn and escape into the tunnel.

CHAPTER FIFTY

Roman passed his torch to Nate and dragged Natalie over the edge of the well. "Where the fuck is Eliza?"

Natalie looked back at the well and pointed. "That thing from Purgatory is down there."

Roman grabbed the torch back and leaned past her. He shone the light down the shaft, the beam cutting through the darkness but not strong enough to reach the bottom. It didn't matter. Two flares burned bright enough to show him how deep the well was.

"What the hell were you doing down there?"

"Eliza's brother..." She paused. Took a breath. "My men threw him down there."

"You mean you ordered them to." Roman turned away from her.

"There's something down there," she said.

Roman spun back around to face her. "Something? You mean the Sheriff?"

"No. I mean something else. It is white and climbs the walls. It is attacking everyone."

Roman glanced at Nate. "I'm going down."

Nate nodded. He turned to Natalie. "I need some lighter fluid. Do you have some?"

"In my backpack."

Nate spun her around and pulled the rucksack off her shoulders. He unzipped the top and emptied the contents over the ground.

Eliza's voice echoed up through the shaft.

Roman stopped dead in his tracks. He leaned over the edge of the well. "Eliza? Eliza!"

Eliza didn't reply.

"Eliza!" When no reply came, he climbed over the edge of the well. He glanced at Nate. "You got this?"

Nate nodded. "Just go get her."

Roman started to climb down. He paused and looked back up at his brother. "Burn that fucker back to Hell."

Eliza struggled along, Billy limping along beside her, his arm hooked around her shoulder.

She glanced behind her. She couldn't see the Sheriff, but she heard his heavy steps chasing them down. She couldn't keep going at this pace. She was exhausted and getting absolutely nowhere. She didn't want to venture into these tunnels, especially if more of those things that had killed André were down here. Her foot caught something and she tumbled to the ground, taking Billy with her.

She shone her torch around. Beau lay beside her feet, his mouth frozen mid-scream. His right arm had been ripped clean from his shoulder. His ear had been gnawed from his head. Intestines flowed from his exposed stomach.

Eliza turned away. She covered her mouth, but the vomit still came. She wiped her mouth. Shit. They were in serious trouble. She rolled Beau onto his front. A small, handheld axe remained hooked on his backpack and she quickly slipped it free.

A white figure landed between them and lunged for Billy. Eliza screamed. She swung the axe down into the creature's back. A deafening shriek rocked through the passage and Eliza pulled the weapon free. She raised it, ready to swing again, but the figure collapsed.

A second creature leapt to the ground and pounced on Billy. A third landed on Billy's right and seized his leg. A fourth lunged for his back and bit down on his ear.

Eliza cried out. One of the figures lifted its head, Billy's severed ear held in its mouth, and looked at her. The creature cocked its head to one side then started to chew, squatting back on its haunches like a baby monkey nibbling on a slice of orange.

Eliza yelled again. The thing glanced up and Eliza swung the axe forward. It embedded itself in the creature's neck but didn't quite remove its head. Eliza ripped the blade out, now swinging for the monster that clawed Billy's leg. The axe head jammed between the creature's shoulder blades and the creature screamed. The last figure looked up from Billy's arm. Blood reddened its white mouth.

"What the hell are you?"

The creature tilted its head, a curious look upon its face. Eliza looked harder. A layer of skin covered its eyes. Was it blind? Eliza waved her palm in front of it. The figure sniffed and followed her hand back and forth. It snarled and turned back to Billy.

Eliza swung the axe. This time she took the head clean off.

Another figure landed behind her. Eliza spun, the light on her hard hat spinning with her. Several other creatures hobbled up behind it. She turned back to Billy. Several figures had circled him. Eliza raised the axe again. Felt it whack against the side of the cavern. When she turned, she saw it had embedded a small crevice. She tugged with all her might, but the axe didn't come free.

More creatures crawled down the walls. Eliza released the axe and spun in a circle. She and Billy were surrounded and she had nothing to use against them. She stepped back. Felt the uncertainty of the bones beneath her feet and knelt beside her brother, cradling him close. She squeezed her eyes shut and thought of Roman. Of the motel room. Of how she'd felt when he held her.

The bones clattered together as they rose from the ground. She imagined them flying towards the creatures like darts. A succession of shrieks and yelps echoed through the darkness. Eliza hugged Billy tighter. She opened her eyes and watched the bones spear the figures. One by one, white bodies fell to the ground. Those that weren't hit fled up the walls until she was alone again.

She glanced at her brother. His whole ear had been torn away and blood gushed from the side of his head.

Eliza flung her backpack to the ground and rummaged inside. She found the roll of gauze and tried to stem the blood flow.

She shone her torch over the pile of white bodies. Some creatures were injured, but most were dead. They looked like children. Smaller. Skinnier. Their ashen skin paler than snow itself. She reached out and touched a dead one. Leathery skin so cold it felt like ice. Were these things proof Dax's folklore tale was true?

Above her, hundreds of creatures hovered on the walls. Eliza swallowed. She needed to get herself and Billy the hell out of here. Once again, she dragged Billy up and positioned herself under his arm. A figure landed behind them and Eliza paused. She heard a second figure land on the bones, then a third, and a fourth.

She swallowed, closed her eyes, and looked for Roman in her memories.

Billy was yanked away from her and Eliza spun around. Her light found him some way back, several figures pinning him to the ground.

Eliza charged towards him. She got within centimetres of him before she was pulled back. She struggled and kicked out, but two long arms wrapped themselves around her chest and held her still. Hot breath warmed the side of her face.

"Now I'm going to make you watch your brother die," the Sheriff whispered.

Eliza screamed and struggled. She closed her eyes but she didn't need Roman. Pure anger lifted the bones from the ground. Like before, they shot towards the creatures who attacked Billy. Torsos, legs, arms, heads – no body part was safe. Creatures dropped around Billy's body. Those who escaped being hit scurried back up into the darkness. But it was only a matter of time before they descended again.

The Sheriff laughed. "You think that's going to save him?"

The bones turned on the Sheriff and darted towards him.

His hold around Eliza tightened and he held her close to his chest. The bones halted inches from her body.

"To spear me, you have to spear yourself. You will die and your brother will become fair game to the things living down here. Are you willing to put him through that just to hurt me?"

"She isn't. But I am."

The Sheriff turned, spinning Eliza with him.

Roman lit up under her lamp.

He winked at her. "Can't leave you alone for a minute, can I?"

Eliza wanted to laugh. She wanted to cry. She wanted to run to him. She wanted to kill the Sheriff. Hell, right now, she wanted everything.

"Help Billy."

Roman looked past them. He spotted Billy and his face hardened.

The Sheriff shuffled Eliza a little to the left, presumably to block Roman's view of her brother.

"You're just in time for the party." He squeezed Eliza tighter and ran his tongue down her cheek.

"The only party around here is gonna be at your wake." Roman stepped forward. "I found your bones."

The Sheriff's hold on Eliza loosened. She closed her eyes and searched the darkness for the motel room. But, truth was, she didn't need the motel anymore. She had Roman standing in front of her. She opened her eyes again and stared at him, his blue eyes sparkling under the light from her hard hat.

Her heart yearned for him. Her arms ached to hold him. She heard the bones behind her lift from ground again. They catapulted towards the Sheriff, spearing him in the back. He released his hold on her and Roman pulled her to safety.

"Help me get Billy," she said, rushing back for her brother.

Roman followed. He lifted Billy from the ground. Blood covered the cop's clothes and he groaned when Roman tried to get him to stand.

"How's about we get the hell out of here," Roman said.

A white figure landed in front of them.

Roman paused. "What the hell is that?"

The Sheriff pulled a bone from his back. He yelled and swung at the creature, spearing it through the head. The creature stumbled backwards and the Sheriff pushed it aside. His face reddened. His eyes glowed. He marched forward, now gunning for Roman.

Roman edged back and Eliza went with him.

Fire ignited around the Sheriff's feet. He took another step. The fire moved with him.

He glanced down at the flames and, when he looked up, his face was full of fear. "Who has them?"

Roman smiled. "My brother."

The Sheriff darted past them and began to sprint towards the well.

The fire sizzled up his legs. The Sheriff collapsed onto one knee. He tried to stand. The fire rose to his waist. A cry whimpered past his lips and he fell forward. He clawed at the bones, trying to pull himself onward. The flames engulfed his coat and upper body and he rolled onto his back.

Roman and Eliza shuffled closer. They stood over him.

Roman looked him in the eye. "I'm the last thing you will ever see, you piece of shit. How's it feel knowing you lost?"

Flames burned through the Sheriff's head, scorching his hair until it was little more than char. Skin melted from his face like hot wax and his scream reverberated throughout the passage. He collapsed onto all fours, his cries fading. The stench of his rotting flesh filled the air and he crumpled onto his front, the flames still eating him until he was nothing but a pile of smouldering embers glowing in the darkness.

Eliza glanced up at the creatures above them. They seemed frightened of the fire, but she knew it wouldn't hold them back for long.

"We need to get going," she said, "before they attack again."

Roman shuffled forward, Billy's arm around his shoulder, his feet dragging.

Eliza heard something descend the wall beside her.

"Keep going," she said to Roman and turned.

Her hat's beam caught several creatures and they scampered away from the light.

She hurried back to Roman, relieved to see the glow of the sticks at the bottom of the shaft. "How're we going to get Billy up?"

Roman reached for the rope and tugged it. It was still secure. He tied it around Billy's waist and looked up the shaft.

"Nate?" he called. "Pull Billy up."

The rope tightened and Billy slowly rose from the ground.

Eliza watched him travel up the shaft, hardly wanting to believe they were going to get out of this.

She glanced back at Roman and saw several figures creep into the light. "Behind you."

Roman turned. A creature leapt towards him. He caught it and threw it back against the wall. A second pounced. Eliza rolled Dax's body onto his front and found a flare in his back pocket. She struck it and jabbed the flame towards the figure.

A shriek echoed through the air and the figure scurried away.

Roman moved her towards the shaft. "Start climbing."

"What about you?"

"I'll be right behind you." He lifted Eliza into the shaft.

She passed him the flare, spread her arms and legs, and started climbing. A few metres up, she glanced down. Roman was following.

Figures were gathering at the bottom of the shaft. Some pulled themselves onto the well and started to climb. Roman saw them too. He dropped the flare, causing the creatures at the bottom of the well to scatter.

An ashen figure grabbed his ankle.

Eliza stopped climbing. She watched, helpless, while Roman tried to kick the figure away.

"Get higher," she called. "They can't breathe up here."

Roman stared up at her, grit his teeth, and pulled himself up. The figure still clung to his leg. Eliza turned and continued to climb. Nate hauled Billy out of the well above her.

The rope tumbled down past them and Eliza grabbed it.

"Lower me," she called up to Nate. "Okay, that's enough."

She kicked out at the creature that clung to Roman, planting her wellie into its stomach over and over until the figure released him and fell to the ground.

Roman glanced across at her, fury in his eyes. "Nate, pull her up."

"No," Eliza argued, but the rope started to rise – and Eliza rose with it.

She stared down at Roman. He'd started climbing the wall again, but the figures were closing in on him.

Eliza reached the top of the well. She climbed out and saw Natalie was tending to Billy.

She turned to Nate. "Get Roman out of there."

Nate threw the rope back into the shaft. Roman reached for it and grabbed hold. Nate started to haul him up. Eliza got behind him and pulled as well.

Roman's hands gripped the top of the well and Eliza ran to him. She grabbed his arm. Nate grabbed the other and together they pulled him out. Roman collapsed on the ground beside the well and Eliza fell to her knees beside him. He cupped her face and pulled her close until her cheek rested against his.

After a moment, she pulled away from him. "I need to check Billy."

A creature climbed over the wall and fell onto the ground beside them. A second figure followed.

Roman jumped to his feet, but they didn't attack. They writhed and gasped for air. Reaching for the wall, they tried to pull themselves back into the shaft. Nate lifted one and threw it over.

Roman did the same with the second. He looked down at Eliza. "Are you going to tell me what the fuck those things are?"

Eliza smiled weakly. "Nothing but a myth."

CHAPTER FIFTY-ONE

Eliza crawled over to Billy.

Natalie had removed her jacket and had it rolled beneath his head. She pressed her palm against the side of Billy's face. "We need to get him to a hospital."

Blood soaked Billy's tattered shirt. Eliza lifted it to see claw marks covering his body. Bite marks covered his arms, not too deep but enough to draw blood.

Eliza gently shook him.

Billy's eyes flickered open. The faintest of smiles turned up the corners of his mouth when he saw her. "Did we win?"

Eliza nodded. Tears fell from her eyes and wet his cheeks. "Can you stand?"

Billy rose onto his elbows, but fatigue quickly took hold and he collapsed onto his back.

When he made no further attempt to sit, Eliza looked at Roman. "Is he going to die?"

Roman shook his head. "He's a tough, old git. I'll give him that."

One long breath exhaled Eliza's relief. She turned to Nate, currently the strongest of the two brothers. "Can you carry him?"

Nate turned away from the well and hurried over. The ceiling was too low to lift Billy over his shoulder. Eliza went to help, but he stopped her.

"You and Roman grab the bags." Nate motioned to Natalie. "Get his arm."

"No," Eliza argued. "She's the reason he's hurt. I don't want her anywhere near him."

"You've just been through hell and she is stronger than you. Help Roman get the bags. We're going to need the supplies to get out of here."

Eliza stood fast. This situation did not sit well with her.

"What's more important? Your pride or getting your brother the help he needs?"

Natalie turned to her. "I can have a helicopter here ten minutes after we get out."

Eliza closed her eyes and sighed. She stepped back, allowing Natalie to replace her alongside Billy. She watched them lift Billy to his feet and walk him towards the chalk man.

Eliza knelt and grabbed a bag from the ground. Roman crouched beside her.

He leaned close. "Do you buy her sudden rush of helpfulness?"

Eliza pursed her lips. "I don't know. She's a smart woman. Maybe she just knows when she's beat."

Roman wrapped his arm around her. "Let's get out of here."

Eliza flung her bag onto her shoulder. Getting out of here was something she wanted more than anything.

They reached the chalk man and didn't bother to stop. Glow stick by glow stick, they made their retreat through the passages. An hour in, they rested before Roman took Billy from Natalie. Eliza watched the two brothers walk side by side and she wondered what relationship they'd have now. Would they finally be able to lay their past to rest? And what was in store for her and Billy? Neither she nor her brother could return to England – not while the police thought they were murderers. Nate was no longer a reaper. Would he even want to go back to the life he had at the church? And Roman? He was still a wanted man as far as Purgatory was concerned. Would there be repercussions for killing the Sheriff?

Billy's feet dragged along the ground. He'd passed out shortly after they'd started walking. He looked pale from the blood loss and Eliza wanted to reach for his wrist and check his pulse. But, fact was, she was terrified she wouldn't find one. Roman had promised he wouldn't die, but had that been the truth speaking or just a ruse to get her out of the Catacombs?

Natalie joined her. "Would you like me to carry your bag for a while?"

Eliza nodded. Its weight was causing her back to ache. She swallowed her pride, slipped it off her shoulders, and passed it to the French woman.

"I am truly sorry about your brother. It was not my intention to hurt—"

Eliza cut her off. "I am not interested in anything you have to say."

"You will not give me the chance to explain?"

"No. You hurt my brother and you tried to kill Roman."

Natalie looked straight ahead. "I never wanted to murder anyone, just imprison."

Eliza scoffed. "It means the same thing when you are talking about Hell."

"So, what now?" Natalie asked.

"Now nothing. In a couple of hours, we'll be out of here. You get Billy to the hospital and that's us finished."

Eliza left her.

She caught up with the boys and positioned Billy's arm around her shoulder, taking her brother's weight from Nate.

Roman glanced across at her. "How're you holding up?"

"Be honest. Were you telling the truth when you said Billy would make it?"

"I was."

"You sense it?"

"I do." He glanced at her. "I need to apologise."

"You? What for?"

"The way I treated you back at Nate's."

Eliza shook her head. "You have nothing to apologise for."

"Eliza, let me say this." He inhaled slowly. "I struggle to see why you hold affection for me. You're smart and beautiful, and I'm—"

"Annoying, pig-headed, and the man who saved my life numerous times?"

Roman chuckled.

"Can the Sheriff come back?" she asked.

Roman shook his head. "He's gone."

"So, we're free?"

"Uh-huh." He looked at her. "So, what do you want to do with this newfound freedom? I feel a sunny beach calling out my name."

"I need to find out who my real mother is," she said slowly.

"Sounds reasonable. Want some company?"

"Maybe."

Roman said nothing and Eliza felt she should expand further. It wasn't that she didn't want Roman to go with her. She just needed time to get her head around the fact that her real mother hadn't died years previously.

Instead, she changed the subject. "It would be good if you put things right with your brother."

"You mean after finding out he was planning on trapping me in Hell?"

"Everyone deserves a second chance, Roman. After all, isn't that what you want him to give you?"

Silence fell between them. She wanted to push for an answer, but it was the wrong question at the wrong time.

"What are you thinking?" he asked

"Nothing."

He chuckled again. "Eliza, that brain of yours never switches off."

"I was wondering if you think Nate will return to England."

Roman sighed. "You want me to have a word with him about that?"

Eliza nodded. "It would be nice having him around, at least while Billy recovers."

The first glimpse of the outside felt like all Eliza's Christmases had come at once.

The breeze swept through the tunnel, freshening her face and energising her lungs. It was a feeling she'd doubted she'd ever feel again. The five of them trudged on, the light becoming brighter the closer the entrance became.

They reached the outside and sunlight warmed her skin. Tweeting birds sat high in the trees, their song music to her ears. As promised, Natalie called for immediate help and they all sat in silence waiting for the helicopter. It didn't take long to arrive, and not the white one they had arrived in. This one was larger. The birds emptied the trees, taking their song with them, as the aircraft hovered above the railway line, unable to land in the narrow ditch. Two paramedics abseiled down onto the train tracks and quickly laid Billy out on a stretcher. They placed an oxygen mask over his nose and mouth, strapped him in tight, and signalled for the stretcher to be winched back up.

"I want to go with him," Eliza said.

Roman held her back. "He'll be fine."

"But I can help them."

Roman looked at her. He didn't loosen his grip.

Natalie approached. "We can take one of the cars." She pointed at the limousines they'd arrived in.

Eliza wasn't happy with the idea. It would take longer to reach the hospital and Billy needed her now. She glanced up. The stretcher had already been pulled inside the helicopter's cabin. The two paramedics climbed in beside him and the helicopter rose higher. It swung left and drifted away.

Eliza watched until it disappeared behind the trees. She glanced at Roman. He remained beside her like a loyal dog.

"I guess we're travelling by car, then," she said.

They turned. Nate and Natalie were already sat inside the furthest limousine.

Roman nodded and took her hand. "Looks like all of us are."

DEAD IN THE WATER

Read on for an extract from the first novel in the
Dead series.

PROLOGUE

8 MONTHS AGO
Peckham, London

Jason Wade removed his mask and breathed in the night air.

The April evenings had become surprisingly warm of late and being able to return to wearing only a T-shirt and fleece pleased him no end. He glanced back at the house. One of his colleagues knelt by the open front door. Two police officers appeared from the living area and waited for him to close the lid on his work box, then exited behind him – their questioning of the aggrieved occupant inside complete and the lure of a brew calling them back to the station. For Jason, it was the lure of a pint down the pub.

Jason peeled off his latex gloves and threw them – along with the mask – into the back of the Ford Transit parked beside him. He found dusting for prints monotonous at the best of times, but at the scene of a burglary? Heck, it was bloody tedious. He unzipped his white overalls and stepped out of them.

His colleague, Ben, reached him. He pulled the mask from his face and wore it like a bow tie. "Don't think there's much hope of linking these to anyone."

He referred to the minimal prints they'd lifted from the open window in the kitchen where the thieving bastards had levered their way inside.

Yep. Jason bloody hated burglaries.

Ben slid his box into its niche, placed his gloves on top of it, and pulled off his overalls. "Fancy a beer when we're through?"

Jason closed the van's doors. The guy was a bloody mind-reader.

The radio in the front of the van crackled. "We've got a body on the south side of the Thames. Outside the Tate Modern. We need you to attend."

Jason's ice-cold beer slipped away. A dead body was not what he needed right now. He headed round to the front of the van and leaned in through the driver's side. Swiped the radio from the dash. "On our way."

Jason made it to South Bank in just under ten minutes, which, everything considered, wasn't too bad for the time of evening. He followed Holland Street around the Tate Modern – a route, it soon became apparent, the majority of the London Met had also taken – and parked as close to the river as he could get before two bollards stopped him.

He unclipped his seatbelt, climbed out of the van, and headed to the back doors. Pulling out a kit box identical to the one Ben had put away ten minutes earlier, he grabbed a camera and a clipboard of paperwork.

He leaned around the open door and tossed Ben a fresh set of overalls. "See you up there." Then strolled over to where two officers stood by a cordon of crime scene tape.

Neither of the men looked familiar to Jason so he pulled out his lanyard and flashed his ID. The officers glanced at it briefly. The one on the left scribbled Jason's name onto the scene log and, once done, the officer on the right stepped aside, pulling back a piece of tape and opening up access to the path behind them.

"Cheers, guys," Jason chirped and followed the immaculately trimmed hedge to the top of the walkway.

Police presence was much more visible up here. Jason caught the eye of the nearest officer – a young chap, his shaken demeanour suggesting he was still a probationer who'd just seen his first corpse.

"Which way, fella?"

"She's down there." The officer pointed left towards a tree-lined tunnel that led to the Thames. "It's not a pretty sight."

"Dead bodies never are, pal. Not even the female ones."

Jason wanted to smile to put the kid at ease but, however bad it was up there, a new day always brought something worse with it. Best the kid grew a pair now if he wanted to survive his thirty years of service.

Halfway through the tunnel, Jason saw the rotund figure of a man waiting for him at the other end. "Hey, Ed. What we got?"

But Ed didn't look right. He patted Jason on the shoulder, the same way he always greeted him whether at the station, a crime scene, or even down the local. But this embrace was different. Strained. Something was off.

Ed's hand trembled but remained on Jason's shoulder. "Not much. We have things covered. You don't really need to be here."

He started for the tree tunnel, his unsteady hand urging Jason to move with him.

"What's going on, Ed?"

"Nothing."

His reddened eyes said different and continued to turn Jason from the scene.

Jason halted a quarter of the way in. "What the fuck's going on?"

Ed swallowed. Beads of sweat caught the moonlight. "Jason…" He swallowed again and glanced over his shoulder.

Jason pulled away from his friend's grip. He waited for Ed to finish the sentence.

Ed didn't.

"Tell me."

Ed turned back to him. "Let's just head back down to the car."

"Why?"

"I'll tell you back at the car."

"Tell me now."

Ed shifted his weight. "Not here."

"Not here? What do you mean, not here?" He stared over Ed's shoulder and back through the tree tunnel. Saw the glow of lights, heard the murmur of police. Nothing looked out of the ordinary – at least not for a crime scene. Except Ed. Ed looked like he'd swallowed a pint of green tea and couldn't spit the shitty taste from his mouth. Jason pushed past him. Ed called out and made after him, but Jason quickened his pace to an anxious jog. He exited the tunnel and the open air hit him in the face.

Ed's hand caught his shoulder. "Mate, please, come back to the car."

"Who'd they pull from the river?"

Ed's eyes glazed over. He chewed his lip but no words came.

Jason's grip tightened around his kit box and he shrugged himself free. "Do I know them?"

Ed reached for him again, but Jason stepped back. He looked left to where a crowd of onlookers were held back behind more tape. Then right. Police and paramedics were dotted everywhere. He saw the SIO in charge and then, along the river's edge, the scene tent.

"Fine," Jason said. "I'll go see for myself."

He marched towards the tent, his chest tightening with every heavy step.

"Jason," Ed called out behind him. "Don't be stupid."

Jason didn't stop. He reached the tent and pulled back a flap. Two investigators dressed in white scene suits didn't bother to look up. A body lay on the ground, partially hidden behind them. Female. Only one shoe – a red stiletto. Red-painted toe nails, unchipped and newly applied given the lack of new growth. Dirty, scratched calves showing through ripped tights.

Jason stepped forward, ignoring the distant warning bell at the back of his mind about the risk of contamination.

A black skirt, soaked through and crinkled to her thigh. A small mark, mid-way between her buttock and her knee, the shape of a butterfly.

Jason froze. Bile reached his throat. His shoulders stiffened.

"Jason?" Ed was behind him again, his voice low and soft. "Come with me, mate."

Again, his hand touched Jason's shoulder.

Jason threw the clipboard. He spun, hooked Ed's arm and held him still. "Why the fuck didn't you say?"

One of the investigators stood. "Hey! Take your shit outside."

Jason pushed him back down.

He turned back to Ed, dropped the kit box and grabbed his friend by the scuff of his neck. Disgust filled his veins. Ed mumbled something, and Jason shoved him away.

Ed stumbled out onto Southbank and the flap fell shut.

Jason whirled back to the body. The girl. The victim.

"Jason!" Ed was back at the tent's entrance. "Let them do their job."

Jason dropped to his knees. Now he saw everything. Her dark hair matted with water and grime. Her eyes open, clouded blue and staring up at the fabric ceiling. Her delicate neck lined with bruises. Needle marks dotting her arm. Jason reached for her hand. Ice cold.

He'd touched so many dead bodies. Knew the freezing temperatures they reached when the blood no longer warmed their skin. But to feel Leah like this? His own sister? It was wrong. This was very, very wrong.

Footsteps approached the tent but Jason heard Ed hold the newcomers back.

He cupped his sister's face, her cheeks just as cold as her hands.

"I'm so sorry, mate." Ed's voice was little more than a whisper. "But you need to come outside now."

Tears filled Jason's eyes. He crumbled forward, burying his head into her chest. He wrapped his arms around her neck and pulled her close. He waited for her body to warm. For the next gasp of life to enter her lungs. Instead, she hung in his arms, a dead weight.

"What happened to her?"

"Come outside and we'll talk."

Ed was right. Jason shouldn't be in here. Touching her contaminated the evidence. His falling tears contaminated the evidence. Heck, being in the vicinity of her contaminated the evidence. But you know what? He didn't give a shit. The only way he was going to leave her was if he was dragged out – and Ed wouldn't risk the scene any further by doing that.

A moment passed before Ed spoke again. "She was pulled from the river."

"But what happened?"

Ed sighed. "We don't know. It looks like she may have fallen in."

"How long ago?"

"Less than an hour ago. Some men found her."

Jason glanced up. "What men?"

"Just some passers-by."

Jason gently laid his sister's body back on the ground and stood. "Show me."

Now Ed blocked him from leaving the tent. "Jason, my boys have already questioned them. They don't know what happened. You know better than anyone that it's the forensics that'll give us the answers."

Jason pushed past him. "You don't have to be sodding Sherlock Holmes to see she was strangled."

He glanced around. Four men, suited but dishevelled, stood on the far side of the scene, two officers with them.

Jason marched towards them.

Ed pulled him back. "My men'll handle it."

Jason snorted and shrugged his friend away. The officers beside Ed straightened like two dogs ready to pounce on their boss's command.

Jason turned from them and looked at Ed. "This how you want it to go down?"

"You're leaving me with little choice."

"I'm asking those idiots a fucking question. One fucking question."

Ed swallowed and took a deep breath. When he exhaled, it was long and steady. He glanced first at the copper to his left, then the one to his right. "Take him to the car."

Jason hit out. His first punch connected with the officer on Ed's right. Arms wrapped around Jason from behind and he head-butted backwards. His skull cracked the cop's nose.

The officer released his grip and Jason made a run for the four men. "What happened?" he shouted. "Did you bastards kill her? Rape her?"

He was three or so feet from them when more officers pounced and took him to the ground. Jason struggled. He caught one in the nuts and pushed him away. Head-butted another. He could just about taste freedom when further police joined the heap. Black fabric swarmed him from all sides, and the four witnesses disappeared from view.

"I'll fucking find you!" he screamed as the constables rolled him onto his stomach.

They forced his arms behind him and cuffs swiftly imprisoned his wrists, but the quantity of men around him still didn't lessen. They lifted Jason from the ground, the tips of his shoes scraping the pavement as they dragged him towards a police car. He struggled, but the only place he was going was back to the station.

And his sister, Leah, would be left out here all alone

CHAPTER TWO

Tavish Finley threw his keys at the valet and straightened the jacket of his made-to-measure suit.

Light tremors rocked his body and his heart pounded with excitement at what the next couple of hours could bring him. He jogged up the steps, ignored the welcoming nod from the doorman as he opened the door, and stepped inside the foyer.

He was immediately greeted by a young blonde. "Mr. Finley. So nice to have you back with us."

Red-painted lips smiled at him. This welcome he did not ignore.

"I'll have a seat prepared for you at the poker table."

"It's blackjack that's calling me tonight, Nicki."

The red lips widened and the girl mumbled into a tiny headset. Then her eyes met Tav's again. "Follow me, Mr. Finley."

She turned and led him through a pair of doors, across the casino floor, and to the high stakes room on the north side of the building – his favourite room.

A croupier – brunette – waited for him. She glanced up. Only a small smile scratched her lips before her focus returned to the green, felt table in front of her. Tav released the button of his single-breasted jacket and took the seat opposite. Slipping five fifties from his wallet, he placed them on the table. The croupier spread them out. Calling out the total, she replaced them with chips, then slid two sealed card decks towards him. Tav tapped the pile on the right.

"Is there anything I can get you, Mr. Finley?"

Nicki still waited beside him. He glanced down at her slender legs. Wondered how they'd feel under his touch.

"Scotch, please, Nicki."

"I'll have a waitress bring it straight over to you."

She smiled, then turned and left the room.

Now the croupier had his attention again. He watched her break the cellophane wrapping on his chosen deck, shuffle, and slide the top two cards across the table. A ten and a two.

He nodded and she turned over a third card. Another ten. Bollocks.

The door behind him opened and a blonde waitress sauntered through, a small tray balanced expertly on her palm. She smiled and placed a napkin on the table beside him, a tumbler of scotch and soda on top of that.

"Compliments of the house, Mr. Finley." She hovered. "Mr. Corrone assumes his order is complete?"

Tav nodded. "Rubber-stamped it myself, sweetheart."

He didn't know why, but he'd assumed he'd have a face to face with Corrone himself tonight.

The girl slid a marker towards him. "Your winnings have been deposited with the cashier. You may pick them up whenever you are ready."

She turned to leave, but Tav caught her arm. "Bring me another."

He swallowed the drink and placed the empty glass on her tray.

The waitress nodded and turned to leave, but Tav stopped her again. He opened his wallet and placed a fifty-pound note on her tray. "The change is for you."

She smiled and nodded, then left the table.

Tav watched her retreat through the crowd. She looked classy, a black dress hugging the slender figure beneath. He'd definitely have to tap that later.

He glanced at the marker, the voice inside his head telling him to cash in the payment and leave. That payment, after all, was promised to others.

"Deal," he said to the croupier.